Egg Shooters

·LAURA CHILDS·

Egg Shooters

BERKLEY PRIME CRIME

New York

BERKLEY PRIME CRIME
Published by Berkley
An imprint of Penguin Random House LLC
penguinrandomhouse.com

Library of Congress Cataloging-in-Publication Data

Names: Childs, Laura, author.
Title: Egg shooters / Laura Childs.
Description: First edition. | New York: Berkley Prime Crime, 2020. |
Series: A Cackleberry Club mystery
Identifiers: LCCN 2020012962 (print) | LCCN 2020012963 (ebook) |
ISBN 9780425281741 (hardcover) | ISBN 9780698197466 (ebook)
Subjects: GSAFD: Mystery fiction.
Classification: LCC PS3603.H56 E343 2020 (print) |
LCC PS3603.H56 (ebook) | DDC 813/.6—dc23
LC record available at https://lccn.loc.gov/2020012962
LC ebook record available at https://lccn.loc.gov/2020012963

Printed in the United States of America
1   3   5   7   9   10   8   6   4   2

Cover art by Lee White
Cover design by Sarah Oberrender

Acknowledgments

A special thank-you to Sam, Tom, Terrie, Brittanie, Jessica, Elisha, Fareeda, M.J., Bob, Jennie, Dan, and all the amazing people at Berkley Prime Crime and Penguin Random House who handle editing, design, publicity, copywriting, social media, bookstore sales, gift sales, production, and shipping. Heartfelt thanks as well to all the bookshop folks, book clubs, librarians, reviewers, magazine editors and writers, websites, broadcasters, and bloggers who have enjoyed the Cackleberry Club Mysteries and helped spread the word. You are all so kind and you help make this possible!

And I am forever filled with gratitude for you, my very special readers, who have embraced Suzanne, Toni, Petra, Sheriff Doogie, and the rest of the Cackleberry Club gang as friends and family. Thank you so much!

Egg Shooters

CHAPTER 1

SUZANNE caught a strobing red blip in her rearview mirror and hoped it wasn't an ambulance.

It was.

The siren let out a piercing *whoop whoop* as she hastily pulled her car to the side of the road and watched the emergency vehicle steam by.

Another patient for Sam.

Suzanne Dietz was engaged to Dr. Sam Hazelet who, at this very moment, was probably on the radio having a tense talk with one of the EMTs.

So much for bringing Sam a late Sunday supper of chili and cornbread.

What had felt like a languid spring evening now seemed infused with tension. And Suzanne fervently hoped that, whatever unlucky soul was strapped to the gurney in that ambulance, they weren't pumping out their last pint of blood or gasping a final breath.

Suzanne lifted her hands from the steering wheel momentarily and breathed out.

Okay. It's still better to stick to my original plan. Sooner or later Sam's going to be hungry.

Suzanne was a tick past forty with ash blond hair, a practically flawless complexion, and just a hint of crow's feet at the corner of her eyes. Character lines, that's what she told herself when she washed off her makeup and studied herself in the magnifying mirror. Those tiny lines helped make her oval face more interesting, right? On the other hand, slathering on gobs of moisturizer might keep them in a holding pattern for as long as humanly possible.

The rest of Suzanne was fairly streamlined. If she lived in New York instead of small town Kindred, she could have probably passed for one of those real-people, middle-aged TV models who were enjoying a brief renaissance in this age of supposed non-ageism. Suzanne was always polished, engaged, and upbeat, though she generally stuck to a casual wardrobe of white cotton shirts knotted at the waist of her faded blue jeans.

Her first husband, Walter, had died four years ago. And now—through some fabulous miracle, probably brought about by fairies and unicorns—she found herself engaged to Sam Hazelet, the town doctor. Engaged and soon-to-be-married. Very soon, as they'd already reserved the backyard patio of Kopell's Restaurant.

A gentle wave of euphoria swept over Suzanne as she turned into the hospital parking lot, for she understood how lucky she was to have found love a second time. Smiling, humming along with the radio now—Adele was singing "Set Fire to the Rain"—she ignored the visitor parking spots in front and pulled all the way around to the back of the building, to the ER entrance. That's where she'd find Sam. And hopefully, if he wasn't up to his ears in X-rays, CBCs, and EEGs, they'd have a few minutes alone together. And she could deliver his dinner. Along with a long, lingering kiss.

The small ER waiting room was empty tonight. Lights were dimmed, chairs empty, magazines arranged just so on low tables. It was a place that felt quiet and hushed. Where everyone walked around in crepe-soled shoes and there was just a tinge of antiseptic in the air.

"Hey, Ginny," Suzanne said as she walked up to the desk. "You're working late."

"I was supposed to leave fifteen minutes ago, but then we got a call. Ambulance just came in, family's on the way." Ginny Harris was fifty-something with a swirl of gray hair and a kind face. Her glasses hung on a silver beaded chain and she wore a blue polka dot dress. She looked like everybody's favorite aunt and, in her free time, worked as a docent at the Kindred Library.

"The ambulance passed me as I was driving in. Is it bad?" Suzanne asked.

"Car crash. Victim has a possible broken pelvis."

Suzanne made a commiserating face. "Sounds nasty."

"But he'll live. They mostly do." Ginny lifted a hand and pointed at Suzanne's wicker picnic hamper. "What wonderful treat did you bring Dr. Sam tonight?"

"Chili and corn bread. But it sounds like it might be some time before—"

Suzanne's words were cut short by an ear-piercing scream followed by a piteous cry and the thunderous sound of breaking glass. A lot of breaking glass.

"What . . . ?" Suzanne said, turning her head in the direction of the outrageous, unnerving cacophony of noise.

And there, loping toward her down the hospital corridor, was an armed man. He wore a matte black jumpsuit of some kind and was brandishing a shiny black pistol.

Like a Navy Seal, was Suzanne's first thought. Like one of the guys who stormed that compound in Abbottabad and killed Osama bin Laden. She watched, feeling as though she was help-lessly trapped in a slow-motion dream sequence, as the man strode toward them. Out of the corner of her eye she saw Ginny's hand moving slowly, inching over to try and press the panic button on her console.

"Don't!" the man shouted at Ginny. He was right there in front of them now, his dark eyes pinpricks of intensity above his gray half mask. His breathing sounded a little uneven, betraying his stress. But the hand that pointed the gun at them never wavered.

As shocked as Suzanne was, she fought hard to steady herself and try to take it all in, to memorize as many details as she possibly could. The man wore a fabric mask, like a cold-weather mask that covered the lower half of his face. He wore a jumpsuit with zippers and snaps. And shiny black boots. He carried a duffel bag that bulged at the seams.

"Don't either of you move." The gunman's voice was low and threatening as he reached across the front desk, grabbed the console, and ripped it from its moorings. Panic button dead, lights gone dim, and thick gray wires dangling, he tossed it to the floor.

Robbing a hospital? Suzanne thought. Then it dawned on her. *Drugs. He just hit the pharmacy and he's got a bunch of drugs stuffed in that bag.*

The sound of running footsteps caused them all to turn and look. It was the night guard, rushing toward them, a look of sheer terror on his hangdog face.

"Hands up!" the gunman snapped.

The guard, a sixty-something ex–police dispatcher named Harold Spooner, who'd never been on patrol, had never confronted real danger, ignored the command and fumbled for the gun on his hip.

The gunman lifted his gun and shot Spooner as casually as if he were shooting rats at the dump. Spooner's hands flew up and he let loose a high-pitched gurgling sound. Then he spun around in a complete three-sixty circle and fell flat on his face. Dead.

"No!" Ginny screamed. Horrified by the wanton murder of Spooner, she jumped to her feet, causing her chair to flip over backward. At the same time, Suzanne scrambled around the reception desk, ducked low, and tried to pull herself into a tight ball.

Improbably, another shot rang out and Suzanne glanced up just in time to see Ginny grimace, then collapse forward onto her desk. Ginny's eyes rolled back in her head and her face blanched white as a glut of blood burst from her left shoulder.

Dear Lord, he shot Ginny, too?

Anger exploded in Suzanne's brain like a white-hot flame. Suddenly everything was needle sharp—the spattered blood, the smell of cordite, the savagery of the attacks. That's when Suzanne clicked into hyperdrive and she grabbed her thermos full of chili. She popped up from behind the desk, and, like a street fighter hurling a Molotov cocktail, threw it hard at the gunman. Her aim was good and true and she struck him squarely in the forehead. The lid blew off the thermos on impact and a geyser of hot, spicy chili erupted, splattering the gunman in his face and spewing gobs of red goop everywhere!

Staggering momentarily, the gunman gasped and wiped frantically at his face. Suzanne saw his lips moving, cursing her. His eyes were filled with rage as he cast a frantic, wild glance at her. Then he took off like a broken field runner, dripping chili—his feet practically slipping in the thick, red stuff—as he ran through the motion-activated door and out into the parking lot.

"Help!" Suzanne shouted. "Two people shot!" She heard footsteps pounding in her direction as she ripped off the scarf that was tied loosely around her neck. Kneeling down, she bunched up her scarf and fought to stanch the flow of blood pouring from Ginny's shoulder. When two nurses appeared from around the corner, she shouted, "Gunman! He shot Ginny and Harold Spooner."

As another half dozen nurses and med techs rushed in to care for the two victims, Suzanne launched herself out the door and into the parking lot.

An avenging angel, she was feverish to catch a glimpse of the fleeing gunman. Or at least his vehicle.

But as she stood in the middle of the parking lot, arms askew, slowly spinning in a circle, she saw . . . nothing.

Where had this mysterious gunman disappeared to? There was no getaway car speeding away, no motorbike, no lone runner cutting through the stubble of the nearby alfalfa field. Nothing to see but a sliver of moon dangling in a blue-black sky, nothing to hear but the drone of something mechanical up on the roof.

CHAPTER 2

RED stuff was still spattered everywhere. In the hallway, on the front desk, the rubber floor mats, waiting room chairs, six-month-old magazines, the windows, and even the curtains. Some of it was blood, most of it was chili con carne.

Ginny would live, it turned out. She'd sustained a flesh wound in her right shoulder. But Harold Spooner had been hit center of mass, directly in his heart. Sam, who'd come running out with the rest of them, had tried his best. But after frantic efforts that included pumping multiple bags of blood into Spooner, he shook his head sadly and said the hapless guard was probably dead before he hit the floor.

Five minutes after that, Sheriff Roy Doogie arrived.

"What the hell happened?" Doogie demanded. He'd gotten the emergency call over his car radio and come blasting in with Deputy Eddie Driscoll right behind him. "It looks like a bloody massacre in here." He gazed in Suzanne's direction. "You saw it all go down?"

Suzanne nodded. "Most of it. Except for the part where the pharmacy got robbed."

"Going for the drugs," Driscoll said.

"How many people shot?" Doogie wore a khaki uniform with a gold SHERIFF badge on his chest and a Smokey Bear hat set straight on. He was a large man, broad in the shoulders and jiggly in the hips, with steel-gray rattlesnake eyes that took everything in. Doogie was no pushover. He knew his job and did it well.

"Two people shot," Suzanne said. "The security guard and the desk clerk. The security guard . . . Harold Spooner, you know Harold . . . is dead. He wouldn't give up his weapon. I guess he thought he could get a jump on the gunman, but he wasn't fast enough."

"And the desk clerk?" Doogie asked.

"Ginny Harris was hit in the shoulder, but Sam says she's gonna be okay. Just a flesh wound. He called it a through and through."

"Still, this place resembles a war zone. That stuff over there . . ." Doogie gestured at the rubber mat near the door. "Looks as if somebody's guts exploded."

"That's mostly chili," Suzanne said.

Doogie turned a crooked gaze on her. "Whuh?"

"Chili con carne. I brought it for Sam's dinner tonight. But I ended up throwing a thermos full of it at the gunman's head."

"Quick thinking, huh?" Deputy Driscoll said it with almost, but not quite, a chuckle.

"Not quick enough," Suzanne said. "And, in hindsight, not much of a weapon."

"Where are the shooting victims now?" Doogie asked.

"Ginny's still in the ER with Sam. But Harold . . ." Suzanne shook her head. "The morgue I guess."

Doogie holstered his pistol. "Oh jeez." He took off his hat and ran a hand through his cap of graying hair, riffling it gently. He suddenly looked older than his fifty-two years. He cocked an eye at Suzanne. "But you witnessed it all? The whole enchilada? Break it down for me, tell me what happened."

"I was standing at the front desk, talking to Ginny, when we heard these horrible crashing and smashing sounds. Like doors being battered down and windows blown out. Then this guy, dressed all in black like some kind of commando, came running down the hall."

"A commando?" Doogie looked skeptical.

"That's how he was dressed, in a kind of jumpsuit, like maybe a paratrooper would wear," Suzanne said. "It struck me that maybe he had some sort of military training or background."

"What makes you say that?"

"From the way the gunman handled himself. He was extremely menacing yet fairly cool under pressure. Until I thunked him with the thermos that is."

"So he shot Ginny . . . why?"

"Because she tried to call for help."

"You're lucky he didn't shoot you, too," Doogie said. He rocked back on his heels. "What else can you tell me about him? I mean, it sounds like you were practically face to face with the guy, right?"

"He was wearing a mask." Suzanne said. "And, I think, carrying the stolen drugs in a duffel bag."

"So this guy suddenly appears, shoots Spooner and Ginny, and then runs out."

"And disappeared," Suzanne said. "Like, poof. No car, no motorbike, not even a skateboard."

"I can hardly believe that," Deputy Driscoll said. He'd been standing there, listening carefully to Suzanne's conversation with Doogie. "He must have had a car or bike or something."

"Accomplice," Doogie said. He looked around once more, then said to Deputy Driscoll, "Eddie, you grab the camera and forensics kit out of my cruiser. I'm gonna have a look at that pharmacy office. What's left of it anyway." He stood there, hands on hips, and blew out a glut of air. "Just what I need. Those truck hijackings and now this happy crap."

WHILE Doogie shot photos, Deputy Driscoll got busy stringing up bright yellow crime scene tape. DO NOT CROSS, the tape read. Though all the damage had already been done and the blood already spilled.

Another deputy showed up, Deputy Robertson, who asked Suzanne a few more questions, then set about taking prints. He focused on the damaged console and the pharmacy office. Doogie and Driscoll pulled out their notebooks and began the long process of interviewing the hospital's night crew.

Suzanne, meanwhile, snuck back into the ER to find Sam. He'd already finished with Ginny as well as the nurse who'd been accosted in the pharmacy. Her name was Birdie Simmons and she was sitting on an examination table as another nurse placed two butterfly tapes over her right eye. Birdie looked scared to death and was clutching a floral tote bag as if her life depended on it. She looked like she couldn't wait to go home, although Suzanne knew that Doogie would want to go over every step of the robbery with her.

When Suzanne finally located Sam, he was stuffing a blue paper gown into a trash bin outside a room labeled IMAGING.

"Hey," she said.

Without hesitation, Sam wrapped his arms around Suzanne and pulled her close.

"I'm sorry," he said. "So sorry you had to be part of this."

"I'm okay," Suzanne assured him. But tears sparkled in her eyes and a hard lump had formed in her throat.

"I feel awful that you were right there when the bullets started flying. That I wasn't there to protect you."

Suzanne managed a crooked grin. "I ducked."

"I understand that's not all you did," Sam said. He pulled back and stared at her earnestly with his boy-next-door good looks.

"I guess you heard about the chili?"

"The chili bomb," Sam corrected. "The news ripped through here like wildfire, that you tossed a thermos like some kind of revolutionary guard." Now his blue eyes danced with amusement and Suzanne all but melted back into his arms. Sam was tall, with chiseled features and tousled brown hair. His specialty was internal medicine, he was not yet forty (yes, a couple of years younger than she was), and he wanted to marry her.

"I . . . I was so furious. I had to do *something* that would stop the gunman or at least derail him." Suzanne shook her head. "But I don't think I did."

"You don't know that," Sam said in a soothing voice. "Maybe you slowed the gunman down a step or two and gave someone else a chance to get a look at him as he made his escape."

"I don't think so. I ran after him and when I got to the parking lot there was nothing there."

Sam's brows pulled together. "What do you mean?"

"I mean that he was gone. Vanished."

"There's gotta be a clue somewhere," Sam said. His hands were making soothing circles on Suzanne's back. "A witness maybe. Or tire tracks if his car peeled away fast."

"Maybe," Suzanne said. A shiver ran up her spine as she recalled the whole bizarre incident as well as the blazing eyes and set of the gunman's jaw just before he'd run outside. He'd looked as if he wanted to kill her.

CHAPTER 3

PETRA cracked a half dozen speckled brown eggs into her giant cast iron frying pan and cast a worried glance in Suzanne's direction.

"How are you honey, really?" Petra asked. She was a big-boned Norwegian woman with a kind face, no-nonsense short silver hair, and warm hazel eyes.

Suzanne pulled an orange into sections. "Doing okay, I guess." She took her sections, placed them on eight white plates that sat on the butcher block counter, and added plump strawberries. It was 8:00 A.M. at the Cackleberry Club Café and breakfast service was about to kick off any minute. Customers would be arriving to order scrambled eggs, pancakes, omelets, and hash browns. As if it were any ordinary day.

Only it wasn't. Not for Suzanne anyway. Because she still hadn't shaken off the frightening mantle of last night's chaos. First things first, she'd blurted out the news of the terrible hospital shootout to her partners, Toni and Petra. They'd already gotten a CliffsNotes version from the morning news on WLGN radio, but were desperate to hear the full story. As Suzanne delivered her horrifying play-by-play account, Petra was aghast, Toni was intrigued.

"What else can you tell us about Mr. Tall, Dark, and Dangerous?" Toni asked. She was a middle-aged hottie-patottie who favored cowgirl shirts bedazzled with rhinestones and wore super tight jeans and hand-tooled buckskin cowboy boots with silver toe guards. Her frizzled red-blond hair was piled on top of her head like a show pony. Toni was also a world-class flirt.

"Honey, you don't want to know any more." This from Petra, a churchgoing woman who wasn't afraid to wear her age like a badge of honor.

"The sad thing is, I do," Toni said. "I'm so starved for male companionship these days that the bag boy down at the Pixie Quick is starting to look good to me."

"The guy with the mole on his face?" Petra asked.

Toni nodded. "Now I'm ready to live vicariously through the antics of a vicious gunman." She puffed up her cheeks and blew out air. "Does that officially make me a crazy lady?"

"Most definitely," Petra said. "I think I'd better say a couple of prayers for you. Maybe light a candle in church."

"Wait a minute. I thought you and Junior were trying to resolve your differences?" Suzanne said. She was suddenly relieved to change the subject. To give her overwrought mind a rest. "Weren't you going to give your marriage one last shot?"

Toni had married Junior Garrett, the town screwup, in a hurry-up-roll-the-dice Vegas wedding. The ink hadn't dried on their marriage certificate before Junior's wandering eye had led him into a compromising position with the slutty waitress at the VFW, the one who wore low-cut fluffy mohair sweaters and hot pink extensions in her hair. Toni, doing what any reasonable woman would do, promptly ousted Junior's skinny butt from her apartment. Their marriage-separation-divorce had been in limbo ever since. It had been four years.

"Junior and I tried having a sit-down, eyes-on-the-prize meeting a few days ago," Toni said. "Only trouble was, while I was sitting on the sofa, explaining my position point by point, Junior wandered into the kitchen and polished off a six-pack of Bud Light."

"Marriage counseling?" said Petra.

Toni waved a hand. "Nah, I think I'm just gonna go on the Internet and download some boilerplate divorce papers from that website Dumpthatchump.com."

Petra looked to the ceiling as if searching for heavenly guidance. Then she turned her gaze on Toni and said, "An Internet divorce. What could possibly go wrong?"

"Exactly my thoughts," Toni said. "Why waste money on some pond scum lawyer when everything I need is right there on my laptop?"

"You better be careful," Suzanne cautioned. "You could pay money to this website only to find out years later that you're not legally divorced."

Toni lifted an eyebrow. "You mean I might get scammed?"

"Don't give me that look. It happens," Suzanne said mildly.

"Yeah, I remember that deposed Bulgarian archduke who wanted to be my pen pal and send me a whole bunch of foreign currency." Toni shrugged. "Didn't work out."

Petra glanced at the clock and said, "Ladies, customers will be banging on our front door in less than five minutes."

Suzanne and Toni exchanged looks and dashed out into the café. Toni flipped the big red sign on the door from CLOSED to OPEN, while Suzanne gave the room a quick once-over.

"I think we're good," she murmured to herself. The rustic wooden tables were set with cups and saucers, the better to jump-start everyone's day with a nice, hot cup of coffee. Silverware and paper napkins were arranged neatly in wicker baskets, and each table had a ceramic pot filled with fresh flowers. The breakfast menu was printed on the chalkboard.

"We're better than good," Toni responded.

Then the door swung open and the day officially began. Regular customers scurried in for their regular seats and, immediately, a loud buzz rose up.

"Did you hear what happened at the hospital last night?"

"Poor Harold Spooner, who would have thought?"

"Looks like the outside world is catching up with our little town."

Suzanne smiled, took orders, and delivered them to Petra. But all the while she listened carefully to the worried whispers of their guests. And worried a little herself. How was Sheriff Doogie managing? Had he uncovered any leads yet? As a sort-of witness, was there anything she could do to help move the investigation along?

When Toni ran into Suzanne refilling her coffeepot at the service station behind the counter, she said, "Hoo boy, it's a good thing nobody knows *you* were at the hospital last night, or our customers would be practically manic. They'd be stampeding after you for juicy details and I'd be forfeiting my tips."

Suzanne put a finger to her mouth. "Then don't tell anyone."

"Honey, you can count on me not to Twitter the news, Facebook it, or spill the tea to Radar Online," Toni said. Then her eyes slowly moved to the door, where two men dressed in jeans, cowboy shirts, and cowboy hats walked in.

"Yippee kai yay," Toni said under her breath. She scooted over to greet them and seated them at a table.

"The menu's on the chalkboard, fellas. See anything that trips your trigger?"

"You," the man in the red shirt said. He reached out a big paw to give her a little squeeze.

Toni danced away from him, shaking her head. "No, no, no. You can look, you can flirt, but please don't touch the merchandise."

"You're no fun," the man in the blue shirt said.

Toni pulled out her order pad, all business now. "Okay, gents, what's it to be?"

Blue shirt squinted at the menu board. "The sausage scramble."

"And you?" Toni asked the other man.

"Eggs and hash browns," red shirt said, still eyeing her with a lustful look.

"Want anything on those hash browns?"

"Make 'em cheesy."

"Same as your pickup line?" Toni said as she bounced away.

By mid-morning, Suzanne noted that their scattering of customers was happily munching away on peaches-and-cream pancakes, egg scrambles, and heart-healthy turkey bacon that Petra liked to slip in to ensure that not all Kindred's men succumb to wicked coronaries. So she wandered into the kitchen, where Petra was carefully stacking baked goods into a large wicker basket.

"That's a lovely gift basket. Who's it for?" Suzanne asked. Petra was forever putting together special baskets filled with fresh-baked blueberry muffins, lemon scones, and banana nut bread for distribution to friends and worthy causes. Petra was the social conscience of the Cackleberry Club, while Toni served as court jester and Suzanne was CEO, marketing guru, and chief problem solver.

"Reverend Yoder and his assistant Reverend Jakes are kicking off a new social services program at their church," Petra explained as she wrapped clear plastic film around the basket, gathered it at the top, then tied a pale blue ribbon into a neat, perky bow. "They're both such good men, always doing their best to help out in the community."

"Hey!" Toni called through the pass-through. "Do you want me to run that basket over to the church?" The Journey's End, a gray stone edifice with a white steeple and cross, was just a hop, skip, and a jump across their back parking lot.

"I thought you were busy setting tables," Suzanne said. With the breakfast rush over, they were slowly coasting toward lunch.

"I finished that, now I'm doing crunches," Toni yelled back.

Petra looked impressed. "Toni, you're doing morning exercises?"

"Not exactly," Toni called back. "I'm basically having a meaningful relationship with a bag of Ripple Chips."

Suzanne looked at Petra and raised a single eyebrow. "Crunches. Go figure."

Toni whipped through the swinging door, took one look at Petra's gift basket and said, "Consider that baby de-livered."

"Thank you," Petra said, as Toni grabbed the basket and headed out the back door. One second later, she skidded to a stop, flattened herself against the door jam, and yelled, "Whoops!" in a loud voice. She'd almost run headlong into Jimmy John Floyd, their new egg, cheese, and produce vendor who was making his Monday morning delivery.

"Pardon, pardon," Toni said as she bumped and slithered her way past Floyd. "Didn't mean to butt butts with you."

"Toni!" Petra cried.

"Can I give you a hand with that basket?" Floyd grinned at Toni. He was tall and forty-something with sandy-colored hair and a perpetually wide grin. Much like an agile cat, he'd also managed to execute a quick spin away from Toni and avoid a collision.

"Thanks a bunch, but I'm fine." Toni was already down the three steps and running across the backyard.

"Here, let me . . ." Petra began. She hurried over to Floyd, propped open the door with her foot, and grabbed a cardboard carton out of his hands.

"I got more," Floyd told her. He also possessed the earnest look of someone who was super conscientious about his job.

"Excellent." Petra set the first box on the counter. "We're low on everything and we've got a big week ahead of us."

"Let me help, too," Suzanne said.

"No problem, I got it," Floyd called back.

Petra turned to Suzanne as Floyd staggered through the door carrying two more large cartons filled to the brim with produce. "Oh my, oh . . . Suzanne, you know Jimmy John Floyd, don't you?"

"Sure, we've met," Suzanne said. "Nice to see you again, Mr. Floyd. Are you sure I can't help you with that? It looks heavy."

"Call me J.J.," Floyd wheezed. "Just about everyone does." He eased his box onto the counter, relaxed, and tipped his red baseball cap at Suzanne. Then he reached into the box, pulled out a wedge of cheese, and handed it to Petra. "Got something special for you. With your flair for farm-to-table fare, this bleu cheese is something that should fit right into your menu. It's from that new place, Pickery Bleu Farm, over in Deer County."

"We'll give it a try. And you brought more of those speckled eggs that I like?" Petra asked. "The Welsummers eggs?"

Floyd bobbed his head as he bent over the carton, looking again. "Five dozen beauties, just like you ordered."

Petra paused. She was running some sort of mental calculation. "Actually, I could use eight dozen."

Floyd's eyes crinkled. "Well, the thing is I got 'em in my truck. Fact is, I got more of everything." He shook his head. "I just came from the hospital commissary where I was supposed to make a delivery. But they're so shook up over there that they never did get their order straight. I'll have to go back later I guess."

"So you know about the people getting shot?" Suzanne asked.

"Heard bits and pieces of it," Floyd said. "Just an awful thing for this community."

"People are fearful," Petra said.

"I can understand why," Floyd said. "A crazy person comes in and knocks over a hospital like that? It's the one place you'd think would be absolutely safe."

"Personally, I won't feel safe until that gunman is behind bars," Petra said.

"And there have been truck heists, too." Now Floyd looked shaken. "Did you hear about those?"

"Just a few rumors," Suzanne said, wondering if there might be any sort of connection.

"HE's such a nice fellow," Petra said once Floyd had gone. "I was worried about who was going to take over Mr. Coogan's route after he and his wife retired and bought a condo down in Boca La Roca, but Mr. Floyd is so caring and nice."

"Glad to hear it," Suzanne said. "We seem to be woefully short on caring and nice these days."

"Tell me about it."

"So. You have today's lunch menu for me?" Suzanne asked.

Petra pulled a recipe card from her apron pocket and handed it to her, looking slightly apprehensive as Suzanne scanned it quickly.

"Everything okay?" Petra asked. "Up to your impossibly high standards?"

"Are you kidding? It's perfect. Our customers will love it."

Out in the café, Suzanne wiped the chalkboard clean, grabbed a few pieces of colored chalk, and got busy. Petra's luncheon offerings today included kickin' chicken tacos, chicken panini, ham-and-Swiss crepes, and spring pea soup. There were orange bars and slices of blubarb pie for dessert, as well as Petra's standard array of homemade cookies, scones, and donuts.

Suzanne printed out the menu with pink and yellow chalk, then drew starbursts, exclamation points, and a few smiley faces to liven up the board. When she finished, she put down her chalk and gazed around the Cackleberry Club, a look of supreme satisfaction on her face.

The place itself was an old Spur station that she'd whitewashed, refurbished, and generally instilled with a veneer of country French and shabby chic, along with slight touches of kitsch. There were rustic wooden tables, bentwood chairs, and polished wood floors. Two small crystal chandeliers dangled from the ceiling, calico curtains hung at the windows, and vintage china and silverware resided in old-fashioned country cupboards. A few antique tin signs graced the walls and Suzanne's extensive collection of ceramic chickens and roosters were perched on a high wooden shelf that extended halfway around the café. Ceramic jars filled with fresh flowers, some augmented by dried flowers, sat on each table.

Two smaller rooms formed the Book Nook and Knitting Nest. A cooler sat in a hallway. It was filled with homemade pickles, sausages, potato rolls, and apple sauce that customers had brought in. Suzanne claimed a small percent of sales and gave the larger share to her producers. One woman was able to send her daughter to junior college just on sales of her canned peach jam.

I love this place, Suzanne told herself. *It saved me.*

Right after Walter died, Suzanne had quit her job as an elementary school teacher, thrown caution to the wind, and bought the place. She plotted, planned, schemed, and dreamed, making the Cackleberry Club her number one priority. She talked Toni and Petra into hopping on board and they all committed (pinky swore) to serving fresh-never-processed foods along with a farm-to-table menu. Amazingly, the Cackleberry Club proved successful from the get-go. Now, afternoon tea parties, event catering, specialty cake orders, pizza parties, and gourmet dinners were a regular part of their repertoire. The three of them were nothing if not adaptable and hardworking.

CHAPTER 4

THE kickin' chicken tacos proved to be an enormous hit with their luncheon crowd, followed by the ham-and-Swiss-cheese crepes. Suzanne and Toni took orders, spun across the café floor like a couple of prima dancers from the Bolshoi Ballet, delivered their order slips to Petra, then came boomeranging back again to pick up and deliver the food.

This was the time Suzanne reveled in. Customers enjoying their lunches, offering compliments, and feeling so happy and sated that they often wandered into the adjacent Book Nook and Knitting Nest.

The Book Nook was small but potently literate. They'd managed to maximize floor space with floor-to-ceiling bookshelves as well as squeeze in two upholstered rump-sprung chairs for cozy seating. Suzanne was both book buyer and bookseller and had carefully labeled each of the shelves. Mystery and romance were their two most popular categories, followed by sections devoted to children's books, cooking, history, crafts, science, and sports.

They also carried a few knitting, crafting, and cooking magazines. And, through Sheriff Doogie's continued urging, also carried *Sports Illustrated*.

"Busy today," Toni said. She was standing behind the marble soda fountain counter they'd scrounged from a defunct drugstore, fixing ten box lunches to go. Suzanne had slipped back there to grab a fresh pot of Kona roast coffee.

"Those are for . . . ?" Suzanne asked.

"The Twisted Scissors Beauty School," Toni said as she scooped potato salad into small containers. "They're having a Curl Up and Dye workshop." She glanced at the large clock overhead. "Supposed to stop by for these boxes in about five minutes."

"You need help?"

"Almost done." Toni took a gulp of coffee from her mug and said, "Coffee, do your job."

At that exact moment, the bell over the front door da-dinged loudly and two more customers walked in.

"Uh-oh." Toni gave Suzanne a nudge. "Look at that. It's old Moby Dick himself come for his noon feeding."

Suzanne turned to find Mayor Mobley heading for a window table, looking very self-important as he waved his arms about, greeting a few customers and gesturing to the man who followed a few steps behind him.

Toni held up two red and white striped straws. "You or me. Pick one."

Suzanne grabbed one of the straws and saw that hers had been sliced in half.

"You drew short straw," Toni said. "Which means *you* get to wait on Mobley and company."

"Rats," Suzanne said as she grabbed two glasses of ice water and hustled over to where Mobley and his guest were sitting.

"Good afternoon, gentlemen," she said. "Welcome to the Cackleberry Club."

Mayor Mobley favored her with a faux-friendly smile. With his florid face, salmon pink golf shirt straining to contain his belly, and low-slung khaki slacks, he looked like a cardiac patient-in-waiting.

"Suzanne," Mobley said. "Always nice to see one of my constituents and local entrepreneurs. Especially when I'm working so hard to promote economic development for our fair city."

"Aren't you just a pistol," she said.

Mobley licked his lips and continued to smile broadly. "I'd like to introduce Robert Stryker. I've been showing Bob all around town, trying to convince him to set up shop right here in little old Kindred. He's looking at warehouse space and, as luck would have it, we've got that brand-spanking-new office park out on Sparks Road." He put his thumb and forefinger together. "He's this far from inking a deal."

"Welcome, then," Suzanne said to Stryker. "What kind of business are you in?" He was a good-looking man. Tall, dark-eyed, big-shouldered, with a gold Rolex circling his wrist. He had on high-polished oxblood brogues and an expensive suit that he wore with attitude.

"I'm a distributor," Stryker said. "Wine, olive oil, and a few mostly midwestern products."

"That's so interesting," Mobley said in a fawning voice.

"What kind of midwestern products?" Suzanne asked. Unlike Mobley, she was genuinely interested.

Stryker smiled at her. "For one thing—pickles. Because growers and manufacturers still prefer to pack pickles in glass jars, the extra weight prohibits their shipping to a large distribution area. So a product like pickles generally has a mostly regional distribution."

"I never thought of it that way, but your mechanics of doing business sound interesting," Suzanne said. Every aspect of business fascinated her. Developing new products, source of revenue, sales and marketing. She followed the stock market, too.

"I do like your town," Stryker continued. "But I'm a little put off by that armed robbery last night."

Suzanne offered a faint smile. "It's probably the first one we've had in years. Though I'd think you'd be more concerned about the spate of recent truck hijackings in the area."

"Not really," Stryker said. "We have excellent security in place. Dash cams, special door locks, and run flats. Some of our drivers are even armed."

"We really should order now," Mobley said, shoe-horning himself back into the conversation. "After lunch, I'm taking Mr. Stryker around to meet the town council."

"Sounds like a regular social whirl. So, what can I get for you, gentlemen?" Suzanne asked.

Mobley studied the chalkboard. "I know it's not on the menu, but what I'm really lusting for is a grilled cheese sandwich and fries."

"Got it," Suzanne said. She wrote down *Cholesterol Special.* "And for you, Mr. Stryker?"

"What's the report on those kickin' chicken tacos?"

"They're pretty good," Suzanne said. "Petra, that's our cook . . . chef, really . . . whips up her own fresh salsa, so the tacos carry some serious zing."

"Perfect."

When Suzanne went to put in the orders, Toni sidled up to her and said, "Who's the Daddy Warbucks–type sitting over there with our diddly-squat-do-nothing mayor? And is he perchance single?"

"That's Robert Stryker. He's about to locate his business here in town. And you settle down, girl, because you're still married."

"Not happily and not for long. Hey, Petra, how are my crepes coming along?"

"Order's up now," Petra said. She shoved the ham-and-cheese crepes through the pass-through to Toni and glanced sharply at Suzanne. "Let me guess, did that fool mayor of ours go rogue and order off the menu again?"

Suzanne nodded as she handed the order slip to Petra.

"He thinks he's some hotshot politico who can waltz in here like it's the Four Seasons or Per Se and have waiters and chefs fawn all over him," Petra complained.

Suzanne smiled. "So no obsequious fawning today?"

"Not never," Petra said. "Mobley's just lucky I don't add ghost peppers to his grilled cheese sandwich and blow his esophagus to kingdom come."

"Oooh," said Toni. "The woman is nasty."

BUT Toni, married or not, waiting on her own tables or not, was still interested in Stryker. Which is why she grabbed a hefty slice of pie and hustled over to his table as soon as Suzanne finished clearing away their dishes.

"Howdy," Toni said. She'd popped the top two pearl buttons on her pink western-style shirt and now leaned forward provocatively. "I'm Toni, one of the partners." It was Toni's unwritten rule that *she* could be forward and flirtatious even though the customers weren't allowed to be.

"Hello there," Stryker said, gazing at the gap in Toni's blouse. By the smile on his face, he'd decided she was fairly foxy.

"I thought, as a welcoming gift, you might enjoy a slice of homemade pie." Toni set it down in front of him and gave a slow wink. "Give you a taste of our town's fine hospitality."

Now Stryker's grin stretched as wide as the Cheshire Cat's. "It does look tasty."

"It's blubarb pie," Toni continued. "Our own delicious combo of blueberries and rhubarb."

"Clever," Stryker said as he lifted his fork.

"Got a piece for me, too?" Mobley asked.

Toni gazed at the mayor as if he were a pile of camel turds. "I guess," she said in a desultory tone. "Whatever."

Toni cut a small sliver of pie and delivered it to Mayor Mobley. Then she circled back to the counter where Suzanne was brewing a pot of Chinese lapsang souchong tea.

"Is that one of those rare teas that's picked only by virgins by the light of the silvery moon?" Toni asked.

"Something like that. Did Mobley say anything more about the robbery and shootings last night?"

"Nope. Because I don't think he *knows* anything." Toni glanced over at Mobley. "Look at that fool. He's holding his phone six inches up in the air. As if *that's* going to give him better reception. Hey . . ." She slipped an arm around Suzanne's waist and gave her a squeeze. "Are you okay? I mean really okay?"

"Trying to be."

"When I think that you could've been a casualty last night . . . it rattles my world and gives me a bad case of the whim-whams."

"Now I'm going to worry about all those nights when Sam is on call," Suzanne said.

"Don't think about that. Sam is going to be just fine . . . we'll have Petra pray for him. I think she's got a direct line to the Lord. And I know for a fact that you and Sam are going to be happy together for a good long time. You two lovebirds are going to grow old together."

"I'm already middle-aged."

But Toni was bubbling with optimism. "Hey, by the time you guys are super old some hot new longevity drug will probably come along. Longevidrine or Extendolife. Those scientists will come up with *something*."

"Or die trying," Suzanne said.

Suzanne was wiping the counter when Sheriff Doogie sauntered in at the very tail end of lunch. He walked up to the counter, nodded at Suzanne, and sat down heavily on one of the stools.

His eyes were red from lack of sleep and he seemed dispirited. He took off his hat and placed it carefully on the stool next to him. It was Doogie's code for *Sit somewhere else, dummy, and don't bother me.*

"You look beat," Suzanne said.

Doogie nodded. "Been up most of the night."

Suzanne poured him a cup of strong black coffee and placed a chocolate donut on a plate. Set everything in front of him and said, "Well? Did you come up with anything yet?"

Doogie ripped open two sugar packets and dumped them in his coffee. "We dug a slug out of the wall and figured out what kind of gun the guy used."

"What kind was it?"

"A 9mm pistol."

"Is that a fairly common weapon?"

"Not so much." Doogie stirred his coffee and took a sip.

"Anything else? Any fingerprints found?"

"The guy wore gloves."

"Surgical gloves?" Suzanne asked. She tried to remember if she'd noticed the gunman's hands. She hadn't.

"Probably were."

"So it could have been someone who worked right there at the hospital."

Doogie shrugged. "Or somebody who bought a box at the drugstore."

Suzanne's mind was whirling.

"Are there a lot of ex-military or National Guard guys who live around here?" she asked.

Doogie stared at her. "You've got to be kidding, right? This area is full of them. We got all sorts of men and women who served in the Army, Marines, Air Force, and in the Guard. Maybe a couple of ex-Seals and Rangers." He hesitated. "Makes me real proud."

"But not if one of them robbed and shot up the hospital," Suzanne said.

"Well . . . no."

"So how exactly did it go down in the pharmacy?" Suzanne asked. She never did get a full explanation.

"Nothing tricky. Our jackhole robber caught one of the nurses as she was going in and stuck a gun to her head. Threatened to kill her. Thank goodness she was the only one in the vicinity."

"The nurse . . . I saw her last night."

"Birdie Simmons," Doogie said.

"Okay, and I guess I have seen her around town. Was she hurt badly?" Suzanne felt a stab of guilt that she'd failed to inquire about anyone else last night. She'd been so focused on finding Sam.

"Miz Simmons was roughed up some. She says the guy slapped her around until she finally handed over the keys to the drug cabinet."

"Oh no."

"Yeah, she's got some cuts and bruises and will probably have a shiner for a couple of weeks." Doogie stirred his coffee again, looking thoughtful.

"What's percolating in that brain of yours?" Suzanne asked. Then, "Wait a minute, you don't think Birdie Simmons was *in* on it, do you?"

Doogie shrugged. "Probably not. Birdie seemed way too shaken up. She swore that the jerk held a gun to her head and made her sort out all the Schedule 2 drugs."

"The robber only wanted the hard stuff."

Doogie nodded. "Drugs that are in high demand on the street."

"And nobody else witnessed this robbery?"

Doogie shrugged. "You're the best person we have so far."

"And I didn't see that much," Suzanne said with some bitterness. "I was at the other end of the hallway."

"You saw enough," Doogie said.

"Look, if you think there's a chance that this robbery was an inside job—and it feels as if you could be leaning that way—you should re-interview some of the doctors and nurses. Ask them outright who *they* think could've pulled off a stunt like this."

"If they'll give me honest answers," Doogie said.

"You have to impress upon them how important this is. There could be an employee who was recently let go, or someone who's disgruntled about his job or salary."

"I hear you," Doogie said with a yawn. Then he leaned forward, elbows on the counter, and said, "Tell me what happened when the guy took off."

"You really want to go over *that* again?" Suzanne felt as if she'd relived it ten dozen times.

"Indulge me."

"Well, it was strange. I mean, from the time the guy ran out the door and I chased out after him . . . only fifteen or twenty seconds must have elapsed."

"But you say he was already gone." It was a statement, not a question.

"Vanished into thin air," Suzanne said.

"He must have had an accomplice waiting for him," Doogie said. He picked up his chocolate donut and took a bite.

"But wouldn't I at least have seen a car? It was a quiet night, cool and clear, nobody else around. And I never caught a glimpse of tail lights disappearing in any direction."

"Running without lights?" A cascade of colored jimmies tumbled down the front of Doogie's khaki shirt.

"Maybe. Or perhaps a motorbike?" Suzanne said.

"Motorbikes make a ton of noise. Did you hear that kind of throaty rumble?"

"Not really."

Toni sidled over to join them and said, "So maybe it was an inside job," she said. "Somehow the guy ghosted along the side of the building, hiding behind shrubbery and stuff, then ran back inside."

"Could have happened that way, yeah." Doogie rubbed the back of his hand against his cheek. "It surely is a puzzler."

"Or maybe the guy worked some kind of weird magic trick," Toni said.

"I assure you, what I saw was no kind of magic act," Suzanne said as Doogie's radio burped noisily.

Doogie pulled his radio off his belt, glanced at it, and frowned. "Driscoll," he said. "Maybe he's got something." He clicked a button, said "Yeah?" Static poured out as Doogie listened for some thirty seconds, then his mouth contorted and his eyes began to pop. "What? What!" he screamed.

Petra's face appeared in the pass-through. "Something going off the rails out there that I need to know about?" she asked.

"What happened?" Suzanne asked, staring at a suddenly agitated and jazzed-up Sheriff Doogie.

"Something big must have gone down," Toni said. She wasn't just a notorious flirt, she was also a first-class busybody.

Doogie jabbered a few quick words to Driscoll. Then he jumped up from his stool, adjusted his gun belt, and grabbed for his hat.

"What is it?" they all cried.

Doogie looked beyond flustered. He'd moved on to full-blown panic. "A second pharmacy has just been robbed!"

"Rudd's Drugstore? Here in town?" Suzanne asked. She could hardly believe it.

Doogie shook his head. "Next town over. The Blue-Aid Pharmacy in Jessup."

"So you want that coffee to go?" Toni asked.

But Doogie was already out the door.

CHAPTER 5

SUZANNE was on pins and needles for the rest of the afternoon. She was itching to call the Law Enforcement Center to ask what had happened, but knew she didn't dare. Doogie would still be tied up with the Jessup robbery, doing whatever he did in a case like this—talking to witnesses, collecting fingerprints, shooting photos, taking an inventory of what drugs were stolen, cussing up a blue storm.

"Chill, girlfriend," Toni said. She'd just delivered a pot of Assam tea, a platter of raspberry scones, and a pot of Devonshire cream to a table of three ladies. Tea time had become a big deal at the Cackleberry Club. Their customers were gung ho for it, so now they stocked a large assortment of loose leaf teas and had acquired a lovely collection of vintage teapots and teacups. In fact, the Cackleberry Club was hosting a library fundraising tea tomorrow afternoon. An event Petra had helped organize and was dubbed Tomes & Scones.

"I know I'm in a flutter," Suzanne said. "But I can't help wondering what's going on. Two robberies within a twenty-four-hour period? That has to be some kind of record."

"A veritable crime wave," Toni said. "And word about it is spreading like wildfire. In the last hour, the three people who dropped off items for tomorrow's silent auction—that's all they could talk about!"

Petra came out of the kitchen to speak with them. "Kittens, I know you've been knocked cattywampus by this second robbery, and I don't blame you one iota. It's terribly frightening to have some stranger come into our sleepy little town—as well as one town over—and wreak such havoc. But need I remind you that our library fundraiser is tomorrow?"

"Tomes & Scones," Toni said. "We remember."

"And we're on it one hundred percent," Suzanne said. "We know how important this is to you."

"I think most of the silent auction items have already been dropped off," Toni said.

"That's good," Petra said. "Now we just have to arrange everything on the extra tables we shoved into the Knitting Nest and make it all look gorgeous. Oh, and put out bidding sheets and pencils."

Suzanne glanced about the café. All their customers looked fairly content. "I'll run in right now and take a look," she said. "See what's what."

"Thank you," Petra said.

SUZANNE turned on the lights in the Knitting Nest and glanced around. Their cozy little retail spot was beyond stuffed. Besides the usual wicker baskets filled with skeins of colored yarn, displays of knitting needles, and stacks of quilt squares, donations were piled everywhere. Baby clothes, decorative pillows, knit scarves, a mug set, picnic basket, CD player, and a lovely rosewood jewelry box. Plus, there was a small plastic kayak and a kid's bicycle.

"Whoa. It looks like the second coming of Christmas in here," Toni exclaimed. She stood in the doorway, peeking in, ever curious.

"For sure we've got lots of loot," Suzanne said. "Even Carmen Copeland donated a lovely gift basket with four of her romance novels tucked inside along with a teapot and some beeswax candles."

"So the high bidder can read and drink tea by candlelight?" Toni asked.

Suzanne smiled. "That's actually kind of a romantic notion."

"Romance-shmomance," Toni said. "What else we got?"

"Let me see. Twenty-dollar gift certificates from Kuyper's Hardware and the Kindred Bakery. Movie passes from the Cineplex Theatre . . ."

"Where else can you get a good nine-dollar box of popcorn?" Toni said. "What else?"

"A candlelight dinner for two at Kopell's over in Cornucopia. And another dozen or so fancy gift baskets. A couple of the baskets have bottles of wine in them. Rosé, if you're interested in making a bid."

"Where there's a will, there's rosé," Toni said as they walked back into the café together. Suzanne worked the cashier station for the next ten minutes while Toni poured refills on tea.

Just as they bid goodbye to their last customer, they heard Junior's truck with its home-built trailer on back come putt-putting into the parking lot. Seconds later, Junior rushed through the front door.

Junior was an overage juvenile delinquent who generally tried to make a casual I-couldn't-care-less entrance, but today he was all agog. His eyes were the size of saucers, his hair stuck up like he'd plugged his finger into a high-voltage electrical socket, and his pack of Camel straights dangled carelessly out of one rolled-up T-shirt sleeve.

"Did you guys hear about the second robbery?" Junior cried.

"Sure did. And I imagine the news is all over town by now," Toni said.

Junior pulled out a cigarette and twiddled it between his fingers. "It's kinda . . . crazy."

"No smoking in here," Toni warned.

Junior tucked the cigarette behind his left ear and hitched up his saggy jeans. "Yeah, yeah. I know."

Since Junior was so jacked up about this second robbery, Suzanne decided to quiz him. Maybe he actually knew something.

"What did you hear about the robbery at the Blue-Aid?" Suzanne asked. "Was anyone hurt?"

"You bet!" Junior said, practically exploding with energy. "The pharmacist, a guy named Denny something, was roughed up pretty good."

"You mean pretty bad," Toni said.

"Was it one single robber?" Suzanne asked.

Junior's head bobbled. "Same as last night, only this time he scored even bigger. Thirty thousand bucks' worth of drugs is what I heard. And the guy only went for the hard stuff. The drugs you can sell on the street."

"Natch," said Toni.

"How did you find out about this?" Suzanne asked. Junior wasn't the most reliable bulb in the box.

"I ran into Deputy Robertson while I was gassing up my truck at the Pump and Munch. You know, the one just down the road from that little airport where people keep their Piper Cubs and those thingumajigs that look like they're powered by lawn mower engines."

"Stick to the story," Toni said.

"Yeah, okay. Anyhoo . . . Deputy Robertson had just come from the robbery at the Blue-Aid Pharmacy. So that's how I come to have this information."

"Crapola," Toni said. "It really is a county-wide crime spree."

Junior hooked his thumbs in his jeans pockets and postured importantly. "I got two ideas about these drug heists."

Toni shook her head. "The last big idea you had was a ferret farm. And we know how that turned out."

"Hey, give me a chance, will ya?" Junior said.

"Okay, what?" Toni said. "Spit it out."

"You know who uses a lot of illegal drugs?" Junior asked.

"Dangerous people?" Suzanne said. "Dopers?"

"Truckers," Junior said. "Long haul truckers. They're always popping amphetamines and stuff to keep themselves sharp on those cross-country runs."

Toni glanced at Suzanne. "He could be onto something."

" 'Course I am," Junior said. "Those trucker guys use a powerful amount of stimulants to stay awake."

"Interesting," Suzanne said. She'd read something about amphetamine use and what Junior said jibed with what she knew. Maybe he wasn't so far off base. "What's your second idea, Junior?"

"There's this old farm I heard about that some guys turned into a kind of compound. You know, like those Branch Davidians? Or the kooks out in Idaho? Anyway, this place has got a bunch of survivalist-type guys who are supposedly holed up there."

"I think I saw that movie," Toni said.

Junior shook his head. "No, ma'am. This is for real. They're preparing for, like, the big invasion."

"The only invasion we got around here is get-rich-quick developers putting up ticky-tacky townhouses," Toni said.

"Who's supposed to invade us?" Suzanne asked. She couldn't resist.

"These days, it could be anybody," Junior said. "Commies, aliens, zombies, you name it."

"Now I *know* I saw that movie," Toni said.

"And these compound guys are ex-military?" Suzanne asked. In a strange way, both of Junior's theories held water. He could actually be onto something.

Junior hitched up his shoulders. "I *think* so. That's the rumor anyway, that they're heavy into guns and bikes."

"Where is this place?" Suzanne asked.

"About ten miles past Shooting Star Casino. Off County Road Seven."

"How'd you find out about this compound-type place?" Suzanne asked.

"Guy told me," Junior said.

"What guy?" Toni asked.

"Smacky."

"That's his actual name?" Suzanne asked.

"First or last?" Toni asked.

Junior shrugged again. "Dunno. He's just . . . Smacky."

"Where would we find this Mr. Smacky?" Suzanne asked. "If we possibly wanted to talk to him." She still hadn't made up her mind if she should get involved. Her curiosity was running at a fever pitch, but her brain warned her to take care.

Junior squinted at his wristwatch, an old Casio that he'd scrounged for fifty cents at a garage sale. "Double Bubble starts in less than ten minutes, so Smacky will probably be tipping back a cold one at Hoobly's."

"Oh no," Suzanne said. Hoobly's was a roadhouse out on County Road 25. It was a combination honky-tonk bar, grill, and strip club. Unsavory types hung out there. Guys with gun-carry permits hung out there.

"Is that where you're headed now?" Toni asked. Junior wasn't technically employed, except for brief stints when he worked as a part-time mechanic at Bellows Auto Repair. Even then he was your basic goof-off grease monkey.

"Maybe yes, maybe no," Junior said, trying to look mysterious. "But you can't say I don't have good ideas." He tapped his index finger against the side of his head. "If you want to be old and wise, you gotta start out young and dumb."

"I'd say you have an excellent start," Toni said.

Junior held up both hands in a gesture of surrender. "Easy, babe, I'm takin' my leave. Got places to go, people to see. Oh, and I brought something for you."

"What's that?" Toni was immediately suspicious.

Junior pulled a crumpled brown paper bag out of his back pocket. "Here." He handed it over to her.

Toni opened the bag and poked her nose in slowly, as if the bag might contain some kind of infestation. When she saw what Junior had given her, she said, "Firecrackers?"

"Not just any firecrackers. Those are Black Cat firecrackers and Clustering Bee rockets," Junior said. "The primo kind from China. I know Fourth of July is still a ways off, but I got a deal on them."

"Thanks. I guess." Toni wasn't impressed.

"You're welcome, sweet cheeks. Adios, see you guys later."

Suzanne and Toni watched Junior back his homemade trailer house out of the parking lot, holding their breath that he wouldn't hit anything.

"Is he still living in the back of that trailer thing?" Suzanne asked.

"I'm afraid so. He's rigged up a TV, heater, hot plate, and a bed. Basically, he can lay in bed, watch cartoons, and fry an egg at the same time."

"Handy."

"Just being around that boy is like a never-ending episode of that TV show *Jackass*," Toni said.

"At the risk of sounding like a country-western tune, D-I-V-O-R-C-E?" Suzanne said.

"I know, I know." Toni stuck the bag of firecrackers into her oversized purse, walked over to the corner, and grabbed a broom. Then she came back to where Suzanne was standing and said, "So what's the plan?"

"What do you mean *what's the plan?*"

"I mean what's our own Nancy Drew gonna do about these robberies? You're the one with the head for crime solving. You've got the sharpest instincts in town, though Doogie would die a slow death if he ever heard me say that. So. You must have some ideas, right?"

"I wouldn't know where to start looking," Suzanne said.

Toni eyed her carefully. "Sure you would."

Suzanne lifted a single eyebrow. "Oh really?"

"I heard you talking to Doogie before. You gave him this perfect description, almost a reenactment, of what went down last night at the hospital. It was like . . . like you were writing a screenplay for a big shoot-em-up Hollywood blockbuster movie."

"But I never saw the robber's face."

"Suzanne, you still described him to a tee. His outfit, the type of gun, the way he carried himself—those are all good solid clues to go on."

Suzanne thought for a few moments. "You mean like his outfit might have come from a military surplus store?"

Toni cocked a finger at her. "Very good. That hadn't occurred to me. See, you're really starting to cook!"

Suzanne thought some more. "And the gunman definitely had a military bearing. Which could point to ex-military or cops or highway patrol."

"Definitely not just a run of the mill fish and wildlife guy. Or a crossing guard at school," Toni said. She wrinkled her forehead as if she were deep in thought, then suddenly snapped her fingers.

"What?" Suzanne asked.

"I'll tell you what's creepy," Toni said.

"What's that?"

"People stop in here all the time to eat, right? Sure, lots of them are neighbors and friends, people we know. But there's all sorts of strangers who come in, too. People who are on the road, like traveling sales guys, truckers, all different sorts. They stop here at the Cackleberry Club for breakfast or lunch or just afternoon pie and coffee." Toni shook her head and said, in an ominous tone, "I tell you, Suzanne, whoever robbed those pharmacies could easily be one of our customers."

An icicle of fear poked at Suzanne's heart. "I never thought of it like that."

CHAPTER 6

"GUESS what?" Suzanne asked the minute Sam walked through the door. He was wearing a camel-colored barn jacket over his blue scrubs. Instead of his usual New Balance sneakers, he had on driving moccasins. Baxter and Scruff, their two dogs, followed hot on Sam's heels as he came into the kitchen.

"I'm supposed to guess?" Sam asked. "Um . . . you burned the pork chops and we have to eat out?" He walked expectantly toward the stove where Suzanne was stirring a pot.

"Another pharmacy got robbed." Suzanne stopped stirring.

Sam skidded to a stop so fast that Baxter bumped into him from behind.

Sam looked stunned. (As did Baxter.) "Seriously?" he said. "At another hospital?"

Suzanne shook her head. "This time they hit the Blue-Aid Pharmacy over in Jessup."

"You said *they*."

"Well, I should have said he. It was one guy."

"Same guy as last night?"

"I don't know anything for sure, but that's the scuttlebutt going around town."

Sam pulled his cell phone out of his jacket pocket. "I'm going to call Sheriff Doogie and ask him to keep a close watch on the clinic."

She poked her spoon in his direction. "Good idea."

Sam spent most of his time at the Westvale Clinic, except when he was on call at the hospital. Or serving his term as county coroner. The Westvale Clinic didn't have a large pharmacy, but they did have a drug locker.

As Suzanne put the finishing touches on her gravy and pulled her roast chicken and potatoes from the oven, she could hear Sam talking on his phone in the dining room. Then he came back into the kitchen and said, "It's all set. They'll have a deputy cruise by every couple of hours."

"That should serve as a decent deterrent," Suzanne said, even though she figured a clever burglar could still break the lock and slip in unnoticed.

I'm getting too cynical, she decided.

THEY ate at the table in the dining room. Suzanne lit candles and put on music, Sam popped the cork on a bottle of Malbec.

"You getting excited about our wedding?" Sam asked.

Suzanne smiled. "Two more months. Got the backyard garden at Kopell's reserved and the invitations are ready to go out."

"What about your wedding dress? I'm looking forward to seeing you in a fantasy of white. Or at least ivory or ecru."

"Yeah," Suzanne said a little absently. "I better work on that."

"You don't have a dress yet?" Sam looked concerned.

"Well . . . no. Not technically."

"Sounds like not at all. Please don't let this go down to the wire."

"I won't."

Sam set down his fork. "You're not going to get sidetracked by this murder and robbery business, are you? I mean, you're not going to get involved?"

"I'd say I'm already involved."

"Sweetheart, I'd rather you didn't poke your nose in where you could get hurt."

"You know me, I'm always careful."

"Sure you are," he said in a facetious tone. "Just like poor Harold Spooner was careful. And look what happened to him."

But Suzanne really was preoccupied by the robbery. "Doogie and I were talking earlier today, when he came in for coffee and—"

"Wait," Sam said. "This was *before* the second robbery?"

"Yes it was. And I suggested he take another crack at speaking with some of the hospital personnel. Ask them, confidentially, of course, if they could think of any disgruntled employees." Suzanne chewed a piece of chicken and swallowed. "Can you think of any disgruntled employees at the hospital?"

"Yeah, I can."

Suzanne practically pounced on Sam's words. "Who?"

"Pretty much everybody."

"That can't be true."

But Sam explained. "Look, we all work long hours, face life-and-death decisions, and deal with a never-ending parade of the sick and injured. Kids especially take it out of you. Then we leave this microcosm of crisis and come home to our regular lives. Sometimes it's difficult to separate the two. Some people can't."

"What happens to them?"

"They either burn out or they get weeded out."

"But you're able to handle it. You've adapted."

"Now, yes. But you should have seen me during my surgical rotation. Life back then was grueling, to put it mildly."

* * *

Sᴀᴍ helped Suzanne carry the dishes into the kitchen. Then, while Suzanne put everything into the dishwasher and wrapped up the leftovers, he poured them each another glass of wine. Five minutes later they were lounging in the living room on Suzanne's marshmallow of a couch. Sam was curled up with the latest issue of *JAMA*, Suzanne was paging through the latest *Vogue*.

When Suzanne reached over to pet Scruff, who'd somehow weaseled his way onto the couch, Sam said, "This is nice. Feels like home."

"This is your home."

"Not technically. Not until we're married."

"Two more months," Suzanne said as her cell phone rang. She picked it up off the end table and said, "Hello?"

It was Sheriff Doogie.

"Can you meet me at the hospital tomorrow afternoon?"

"I guess so. But, um, why?"

"There's a guy who works there, Ed Noterman. He's one of the orderlies."

Suzanne stiffened and sat up straighter. "And you suspect him of robbing the pharmacy?"

"I'm not saying that at all. I just want you to take a *look* at the guy. Give me your general impression. Can you do that?"

"We're hosting a tea party at three . . ."

"This will take twenty minutes at most. Tell you what. I'll pick you up, then run you back to the Cackleberry Club. Lights and siren all the way if you want."

"Okay, then," Suzanne said.

"Good. I'll see you . . ."

"Sheriff?"

A sigh. "What?"

"The robbery this afternoon at the Blue-Aid Pharmacy. Do you think it was the same person?"

"Could be." Doogie was clearly playing his cards close to the vest.

"Any witnesses? Any clues?"

"Can't really say at this point," Doogie said.

Sure you can, you just don't want to, Suzanne thought.

"Okay, see you tomorrow," Suzanne said as she disconnected.

"That was Sheriff Doogie?" Sam asked.

"Mmn, yeah . . . he wants me to take a look at a guy tomorrow."

"What guy?"

"Do you know Ed Noterman?"

"I'm not sure," Sam said. "But, Suzanne . . ."

"I'd be observing him from a distance. So it'd be safe." Suzanne took a sip of wine and let her mind wander. Could this be it? Was she going to recognize this guy Noterman as the gunman?

"Still sounds risky," Sam said.

"I'll be fine."

Sam set his magazine down. "Pharmacies getting hit is a relatively common occurrence, you know."

"No, I didn't know that."

"There's always a lot of good stuff that can be used, sold, or traded," Sam said.

"Such as . . . ?"

"OxyContin, Valium, Dilaudid, Librium, Demerol, Fentanyl, Adderall, as well as stronger stuff. The Schedule 2 drugs," Sam said.

"They sound dangerous."

"They are. Which is why we try to keep them locked up and out of the hands of junkies."

CHAPTER 7

"What on earth are tiramisu pancakes?" Toni asked.

It was eight-thirty Tuesday morning at the Cackleberry Club and Petra was chuckling over her new concoction.

Toni turned to Suzanne, who was slicing fresh strawberries for a yogurt parfait.

"You ever heard of tiramisu pancakes?" she asked.

"Not until now," Suzanne said. "But they sound wonderful. Almost like a dessert."

"So what's in 'em?" Toni asked Petra.

Petra shoved two pans of poppy seed muffins into the oven, then turned to face her partners.

"I start with my basic buttermilk pancake recipe, then add espresso, dark chocolate, and some mascarpone cheese."

"Hashtag yum," Toni said. "It *is* a dessert. Dare I ask what the calorie count is on a four-stack of those puppies?"

"I'd imagine around fourteen hundred," Petra said.

Toni winced. "And the carbs?"

Petra smiled happily. "Off the charts."

But Petra's sinfully rich pancakes weren't the only item on this morning's menu at the Cackleberry Club. They were also serving scrambled eggs, turkey bacon, cinnamon raisin brioche, yogurt parfaits, and oatmeal with baked apples. And because Petra delighted in whipping up her superhot tomato sauce, they were also offering eggs in purgatory. Which was basically poached eggs in hot sauce.

Out in the café, business had cranked up. Toni delivered several orders, then turned to Suzanne and said in a low voice, "There must be something in the ozone today because we're super busy. We've even got three people waiting in the Book Nook."

"And did you notice? Everyone's talking about the two robberies," Suzanne said.

"They've all got their own crackpot theories. Like Teddy Butters over there thinks it's a roving gang of old hippies," Toni said. "He probably saw a vintage VW bus and hit the panic button."

"Frankly, I thought Junior wasn't far off with his observation on truckers and survivalists."

"Hard to think that Junior's brain could actually be onto something. Although . . ." Toni stopped suddenly and scrunched up her face as if she'd just taken a hit of evil-tasting cough syrup.

"What's wrong?" Suzanne asked.

"Wait a red-hot second. Isn't Daddy Warbucks into trucking?"

"Um . . . I guess so. Where exactly are you going with this?"

"Maybe Daddy's also into stealing drugs."

Suzanne thought for a minute. "I guess there's no sense in discounting Robert Stryker completely. His arrival in town and the pharmacies getting hit does feel strangely serendipitous."

"Is that good or bad?" Toni asked.

"It's a good word to describe a bad thing."

"Gotcha."

SUZANNE and Toni continued to greet customers, take orders, and deliver orders. All the while they kept their ears open, hoping to catch a bit of news or maybe a hint at something extra. Unfortunately, nothing seemed to materialize.

At ten forty-five, Joey Corcoran, their slacker-skater-busboy, arrived. Though Joey dressed like a member of a doomsday cult—black slacks, torn black T-shirt, multiple chains, earrings, and piercings—he was a good kid at heart. He usually worked one or two days a week at the Cackleberry Club, depending on how many events they were hosting. And Joey took his job seriously. He worked diligently and was always saving up money for the newest model skateboard since he hoped to someday turn pro.

"Hey, Mrs. D," Joey called to Suzanne as he clattered his way through the back door and into the kitchen. He waved at Petra, too. "'Sup, Petra?" His greetings were always exuberant.

"Kindly leave your skateboard outside," Petra said as she chopped onions and carrots on the butcher block counter.

"Uh, okay, I guess I forgot," Joey said. He left his skateboard on the back steps and came in again, fairly beaming.

"You look happy and upbeat today," Suzanne said to him. She'd just finished slicing potatoes and was wiping her hands with a towel.

"Got myself a new hobby," Joey said.

"Besides skateboarding?" Suzanne asked.

"Hey, I'm maturing. I'm open to outside interests." Joey grinned.

"So thrill me," Petra said. "What's your big adventure now? Rock climbing? Motocross riding?"

"Paintball!" Joey exclaimed. "And is it ever fun. There's this paintball range outside of town with all sorts of hills and ravines and creeks and broken-down old buildings." He was practically bubbling over with excitement. "It's like playing Army, plus you get to use a special gun and paint cartridges and everything."

"It sounds exciting," Suzanne said.

"The thing is, it's real messy when somebody nails you and you get all splattered with different colored paint. And it kind of hurts. So we gotta wear these jumpsuits that, you know, protect our regular clothing. Hats and goggles, too."

"So you go out there and shoot each other?" Petra asked. She sounded slightly disapproving.

Joey nodded. "Yup, it's a real gas. Like you can pretend you're invading Fallujah." He furrowed his brow and turned serious. "Makes me think about enlisting in the Army."

"You're too young," Petra said immediately.

"Joey, I've got kind of an odd question for you," Suzanne said. "But I don't want you to take it the wrong way . . ."

Joey stared at her with puppy dog eyes. "Yeah?"

"Do you or your friends ever get offered drugs?"

"You mean by dealers?"

"I suppose that's what I mean, yes."

"You're kidding, right?" Joey said. "Because they're everywhere."

"The drugs or the dealers?"

Joey shrugged. "Both. It's no big thing."

"Actually it is. You heard about the two pharmacies that got robbed?"

"You think those guys are gonna start selling the stolen drugs on the street?" Joey asked.

"Maybe. But that's up to Sheriff Doogie to figure out. And, obviously, catch the criminal or criminals."

Joey grinned at her with one eye closed. "Ain't you the sheriff's right-hand man?"

"Aren't," Suzanne said. "And no, I'm certainly not."

"But I thought you . . ."

"Joey," Petra said.

Joey gazed at Petra as she slowly shook her head.

SUZANNE hurried back out to the café to ring up customers and give Toni a helping hand. When she came back into the kitchen some ten minutes later, Joey was slurping a glass of milk and eating a scone, compliments of Petra.

"Eating the profits," Suzanne said, but meant it as a joke.

"Joey's such a good boy," Petra said. Although Petra had no children of her own she should have. She was the mothering kind.

"Do you want me to go out and help Toni in the cafe?" Joey asked.

"Naw, we got it," Suzanne said. "You just focus on getting the dirty stuff into the dishwasher. And take extra care with the silver."

"Do you want me to help serve at your tea party this afternoon?"

"Probably just clear tables," Suzanne said.

"Okay, but if you were in a pinch or anything, I could help pour tea. I promise I'd be real careful."

"I know you would," Suzanne said.

Joey was clearly hoping for something more meaningful than bussing and washing dirty dishes.

"You know, we have a lot of auction items and gift baskets that are still sitting haphazardly in the Knitting Nest," Suzanne said. "It'd be nice if they were all artfully arranged."

Joey brightened. "I could do that . . . make them look all pretty and orderly."

"That would be a great help."

Back out in the café, Toni was making the rounds, a coffee pot in one hand, a teapot in the other. When she'd finished with refills, she sidled up to Suzanne and said, "I talked to Junior again about truckers using drugs, and he said the ones he knows are all speed freaks."

"Sam said that Schedule 2 drugs—the kind that were taken in the robbery—are easily sold on the street," Suzanne replied.

"Kind of scary, huh?" Toni said.

Petra stuck her face in the pass-through and cleared her throat loudly. "Do we need to talk about the world's problems and sins this early in the morning?"

Petra was a Baptist with a strict sense of right and wrong. To her, drugs, gambling, and strip clubs were all hard-core sins. Much like lawmakers had amended the Constitution over the years, Petra thought those particular sins should be amended into the Ten Commandments.

"Enough is enough," Petra said. "We've got to get through breakfast, then lunch, then host our library tea."

"Will do," Toni said. "I shall diligently apply nose to grindstone."

"Me, too," Suzanne echoed. But she was still thinking about truckers and drugs and masked gunmen when Gene Gandle, the jack-of-all-trades feature writer, ad sales guy, and hog prices reporter for the *Bugle*, strolled in. He was string-bean skinny, middle-aged, and balding, with a stalk-like neck and enormous Adam's apple that protruded from his shirt collar. He fancied himself the Woodward and Bernstein of Kindred.

"Suzanne! You're just the person I was looking for." Gandle whipped out a red spiral notebook, grabbed a pen from his jacket pocket, and flew across the café to accost her.

"What's up, Gene?" Suzanne was busy keeping an eye on her tables as she printed the luncheon menu on the blackboard.

"A little bird just told me that you witnessed the hospital robbery Sunday night."

"I was there, yes. But do I qualify as a witness? Hardly."

Gandle waved his hands around. "Come on, Suzanne, this is a major developing story. First, the robbery at the hospital, then the Blue-Aid Pharmacy in Jessup. Our readers are hungry for details. They want to know what happened, who was in danger, and could it happen again?"

"I certainly hope not," Suzanne said.

Gandle's Adam's apple bobbed up and down. "So you surmise that the robber might have moved on? That he's on some kind of crazy spree?" Gandle made quick jots in his notebook.

"I don't think that at all. And please stop putting words in my mouth and then writing them down as gospel truth."

"Fair enough." Gandle grinned at her, all eyes and teeth now, looking like a predatory shark. "Rumor has it that you threw something at the hospital gunman?"

"Well, yes." *Does everybody know about that?*

"A can of chili?"

"Thermos full of chili," Suzanne corrected.

"You were defending yourself?"

"More like making a statement."

Gandle pressed Suzanne for more details while Suzanne tried to gently sidestep his questions. Finally, Gandle put down his notepad and pen, jabbed an index finger at her, and said, "What are you going to do about it?"

"Do?" Suzanne's voice rose in a squawk. "I'm not going to do anything!" *Why is everyone and his brother-in-law asking me what I'm going to do?*

"People are wondering if you're going to get involved. Like you have on a couple of other cases," Gandle said.

"What people?" Suzanne asked.

"Come on, Suzanne," Gandle said, ignoring her question. "You were a hairsbreadth away from getting killed yourself at that hospital. Heck, you were the only one who had the courage to fight back!"

"Harold Spooner tried to make a stand." The vision of Spooner getting shot still haunted Suzanne and played through her head like old black-and-white newsreel footage.

"But you really clocked the gunman!"

"It was a thermos full of chili, Gene, not a gunfight at the OK Corral."

CHAPTER 8

LUNCH today was Italian stuffed meatloaf, herbed eggs in toast baskets, Hawaiian salad with citrus vinaigrette, and chicken rice soup. Most of the time, customers hurried in, grabbed a quick lunch, then rushed back to work. Only a few people sat around and dawdled. Today, everyone seemed to be on a fast track.

"Have you noticed that a lot of people have been foregoing dessert lately?" Toni asked. "I wonder why that is?"

"Maybe because it's April and the weather is getting warmer?" Suzanne said.

"Ah, the age-old fear about swimsuit season. That summer has snuck up on you and your love handles."

"That could be a contributing factor, yes."

"Not for me," Toni said. "I wait until a nice hot, steamy day comes along, then I twist a whole bunch of Saran Wrap around my waist and hips. *Then* I pull on a swimsuit that's one size too small. All that plastic and Lycra helps me sweat away my blubber."

"Toni, you're as skinny as an alley cat."

"Yeah, but plastic wrap is one of those sure-fire beauty tricks I learned from Sheryl-Lynn Hamer. You know she was crowned Miss Hecker's Feed Mill two years in a row."

"An honor that's not to be taken lightly," Suzanne said.

"Sheryl-Lynn gave me another good tip."

"Oh yeah?"

"For really big events, you rub Preparation H under your eyes to tighten up all those tiny little lines."

"Toni!" Suzanne cried. "Just . . . no."

TRUE to his word, Sheriff Doogie swung by the Cackleberry Club to pick up Suzanne. Only thing was . . . he honked his horn, but stayed in his cruiser.

"Who's that out there in the parking lot laying on his horn?" Toni asked. She ran to the window and looked out. "Cripes, I should have known. It's Doogie. Holy Christmas, now he's flashing his light bar. You better hurry up, Suzanne, before he turns on . . ."

There was the high-pitched wheeeeee of a siren.

". . . His siren," Toni finished.

"I'm coming, hold your horses," Suzanne complained as she grabbed her jacket and ran out the front door. Then she was tugging the passenger door open and trying to wedge herself into the front seat of his tan and burgundy cruiser, along with a computer, radio, scanner, dashboard cam, a sixty-four-ounce bottle of Diet Pepsi, and Doogie's brown bag lunch. In the foot well she found herself kicking around empty cans of Diet Pepsi and Sprite while dozens of old HoHos wrappers stuck to the bottom of her shoes.

"You're like a bad date, you know that?" Suzanne said to Doogie as she pulled her seatbelt strap across her. "You show up, blow your horn, don't bother to come in and meet the folks."

"Whatever," Doogie said as he negotiated a fast K-turn, whipped onto the highway, and took off like he was driving an Indy car.

"And you're messy. How can you get anything done with all this junk laying around?"

"I'm actually organized. Just not the same way a Type A person like yourself is organized. My thinking's more linear."

All the way, Suzanne listened as static blatted out of his radio and Doogie talked incessantly into his phone as other voices talked in various codes—ten four, ten five, and ten seven—over his scanner. The cacophony was enough to give her a headache.

Once they arrived at the hospital, Doogie immediately dragged Suzanne into the busy, clattering cafeteria.

"It's still pretty crowded," Doogie said as they plunked down at a small table near the back. "A lot of surgeries and procedures run late, so most times the staff is eating late."

"Sure. Okay," Suzanne said. They sat for a few minutes and then she said, "So what exactly am I supposed to be doing?"

"Just take a look around. Study the faces. Tell me if you see anybody you think could be the guy."

Suzanne's eyes searched the three dozen or so people who were shuffling through the food line, grabbing salads, yogurt, and chicken casserole, the cafeteria's entrée du jour.

"Not really," she said.

"Keep trying," Doogie said.

Suzanne focused on the people who were seated at tables. There were orderlies in green scrubs, doctors in blue scrubs, a few folks wearing pink. She guessed everything was color-coded here. The different floors. The files. Even the people.

"Nobody jumps out at me," Suzanne told Doogie.

Doogie lifted his chin. "What about that guy over there?"

Suzanne's eyes roamed across the cafeteria and stopped on a tall man wearing a paper cap and green scrubs. "Is that Noterman? The guy you told me about?"

"Yeah. Whadya think?"

Suzanne stared at Ed Noterman. He was tall, fairly lanky, and average looking. Middle-aged with brown hair, brown eyes, and a placid face.

"Well, the height's about right," she said.

"But . . ."

"It's difficult to give any kind of definitive answer when I didn't get a good look at the gunman's face."

"The way you explained it," Doogie said, "it sounded like the two of you had a moment."

"Maybe I'd have to look into Noterman's eyes." *And see what?* Suzanne wondered. *Hatred, anger, recognition?*

Suzanne immediately backtracked. "Even if I could look at him face to face, I probably wouldn't be one hundred percent sure."

Doogie sighed. "I'd rather you didn't get too close to Noterman. Just in case."

"In case he recognizes me?" Suzanne asked.

"There's always that."

"Is he . . . ?" Suzanne stopped mid-sentence.

"Is he what?"

"Friendly with Birdie, the nurse who worked in the pharmacy?"

"I understand they used to eat lunch together," Doogie said.

"So you're definitely thinking inside job?"

"Right now I'm just casually considering it. But I'm not ruling anything out."

"Junior—Toni's Junior—has a theory," Suzanne said.

Doogie flicked his eyes toward her.

"Junior thinks it's truckers."

"Truckers," Doogie said.

Suzanne drew a deep breath. "You heard about that trucking company that Mayor Mobley is helping to get headquartered here?"

"Maybe."

"The guy who owns it, a fellow named Robert Stryker, came into the Cackleberry Club the other day. He's . . . interesting."

"How so?" Doogie asked.

"Stryker is intense and extremely sure of himself. Almost aggressively so."

"And you think he bears looking into?" Doogie didn't sound as if he shared her concern about Stryker.

"Maybe." Suzanne hesitated. "There's something else you should know about. A bunch of survivalist-type guys have set up a compound out past the casino."

"And you think they're dopers? Or a gang of armed robbers?" Doogie asked.

"I don't know."

"Suzanne, for somebody who claims they don't know, you sure have given this a great deal of thought."

THEY left the cafeteria then, and walked around the hospital. Took the elevator up to the third floor, walked the halls, and made their way down to the second floor. Along the way they dodged food carts, linen carts, and any number of transport personnel who always seemed to be pushing or pulling something— an IV stand, a gurney, a patient in a wheelchair. But nobody stood out to Suzanne.

As they passed one of the patient rooms, Suzanne recognized a familiar voice coming from inside.

"Ginny?" she called out.

"Suzanne?" Ginny called back.

Suzanne turned to Doogie. "Give me five minutes, okay?"

Doogie nodded. "Yeah, okay."

Ginny was ensconced in a private room, propped up on pillows, talking on the phone while *Days of our Lives* played soundlessly on TV. She had a large white bandage wrapped around her shoulder and her entire arm rested atop another pillow.

Suzanne waited until Ginny hung up, then went over and gave her a careful hug. She pulled up a clunky green vinyl chair and sat beside her bed.

"How are you doing?" Suzanne asked.

"To tell you the truth, I feel awful."

"Do you want me to call a nurse?"

"No, no. I mean about what happened. To Harold Spooner."

"It wasn't your fault. You couldn't have saved him," Suzanne said. "Nobody could."

"But it makes me so sad. Harold was such a good guy, everybody loved him. He was always bringing toys to the kids in pediatrics, or getting wheelchairs for the seniors who were having a tough time. I'd be the first to admit that Harold wasn't exactly your macho-type guard. He was more . . . what would you call it? A hospital ambassador. Always welcoming patients and visitors with kind words and a smile." She reached for a Kleenex tissue and dabbed at tears that had formed in the corners of her eyes. "Harold didn't deserve to die."

"Of course he didn't," Suzanne said. She'd gone over the shooting a hundred times in her head. And still didn't know what anyone could have done differently. It was just . . . a horrible, tragic event.

"And poor Birdie, too," Ginny said.

"I understand she got hit pretty hard."

Ginny nodded. "Rumor has it Birdie's not coming back to work. She's feeling too traumatized."

"You mean she's going to quit?"

"I guess so." Ginny reached out and grabbed Suzanne's hand. "That's why I have a favor to ask."

Oh no.

Ginny said the words Suzanne was dreading.

"I'm hoping you'll look into this."

Suzanne tried to deflect Ginny's request. "That's what Sheriff Doogie is busy doing right now."

Ginny focused sad eyes on Suzanne. "You know what I mean."

Yes, I suppose I do.

"You're so smart at figuring things out," Ginny said. "Look how you put the puzzle pieces together when Allan Sharp was murdered in the theater last Christmas. Nobody else even came close."

And I almost got Toni and myself killed in the process, Suzanne thought.

"Suzanne," Ginny said again. "I trust you. People in this town trust you. Fact is, you might be our only hope."

"Ginny . . . no."

"Promise me you'll just *think* about it?" Ginny asked. "Noodle around some ideas?"

Ginny looked so solemn and wistful that Suzanne almost had to say, "Yes, I'll think about it."

"Thank you," Ginny said. "And please tell Petra that I'm sorry I can't make her library fundraiser this afternoon."

"I'll be sure to tell her."

"You about ready to go?" Doogie's voice boomed from the doorway just as his shadow loomed tall and wide.

"I'll be right there," Suzanne said. She gave Ginny another quick hug and whispered, "I'll do my best. Promise."

"Thank you," Ginny whispered back.

Walking down the hallway, Doogie said, "You'll do your best at what?"

"That's between Ginny and me."

Doogie made a sound that was somewhere between a snort and laughter. "Why do I have the feeling that I'm the guy who's left hanging in the middle?"

CHAPTER 9

THE Cackleberry Club fairly sparkled this afternoon. Tables were set with white linen tablecloths perfectly setting off their Shalimar by Haviland plates and teacups. Silverware gleamed, tall white tapers flickered, and crystal vases were filled with snow white lilies and carnations. There was definitely a feeling of luxury and elegance.

"Everything looks gorgeous," Suzanne exclaimed when she walked in.

"Doesn't it just?" Toni said. "And guess who helped?"

"Joey?" Suzanne said just as Joey pushed his way through the swinging door into the café. He was balancing three pitchers of ice water.

"What?" he said.

"I was just telling Suzanne that you arranged all the flowers," Toni said.

"I'm impressed," Suzanne said. "They look so beautiful."

"Aw, it's no big deal," Joey said. "I help my mom with her garden all the time."

"And the Knitting Nest?" Suzanne asked.

"Perfection," Toni said. "Joey organized all the silent auction items."

Joey set down his clutch of pitchers and said, "That's nothin', you guys oughta see the special food that Petra fixed. She made all these fancy little triangle-shaped sandwiches that she's arranging on these cool three-tiered trays."

"That's our Petra," Suzanne said. "Bless her heart." She looked around again. "Anything last minute that I can do to help?"

"Maybe pick out some music," said Toni. "Then we're all set."

"I've got just the thing," Suzanne said. "A CD by Diana Krall, that jazz pianist with the great voice."

"Doesn't jazz have squawky notes that jump all over the place?" Toni asked.

"This is smooth jazz. And the CD is called 'Turn Up the Quiet.'"

Toni laughed. "Okay, then. Pop it in the CD player and let the quiet rip."

At three o'clock on the dot, the Tomes & Scones tea party officially got under way. Librarians, library docents, and at least four dozen library boosters crowded into the Cackleberry Club. Suzanne knew many of the guests—old friends like Lolly Herron, Pat Shepley, and Bea Strait—and was introduced to those she didn't know by Clara Gilkey, the library's peppy special events director.

"This is so grand of you to help us host a tea," Clara gushed to Suzanne. "We've never done anything like this before. Well, we had a potluck supper once where people brought hot dishes and those colored marshmallow salads. But this tea . . . this is a major event for us!"

"We're happy to have you," Suzanne said. "And I'm impressed that you received so many donations for your silent auction."

"We had a real energetic committee," Clara said. "You can do wonderful things when you have hardworking people who believe in what they're doing." She smiled. "Do you know what Margaret Mead once said?"

Suzanne shook her head. "No, tell me."

"She said, 'Never underestimate the power of a small group of committed people to change the world.'"

"Was she ever right," Suzanne said.

CLARA stood in the center of the café and gave a heartfelt welcoming speech. Then she introduced Suzanne and turned the floor over to her.

"Thank you so much for celebrating your first ever Tomes & Scones at the Cackleberry Club," Suzanne said, her voice ringing out across the room. "We're absolutely delighted to have you join us and we hope that today's menu will meet everyone's expectation of a cozy afternoon tea party."

There was a spatter of applause and then Suzanne continued.

"That said, we'll be serving three different courses on our three-tiered tea trays. First course will consist of cream scones with strawberry jam and Devonshire cream. Second course will be tea sandwiches. Two kinds today . . . crab salad on brioche and chicken salad with chutney on cinnamon-raisin bread. For dessert you can choose from an array of fresh-baked brownie bites, macaroons, and toffee cookies."

There were ooh's and ah's as Suzanne continued.

"We'll also be serving two kinds of tea today, a Chinese black tea and a lovely Darjeeling from India." She paused. "And now, dear Tomes & Scones guests . . ."

That was the signal for Toni, Petra, and Joey to march out into the café, each one of them carrying an enormous three-tiered tray stacked full of goodies.

". . . Please enjoy your tea party," Suzanne finished.

First the guests clapped politely. Then, as the tea trays were placed on their tables and they saw the frosted scones, delightful little sandwiches, and sweets nestled together and sprinkled with edible flowers, they cheered. And when Suzanne and Toni grabbed steaming teapots and began pouring tea, the guests broke into a rousing applause.

Petra, who was watching all this, a grin on her broad face, was positively delighted.

"It's a hit," Suzanne whispered to Petra a few minutes later.

"It's more than that," Petra replied. "We've absolutely charmed them."

SUZANNE carried two vintage teapots, an English Globe rosebud teapot filled with Chinese black tea and a Windsor Sadler blue floral filled with Darjeeling, to the nearest table. "A refill on your tea, ladies?"

Sally Kramer, who worked at the bank, held up her cup and saucer. "I'd love some more Darjeeling."

As Suzanne poured, Sally said, "These are my friends, Elaine and Connie. This is their first time at an actual tea."

"Welcome, then," Suzanne said.

Connie, a brunette who was wearing a heroic pair of gold hoop earrings, said, "Everything is delightful so far. But the cream scones . . ." She pointed at the half-eaten scone on her plate. "You call them that because you serve them with Devonshire cream?"

"Good guess, but no," Suzanne said. "Heavy cream is one of the main ingredients and helps make them super moist."

Suzanne moved around the table, filling teacups and chatting with her guests. She was feeling upbeat about the event until a gray-haired woman put a hand on her arm and said, "Suzanne, how are you holding up?"

Suzanne stared into the piercing eyes of Mildred Roth, a not-all-that-friendly lady who worked part-time at the fabric store.

"Things are good," Suzanne said lightly.

"But after that shoot-em-up at the hospital . . . and poor Harold Spooner getting murdered in cold blood." Mildred's eyes gleamed in a curious way. She wanted more information and seemed determined to get it. "I bet you're still shaking in your boots."

"I don't scare all that easily," Suzanne said as she poured out the last of her tea, then headed back behind the counter. She refilled her teapot and snugged a patchwork tea cozy around it just as . . .

BOOM!

A thunderous, ear-splitting noise—loud as any sonic boom—suddenly erupted outside. The noise bounced off every wall in the Cackleberry Club, rattling the ceramic chickens on their overhead perches and literally stunning their guests. The hum of conversation instantly morphed into a collective, frightened gasp. Nervous shrieks and a few screams followed.

"A gunshot!" someone shouted. "That was a gunshot!"

The realization that a gunman might be standing outside the Cackleberry Club stunned Suzanne. Her brain froze for a moment and the floral teapot slipped from her hands. It crashed to the floor, broke into a dozen pieces, and rendered yet another discordant and terrifying blast of noise.

Standing in a puddle of hot tea, Suzanne's heart thundered inside her chest. *Was that shot meant for me?*

Sally Kramer's friend Connie slipped from her chair like a will-of-the-wisp and disappeared under the table. Other women ducked, a few brave souls frowned and stood up.

Sally rapped her knuckles on the table and said, "Connie, don't be a goose. Did you *see* a gun? Does anyone see a gun?"

At hearing the word "gun," Petra burst out of the kitchen waving a twelve-inch cast iron frying pan.

"Who's shooting? Is everyone alright? Was anyone hurt?" Petra yelped. She was ready to do battle, to defend her turf.

Toni ran to the window just as another horrendous boom erupted.

"Whoa! Calm down, everyone!" Toni cried. Her hands moved up and down in a take-it-easy gesture. "It's just a backfire from an old car."

Petra lowered her frying pan. "A car?" Her voice was a disbelieving squawk.

"Yeah." Toni glanced out the window again. "It's just a couple of guys in a beat-up muscle car." She squinted. "Faded red. Looks like maybe an old Mustang."

"Holy Matrimony," Petra said.

"Ah, they're gone now. Pulled into the parking lot at the Journey's End Church." Toni turned back to face the crowd and dusted her hands together. "Looks like the fun's over. Too bad."

Everyone stared at her in amazement.

Suzanne, who'd managed to pull it together emotionally, now walked to the center of the room, a smile on her face.

"I do apologize if anyone was unduly startled by that disturbance," she said, trying (hoping!) to make light of it. "But there's plenty more tea party left in the day. In fact, we'll be coming around with seconds on scones and refills on your tea. So please . . . sit back and enjoy."

The guests nodded, smiled, and visibly relaxed. A murmur of conversation started up again, then grew to a loud buzz.

"Crap on a cracker," Toni said to Suzanne as they met behind the counter. "That was crazy weird, huh? First thing our guests thought of was terrorists."

"First thing I thought of was a gun," Suzanne said.

"But everything's cool now, so buck up, girlfriend." Toni

winked at Suzanne. "When life gives you lemons, squirt someone in the eye."

Suzanne and Toni poured refills and doled out more scones, thanking their lucky stars that Petra had baked extra. Clara Gilkey stood up, thanked everyone for coming to the Tomes & Scones tea, and cheerfully announced that the silent auction was now open in the Knitting Nest and there were all sorts of wonderful items ready for bidding.

WHEN just a few guests still remained in the Knitting Nest, placing bids on the auction items, while Joey was clearing and Suzanne was looking forward to getting off her feet, Sheriff Doogie walked in.

Suzanne took one look at him and could tell, by the determined look on his face, that something big had happened.

"What?" she said. She was standing in the middle of the café holding a tub full of dirty dishes.

Doogie crooked a finger at her and headed for the counter. Suzanne handed her tub to Joey and followed hot on Doogie's heels.

"What?" she said again as she slipped onto a stool next to him.

"You're never gonna believe this," Doogie said.

"Please tell me you caught the gunman."

"I wish."

"Then what is it?"

Doogie looked around furtively, as if he feared they'd be overheard.

"Just spit it out," Suzanne said. "It's not like you're passing state secrets to North Korea."

"Here's the deal," Doogie said. "You know Holt Wagner? He's got a dairy farm out on Country Trail West?"

"Yeah?"

"Wagner discovered a bottle of OxyContin laying in one of his fields this morning."

"No way!" Suzanne cried.

"Way," Doogie said. "Holt thought it was mighty strange, considering the recent robberies. So he hotfooted over to the Law Enforcement Center and gave the bottle to us. He figured it might be part of the stolen drugs."

"Was it?"

"We're checking now. I had Deputy Driscoll run the bottle over to the hospital, to see if it came from their pharmacy."

"But how weird—this guy Wagner actually found it in his field? Maybe our gunman was riding a motocross bike after all," Suzanne said.

"The thing that plunked my magic twanger was the stuff you told me earlier today. When we were at the hospital."

"About the survivalists," Suzanne said.

Doogie leaned in closer. "Their so-called compound isn't far from where that bottle was found."

"Holy cats," Suzanne said with a slight shiver. Suddenly the investigation felt real. They'd been slogging through a sticky morass, not really getting anywhere. Now there was serious momentum.

"The other thing I thought of," Doogie said. "The gunman . . . the robber . . . could have been riding a horse."

Suzanne thought of her own two horses, Mocha Gent and Grommet, and smiled to herself.

"I don't know," she said. "A gunman making a getaway on a horse? That sounds awfully Butch Cassidy."

"Yeah," Doogie said. "Besides, if he was on a horse, wouldn't you have heard the hoof beats?"

"It's unfortunate that only one bottle of Oxy was recovered out of hundreds of bottles stolen."

"Hey," Doogie said, sounding a little ornery now, his fatigue beginning to catch up with him. "It's what I got."

"And you can fingerprint the bottle?"

"Already did. Nothing there."

"Do you know . . . have there been any other pharmacy robberies in the state?" Suzanne asked.

"Just those two. I checked with the BCA, the state Bureau of Criminal Apprehension, and they didn't know of any recent ones. In fact, they seemed surprised by these two—as well as the murder. Even offered to send an investigator to help out if I wanted."

"Do you want them to step in and help?"

"Not yet."

"So where do you go from here?" Suzanne asked.

"I'm trying to work that out."

"What if you . . . um, spread the word that you located one of the stolen pill bottles, and you found a print on it?"

Doogie squinted at her. "You mean lie to the public?"

"I mean create a kind of trap. If you make it sound as if you're getting close to solving the two crimes, that could force the robber's . . . the killer's . . . hand."

"Might cause him to go underground, too," Doogie said.

"You're right. It's a risk," Suzanne said.

"On the other hand, our guy might not have to show his hand at all. For all we know, he could have already fenced the drugs and is sitting back counting his money. My basic impression is that our guy is a fairly cool professional."

"That's what I thought at first, too," Suzanne said. "But I've changed my mind."

"Why's that?" Doogie asked.

"Because he shot Spooner when he really didn't have to. Spooner couldn't even clear his gun from his holster."

"So with one case of complete overreaction, our guy went from armed robbery to murder one," Doogie said thoughtfully. "Which *is* the mark of a rank amateur."

"Who might eventually become a professional?" Suzanne said.

Doogie shook his head. "Don't even think that."

A half hour later, Suzanne and Toni were straightening up the Knitting Nest, putting everything right and turning it back into a cozy little yarn shop.

Toni pinned two mohair shawls back on the wall and said, "Well, what did Deputy Dawg have to say for himself?"

"Doogie? Not that much," Suzanne said. "A single bottle of OxyContin has been recovered from a farm field, but that's about it. No clues, no suspects, no nothing."

"Doogie's got nothing?"

"So he says."

"But there have to be a few names rattling around in *your* computer brain," Toni said. "Who do you see as potential suspects?"

"You promise not to tell anybody?" Suzanne asked.

Toni pantomimed clicking a lock on her lips. "Mum's the word."

"I'm thinking about Ed Noterman as well as Robert Stryker, Birdie Simmons, and those semi-mysterious survivalist guys," Suzanne said.

"If you want to get a line of those survivalist guys you should talk to Smacky," Toni said.

"I forgot all about Smacky. But you're right."

"Will Sam be at the hospital tonight?"

Suzanne nodded. "What have you got in mind?"

"Maybe see if we can have a word with Smacky?"

"Sounds tricky."

"Could be revealing," Toni said.

"Then I guess we should maybe take a chance."

CHAPTER 10

HOOBLY's was your typical middle-America country roadhouse. A one-story building with fake log siding that had seen better days (and more than a few fights), and a string of yellow bug lights stretched along the roofline. It sported an aggressive purple and red neon sign with a few burned-out letters that spelled out HO BLY' R ADHOUSE. There were several dozen trucks and four-by-fours parked in the gravel lot and raucous music leaked out into the dark night.

"I hope I don't live to regret this," Suzanne said as she and Toni pushed their way through the front door. They found themselves in an entryway with knotty pine walls and a small counter where pull tabs, T-shirts, and lottery tickets were being sold. The place smelled of cigarette smoke, stale beer, burned cheeseburgers, and a touch of eau de diesel fuel. Music thumped incessantly.

"This is gonna be exciting," Toni said. She was all revved up, ready to party, and had added a clip-in piece of reddish-blond

Dynel hair to her own curly locks. She'd also exchanged her sports bra for a hot pink lace push-up bra that now peeped out enticingly from beneath her cowboy shirt.

"You think?" Suzanne asked. She glanced at the dirty red carpet, the row of booths with cracked black plastic seats and backs, and the battered L-shaped bar where customers were lined up two-deep watching the NHL playoffs on a TV that hung above a glistening array of liquor bottles. On a tiny stage in the far corner an exotic dancer pranced around in red lingerie. "Cookie" by R. Kelly pounded out of the speakers. Another corner held coin-operated arcade games. Shuffleboard bowling, pinball, and a *Terminator Salvation* shooting game.

"C'mon," Toni urged. "Let's hurry up and find us a booth. I called Junior right before we left and he promised to meet us here."

Suzanne and Toni elbowed their way through a sea of scruffy (but seemingly interested) men and slipped into a booth that was padded like an old bumper car. Toni immediately grabbed two plastic-covered menus and slid one across the table to Suzanne. The menu offered your basic array of fried foods. Fried catfish, fried onion rings, fried chicken tenders, fried wings, and fried cheese curds. And, just to shake up the status quo, fried jalapeño poppers stuffed with gooey cream cheese. It was all generic bar food that came pre-breaded, pre-formed, and frozen in fifty-pound sacks.

"What looks good?" Toni asked.

"Um . . ." Suzanne was stalling. She'd scanned the menu and decided that nothing looked particularly good to her. "Maybe I'll just order a plain burger." *And hope for the best.*

"I'm gonna get—" Toni broke off her words as she hastily threw up an arm and waved frantically. "There he is, there's Junior!"

Junior sauntered up to their booth like he owned the place. Tonight he was wearing a silver-studded black leather jacket over a ripped sweatshirt that had an image of a ten-point buck on it with the words I LIKE BIG BUCKS. He also had on his usual saggy jeans, motorcycle boots, and had slapped on a few ounces of dime-store cologne.

"Ladies," Junior said, giving a knowing nod. "Great to see you."

"Thanks for coming," Toni said. "Were you able to get hold of Smacky like I asked?"

"Would I let you down?" Junior asked with a smirk.

"Yes," they both answered at once.

Junior looked stung. "That's not true. Who went out and cut you a pile of Christmas greens when you needed them?"

"You did," Toni said in a small voice.

"And who swiped a bunch of hay bales when you wanted to decorate for your Halloween party?"

"You *stole* those?" Toni asked.

"And you guys did ask me to make a wooden model of the Eiffel Tower for your gourmet dinner."

"We get it, Junior, we're pathetically grateful for all you've done and will do for us," Suzanne said. "Now, is your friend Smacky here or not? Because we'd definitely like to have a word with him."

"Smacky's here," Junior said. "But I'm afraid he's *occupado* right now." Junior grinned and dropped his voice to a conspiratorial whisper. "He's busy watching the entertainment."

The strippers, Suzanne thought, feeling more than a little uncomfortable. She hated the idea of patronizing a place where women took off their clothes for men's enjoyment. Even if the women hadn't been *forced* into it, even if they were earning serious cash, it still felt sleazy to her.

"Why don't you ladies order yourselves a cool refreshing beverage and I'll go get him?" Junior said. "Oh, and I personally recommend the Spam fritters."

"Gotcha," Toni said.

They ordered bottles of Miller Lite and burgers with crinkle fries. The beer was ice cold and the burgers arrived medium-rare, just as they'd ordered, so Suzanne was beginning to feel slightly better about the place. Just as she dunked a crinkle fry into a puddle of catsup, Junior showed up with Smacky in tow.

"Here he is," Junior announced. "The man of the hour." He made quick introductions, then gestured for Smacky to join them. "Go ahead, buddy, crawl in there. The ladies want to converse with you."

Smacky plunked himself down next to Suzanne. He was short with jolly pink cheeks, a shock of brown hair that couldn't quite be tamed, and a nubby nose that looked like it might have been broken a few times. He was dressed like most of the other guys, saggy jeans, plaid shirt, leather jacket. Imaginative.

"Thank you for meeting us here," Suzanne said.

Smacky waved a hand. "It's no big deal. This is like my home away from home."

"Convenient," Toni said.

Suzanne leaned toward Smacky. "Junior tells us that you're somewhat acquainted with the so-called survivalist guys who are living out on County Road Seven."

"I don't know for a fact that they're dyed-in-the-wool survivalist guys," Smacky said. "But they do wear Army fatigues and stuff like that."

"How many men do you think are living there?" Suzanne asked.

"I don't know," Smacky said.

"Three or four? More than a platoon?" Toni asked.

"Not sure," Smacky said.

"Do you know if they're into drugs?" Suzanne asked.

"You mean *using* drugs?" Smacky reared back, eyes open wide, mouth pulled into a surprised oval as if the very idea of illegal drugs appalled him. It was an amazingly unconvincing performance. Suzanne could barely keep from laughing out loud. "I wouldn't know about that," Smacky finally mumbled.

"Well, what *do* you know?" Toni asked.

Smacky lifted both hands in a what-can-you-do gesture. "I only ran into a couple of those fellas because I rode my Fat Bob over to Crown Cycle in Jessup to get a new carburetor."

"A Fat Bob?" Suzanne said, not understanding the reference.

"His Harley," Junior explained.

"So these are biker guys?" Suzanne asked Smacky. She was even more interested now.

"The guys I ran into had decent rides, yeah," Smacky said. He puffed out his chest. "Not nearly as nice as my Fat Bob."

"Did you actually talk to these guys?" Suzanne asked.

Smacky lifted a shoulder. "We talked bikes, yeah. For a few minutes anyway."

"Okay, we were under the impression that you *knew* these guys," Suzanne said. She eyed Junior as she said it and frowned at him.

"Um, not really," Smacky said. His eyes wandered in the direction of the stage and he said, almost sheepishly, "Jeez, is that Lucinda up there?"

"Luscious Lucinda," Junior said. He was goggling at the stage where a dusky, raven-haired woman pranced about in a pink teddy and thigh-high leopard print boots. "Our own cat woman. Meow."

Toni made a face. "I think I'm going to be sick."

"Okay, thanks a bunch," Suzanne said as the two men eased their way out of the booth, their eyes never leaving the stage. She gazed at Toni and said, "This turned out to be a big nothing."

Toni shrugged. "Sorry."

"Not your fault."

"That guy Smacky is dumber than a socket wrench," Toni said. "Dumber than Junior."

"He was not particularly . . . helpful." Suzanne decided to leave it at that.

"Do you think we should drive over to the compound he mentioned and take a look around?" Toni asked.

"I think we've done enough investigating for tonight," Suzanne said as a guy in a plaid shirt, leather vest, and string tie strolled up to their booth.

"Care to dance?" plaid shirt asked Toni.

"I'm sorry, we were just leaving," Suzanne said, answering for her.

"We might be able to stay a little longer," Toni said, batting her eyelashes at the guy. Toni's general attitude was: if a reasonably attractive guy puts a move on you, why not give him a little consideration?

"No, we really do have to go," Suzanne said. "It's getting late."

"What are you, her mother?" plaid shirt asked with a curled lip.

"No, her parole officer," Suzanne said smartly.

The guy gaped at Toni. "A bad girl, huh?" Then he gave her a thumbs-up. "Way to go, babe."

They pushed their way back through the crowd and escaped Hoobly's Roadhouse just as a second dancer took the stage and "Rack City" by Tyga began blasting over the speakers.

CHAPTER 11

SUZANNE was busy with breakfast service this Wednesday morning, tempting customers with cheese omelets, apple and pecan hotcakes, breakfast tacos, and ham-and-apricot-jam biscuit sandwiches. But as charming and welcoming as she could be, her brain was still humming a mile a minute as she tried to conjure up a prime suspect for the shooting and pharmacy robberies. She'd thought carefully about Ed Noterman, Birdie, Robert Stryker, and the survivalist guys. She had even given brief consideration to Smacky himself.

Her reverie came to an abrupt end as Reverend Ethan Jakes from the Journey's End Church strolled into the Cackleberry Club. And this morning Jakes wasn't alone as he usually was, ducking in for a modest breakfast consisting of a toasted English muffin and cup of black coffee. No, today Jakes was accompanied by two young men, neither of whom Suzanne had ever seen before.

What's this about? Suzanne wondered as she watched the trio sit down at a table near the window. *Who are these newcomers? Friends? Relatives? Ministers in training?*

She was across the café in a flash.

"Suzanne," said Reverend Jakes, brightening when he saw her. He was a soft-spoken yet stern-looking young man. "Good morning to you. I wanted to stop by and personally thank you for that glorious basket of scones and muffins you folks sent over to celebrate our new program at the Journey's End Church. And then I thought, what better way to express my appreciation than to bring the program directly to you?" He indicated the two young men sitting with him, neither of whom looked more than twenty-one or twenty-two years old.

"Excuse me?" Suzanne wasn't quite following. What program was Jakes referring to?

"These are our first two enrollees," Reverend Jakes said, pride obvious in his voice. "May I introduce Billy Brice and Loren Redlin." He paused. "Boys, this is Suzanne Dietz, a very kind lady and owner of the Cackleberry Club."

"Nice to meet you," Suzanne said, nodding at the two young men. "And welcome to Kindred."

The two young men ducked their heads and mumbled faint hellos.

"Now, what can I bring you gentlemen for breakfast?" Suzanne asked even as her curiosity continued to build.

"What's good?" Billy Brice asked. He was skinny to the point of emaciated, wearing a tight chambray work shirt and slim-cut jeans. His gray eyes were like a pair of ball bearings and his hair was slicked back. He seemed infused with nervous energy and his hands and feet never stopped moving.

Loren Redlin was just the opposite. A taciturn dark-haired young man who barely looked up. Or maybe, Suzanne decided, he'd just rolled out of bed and still had a case of morning brain fog.

"Our hotcakes have been going like hotcakes, and our cheese omelets and French toast with turkey bacon are big favorites," Suzanne said. "But we're also serving a sausage scramble, eggs

Benedict, and our usual toast and English muffins with home-made rhubarb jam."

After a short conversation with Jakes, the boys ordered sausage scrambles and Jakes had his regular English muffin and coffee.

Suzanne dropped the order slips with Petra, grabbed a sticky roll for another customer, boxed up two takeout orders, and put on a fresh pot of coffee. When the orders for Jakes and company were up, Suzanne was happy to see that Toni grabbed the plates and hustled them over to their table. Perfect.

It wasn't until the two young men finished their breakfasts and wandered into the Book Nook to look around that Suzanne circled back to ask Reverend Jakes exactly what kind of program he'd started at the Journey's End Church.

"It's a rehab program for first-time drug offenders," Jakes said in a smooth voice.

"Um . . . excuse me?" Suzanne said. She wasn't sure she'd heard him correctly. *Drugs? Are drugs rearing their ugly head in our community yet again?*

Reverend Jakes favored Suzanne with a tolerant smile. "I know it's not the most popular thing. A lot of people hear the word drugs and they immediately think coke heads, pill poppers, dealers, and outlaws—the whole ball of wax. But these guys, my guys, are first-time offenders and genuinely committed to staying clean."

"Are you absolutely sure about that?" Suzanne asked.

Jakes clasped his hands together. "They're studying the Bible, praying, and working hard to turn their lives around. I think . . . I *know* . . . that they deserve this second chance and will definitely *earn* it."

"Second chance. What does that mean?" Then the answer popped like a soap bubble in Suzanne's brain. "Wait a minute, had they been sentenced to jail terms?"

"I'm afraid so," Jakes said in a solemn tone. "Not jail per se, but court-ordered incarceration at a workhouse. Which is why I hastened to intercede. Those two boys are certainly not going to be rehabilitated and have their lives set straight in any kind of county workhouse. Just the opposite in fact. What they need most at this point is emotional and spiritual guidance."

Suzanne was not only weirded out by this turn of events, she felt totally unsettled. "You do know about the murder of Harold Spooner and the two pharmacy robberies, don't you?" She couldn't help herself. It was important to bring it up whether Jakes was offended or not.

"Suzanne . . ." Now Reverend Jakes's voice carried a distinct *tone*. "My guys have only just arrived and are still feeling their way around. So I know . . . no, I *guarantee*, that my men were in no way involved in either of those events."

"A shoot-to-kill is more than just an event," Suzanne said. "It's a death, a tragedy."

"Yes, of course it is," Jakes said. "But I know my boys. And I can promise you they are fine young men."

"Except they were here," she said. "They were living . . . where? In the downstairs part of your church when the shooting and robberies occurred? Were you with them? Overseeing their every move?"

"I'm not about to stifle these young men, Suzanne. Because I do trust them."

"So you weren't there."

"Like I said, I trust them."

SUZANNE was in the kitchen, dicing onions for Petra's crab tacos, when she got a call from George Draper at the Driesden and Draper Funeral Home. Draper, in his somewhat mournful funeral director's voice ("Sorry, so sorry for this last-minute call"), wanted to know if the Cackleberry Club could cater Harold

Spooner's visitation tonight. Nothing fancy, just coffee, cookies, and bars.

Suzanne put a hand over the receiver while she checked with Petra.

"Is this a paying gig?" Petra asked.

Suzanne cocked her head to one side and said, "Excuse me. Have we met?" Suzanne had a well-earned reputation for watching their bottom line like a hawk.

"Okay, as long as our food costs are covered and there's some spiff in it for us. Then we can surely help out," Petra said.

"We'd be happy to," Suzanne told Draper. "What time? Okay, got it." Suzanne hung up and said, "It's not a huge profit but it's some kind of profit." She was particularly adamant about earning a profit versus just making a living. This was a key concept that a lot of small businesses didn't seem to grasp. Some big businesses, too.

"Speaking of money," Petra said, "between the tea party and the silent auction yesterday, it looks like the library took in almost fifteen hundred dollars."

"That's wonderful."

"Maybe we can do it again some time?"

"I think that's a given," Suzanne said. She gazed through the pass-through at the glass pie saver that held a dozen peanut butter cookies. "We're going to need more cookies for tonight."

"That's a given, too," Petra said. "I think I'll bake a batch of chocolate chip cookies and then a pan of lemon bars. How's that sound?"

"Like a lot of calories. But in a good way."

OUT in the café, Suzanne said, "Toni, can you help out tonight at Harold Spooner's visitation? We've been tapped to do the catering."

"No problem," Toni said. She placed a brownie on a plate, cut it into quarters, and popped one of the quarters into her mouth. Chewing enthusiastically, she said, "How come you were giving the stink eye to those guys Reverend Jakes brought in?"

"Because they're members of his little drug rehab program for first-time offenders," Suzanne said.

Toni swallowed hard, practically choking, and said "Get out of town!" Then, "You know who those dudes are, don't you?"

"What do you mean?"

"They're the motor heads who were driving that old Mustang. The car that caused such a big disturbance yesterday. So. They're in a *program*?"

"Jakes explained the whole thing to me. Said he rescued them from the clutches of the county workhouse and intends to give them spiritual and emotional guidance. Told me he trusted those boys implicitly."

"And Jakes knows all about Spooner's murder and the robberies?"

"Oh yeah."

"And he's still letting those deadbeats *live* in the church?"

"You got it, sister."

Toni was stumbling over her words now. "But they could . . . might even have . . . um . . . shot Spooner and stolen the drugs. I mean, we don't know these guys from Adam and suddenly they're here in town and we've got . . ."

"Trouble in River City," Suzanne finished.

"Along with a whole raft of suspects," Toni said. "Think about it. We've got a trucking guy who specializes in distribution, which is kind of suspicious right there, a bunch of dim bulb survivalists who are preparing for World War Z . . ."

"And we've got an orderly at the hospital who may or may not be a natural-born killer. Now, to top it off, we've got druggies living in the church right next to us," Suzanne said.

"Did we leave anybody out?" Toni asked.

"What about Smacky? And Birdie?" Suzanne asked. "Smacky was playing it cool last night, but he could be tight with those survivalist guys. And we know Birdie is a BFF of Noterman's."

"But you said the guy you saw was tall. Smacky's like the size of a hobbit and Birdie is pretty short, too," Toni said.

"Sure, but they could be accomplices. What if Smacky set up the robbery with his survivalist pals? Or Birdie was a willing partner with Noterman?"

"So the plot thickens," Toni said.

"And my head is starting to hurt," Suzanne said. "If I think about this any harder I'm going to need a brain transplant."

"That's quite futuristic," Toni said. "It could actually happen someday."

"Probably not soon enough."

CHAPTER 12

ALL through lunch, as they served chicken club melts, pecan chicken salad, and mushroom and cheese personal pizzas, Suzanne and Toni were buzzing back and forth.

"What if one of those soon-to-be-rehabbed guys objects to being rehabbed?" Toni asked.

Suzanne couldn't agree more. "What if he suddenly found himself in a small town filled with fairly trusting folks and decided to pull a quick drug heist? And then, because he got away with it so easily—even shooting poor Harold—he staged another robbery the next day? To keep everyone off-kilter."

"That's the exact same scenario that's been rattling around in my brain," Toni said. "And here's another thought—before our outlaw guy pulled those quick and easy heists, what if he hi-hoed himself to the local Army surplus store and bought himself a nice shiny black jumpsuit?"

Suzanne's eyes widened. "Jeez, Toni, we should go over to the local surplus store and check it out!"

"I kind of like that funky old place. Count me in."

Petra slid an order of pecan chicken salad through the pass-through and said, "What are you two plotting now?"

"Nothing," Toni said, trying to sound innocent but looking guilty.

"Okay . . . whatever," Petra said. "But you both promise you'll show up at the visitation tonight and help out, right?"

"We'll be there," Suzanne said.

By two o'clock lunch was over and Petra was in full baking mode. She was chopping walnuts, zesting lemons, mixing flour and eggs together, and preheating her oven. Suzanne propped open the swinging door to the café to keep an eye out for afternoon customers as she, Toni, and Petra talked over the menu for their first ever Saturday night gourmet dinner. Petra had suggested a French brasserie menu and a name for the event—Petit Paris—which Suzanne had eagerly seconded.

"And we're serving oafs?" Toni asked.

"No," Petra laughed, "they're *oeufs*. Eggs. And our *oeufs* will be in the form of egg shooters."

Toni wrinkled her nose and aimed a finger at her mouth in a gagging motion.

"They're not what you think they are," Petra said.

"What do you think I think they are?" Toni asked. Before Petra could answer, she said, "Honey, I *know* what egg shooters are. A raw egg plopped in a glass of whiskey. I saw a bartender make one in a bar once. Blech."

"That's a boilermaker," Suzanne said. "Actually, the egg shooters, the *amuse bouche* that we plan to serve, are more like ultra fancy deviled eggs. You substitute crème fraiche for the mayo, top them with pickled peppers, and add a dollop of caviar."

"*Fish* eggs?" Toni asked. "That's even worse."

Petra waggled a finger at her. "Don't do that gagging thing again."

Toni scrunched up her face instead.

"Then duck wings *à l'orange* followed by mixed field greens with champagne vinaigrette," Petra said.

"Sounds about right," Suzanne said.

"What about our entrée?" Toni asked. "It's gotta be something super special, right?"

Suzanne glanced at Petra, who was expected to take the lead in this. "Petra?"

"I'm still thinking petite filet mignons," Petra said. "But done on a grill outside so they have a nice char on them."

"I think we can arrange that," Suzanne said.

"Then maybe with some kind of sauce and definitely a side of *pommes frites*."

"Fancy French spuds," Toni said.

"And you'd mentioned a peach and almond tart for dessert?" Suzanne asked.

"Let's do it," Petra said as Toni nodded her approval.

"So we're set," Suzanne said. "Petra will draw up an ingredients list and put in our orders. Toni, you call Bud Nolden and see if we can borrow that supersized grill of his. And I'll noodle around ideas for the decorations and wine."

"I guess with this kind of menu we won't be serving any wine coolers out of a box," Toni said.

"Gotta serve the good stuff," Petra said, sliding two pans of cookies into the oven.

"Toni, how many tickets have we sold for Saturday night?" Suzanne asked.

"Almost all of them," Toni said as she ran a finger around a mixing bowl, trying to scrape up the last bits of cookie dough. "We've got . . . um, lemme think, three . . ." She licked her fingers and squinted her eyes. "No, there are four seats left."

"Almost a sellout, then," Suzanne said. She jumped to her feet just as several loud knocks sounded on the back door. "I wonder who . . . ?" She opened the door and was surprised to find the two guys from the Journey's End Church standing on the back steps.

"Reverend Jakes told us to come over here and help out," Billy Brice said. He held a long, curved blade that looked like a machete.

Startled by the machete, practically at a loss for words, Suzanne squeaked out, "Help out with what?" She wasn't sure she wanted these two overage juvenile delinquents anywhere near the Cackleberry Club.

"Jakes told us we're supposed to clear away the underbrush," Brice said. "You know, that big tangle of buckthorn you got in your back woods. And maybe some of that wild grape vine. It's gonna climb up into the trees and strangle the branches if you don't cut it back."

"Spring cleanup," Redlin added. "Helping people out, working in the community, is supposed to be part of our program." He didn't look happy.

Suzanne glanced past the two men. There was a ton of brush that had spurted up in the woodlot that bordered the farm field in back. In fact, the farm across the way was actually her farm, property she owned and leased to a farmer named Ducovny. It was also where she kept her horse, Mocha Gent, and her mule, Grommet.

"Okay, then," Suzanne said, deciding there was no harm in putting a couple of young guys to work. "I guess you fellows can have at it."

"Right, ma'am," Redlin said, shooting her a quick salute.

"I've been ma'amed," Suzanne told Petra as she closed the door. "Those guys ma'amed me. They think I'm old."

"None of us are exactly spring chickens," Petra said.

"I know. But . . ."

"Count your blessings, Suzanne. Because you're engaged to a

younger man." Petra gave a slow wink. "You've got a good thing going there, girlfriend."

SUZANNE waited on a few customers who'd come in for tea and scones, then went into the Book Nook to unpack two boxes of books that had arrived that morning. One box was filled with copies of *Rapturous Rendezvous*, the newest release from Carmen Copeland, a local romance writer. The other box was filled with an assortment of children's books.

Suzanne checked her computer to see what other books were due in, unpacked and shelved the romance novels and kids' books, then grabbed an X-acto knife and broke down the cartons. She hauled them through the café and into the kitchen.

"I'm taking trash out," Suzanne told Petra. "Got anything? Tomorrow's pickup day."

"Just that one bag," Petra said, nodding toward a black plastic bag that was nearly bursting its seams. She'd already put a twist tie on it.

"Okay."

Suzanne hauled the cardboard and bag of trash outside and over to their trash bin. Once she'd stashed it all away, she took a few minutes to stand in the sunlight and savor the day. The temperature was hovering around sixty degrees with just a few poufy clouds scudding across a robin's egg blue sky. Spring had finally arrived after a cold, punishing winter. And did it ever feel good. The wild roses on the back trellis already had tiny green buds and the grass bordering the back parking lot was also greening up nicely. Maybe this was the year for that herb garden she was always threatening to plant. Some basil, dill, fennel, and chives. It would all be wonderful on eggs. She stepped onto the grass, walked past a small grove of poplar trees. In fact, the garden could go right over . . .

"Did ya come to spy on us?" a voice at her elbow asked.

Suzanne spun around and came face to face with Billy Brice. His gray eyes drilled into her and he had a smile . . . or was that the beginning of a smirk? . . . on his face.

"No, of course not," Suzanne said. She made an offhand flap in the direction of the trash bin. "I just brought out a bunch of trash."

"Too bad you didn't bring out a couple of beers," Brice said, edging closer to her. "A cool, refreshing beverage would hit the spot right about now."

She decided to ignore his words and said, "How's the work progressing?"

"It's hard."

"I guess Reverend Jakes is a tough taskmaster, huh?" Suzanne said.

"You sure seem like a nice lady," Brice said.

Suzanne didn't care for the direction of the conversation. "I'm sure Reverend Jakes will be asking about your work ethic," she said in a cool tone. "I'd hate to give you a low grade." She started for the door, but Brice moved quick as a cat to cut her off.

"Aw, don't be like that," Brice said in a smooth voice. "Not when we're just getting to know each other."

"I really don't think . . ." Suzanne began, just as Jimmy John Floyd's white panel truck chugged into the parking lot. *Will you look at this? Saved by an afternoon delivery.*

Brice glowered as Floyd jumped out of his truck and headed for them.

"Suzanne, you're just the person I was looking for," Floyd said. He stopped, saw the nervous expression on Suzanne's face, as well as the look of dismay on Brice's face, and said, "Is there a problem here?" He pulled himself to his full height and moved purposefully toward Suzanne.

Brice slunk away like a weasel from a hen house.

"Mr. Floyd, thank you," Suzanne said. "That guy . . ." She shook her head, decided not to dwell on it. Instead she said, "It's great to see you again."

"I got a call from Petra a little while ago. I understand you ladies have some special requirements," Floyd said. "As far as groceries and produce go."

"For our upcoming French brasserie dinner," Suzanne said. Then, "Come on in and you can talk to Petra about it."

Suzanne led the way inside, chatted with Floyd some more about the dinner, then handed him off to Petra. She slipped into the café, which was thankfully empty.

Toni was using the push broom to clean up any crumbs.

"How are those two dudes doing out there?" Toni asked. "Clearing up that tangle of buckthorn and sumac?"

"Working on it anyway," Suzanne said.

"That's good. I mean for them to keep busy like that."

"Let's hope Reverend Jakes keeps them super busy."

Suzanne went into the Book Nook, grabbed four books on knitting, and placed them on her small display table. Then she went into the Knitting Nest, gathered up some knitting needles, a dozen skeins of yarn, and a half-knitted scarf, and took it all back to the Book Nook. She made a nice arrangement that would hopefully sell a few knitting or quilting books and maybe even encourage a few local ladies to take up knitting. Petra loved teaching classes, after all.

When Suzanne came out twenty minutes later, Floyd was gone, Petra was packing her desserts into plastic containers, and Toni was running the dishwasher.

Okay, looks as if it's all quiet on the western front.

Just as Suzanne was pouring a cup of coffee for herself—she still felt like she needed something to steady her nerves—Sheriff Doogie strolled in. She poured a second cup of coffee and placed it in front of him as he sat down at the counter.

"What's happening out there?" Suzanne asked. "Having any luck?"

Doogie swept his hat off his head. "Not much. Just trying to run down a couple of leads."

She leaned on the counter and faced him. "What kind of leads?"

"Something I got from that new egg and cheese supplier . . ."

"You mean Jimmy John Floyd?"

Doogie nodded.

"He was just here. What about him?" Suzanne asked.

"I found out, by the by, that he was making a delivery to Lilly Anne's Café in Jessup when the Blue-Aid robbery took place. And that he witnessed a gray pickup truck with smoked windows go screaming out of town."

"A gray pickup. He was sure of that? Not a motorcycle?" More and more, Suzanne was convinced that the killer had escaped the hospital that night on some sort of motorbike, albeit a quiet one. Maybe . . . some kind of moped?

"When I talked to Floyd earlier this afternoon, he was quite clear about the truck. But he was nervous about telling me. I think he's afraid of possible repercussions."

"I don't blame him," Suzanne said. The gunman's menacing stare still weighed heavily on her mind. "But it's still a good clue, right? You can tap into the motor vehicle database and see who owns a gray truck."

"You know how many gray trucks there are in the tri-county area?" Doogie asked.

"A lot?"

"A shitload. For some reason black and gray are the hot new colors to come out of Detroit." Doogie pronounced it *Dee*-troit, just like the old Motown artists.

"Do you have anything else?"

"Maybe. The pharmacist at the Blue-Aid, Denny Studer, he . . ."

jeez." Doogie stopped and shook his head. "I shouldn't be telling you all this stuff."

"Yes, you should. Continue please."

"I . . . well when the gunman was knocking Studer around, threatening to beat him to a pulp, he happened to notice a partial tattoo on the guy's wrist."

"What'd it look like? The tattoo, I mean."

"It's weird. Studer said it looked like some kind of chemical equation. And him having a Masters degree in clinical chemistry besides his degree in pharmacy, he thought the equation might've been for cocaine."

"What?"

Doogie pulled a small orange spiral notebook out of his shirt pocket and flipped it open to a scribbled page. It read $C_{17}H_{21}NO_4$.

"That's the chemical equation for cocaine?" Suzanne asked.

"Yup. I looked it up on the Internet. Apparently a lot of guys—dealers and users—are sporting drug tattoos these days."

"This is going to sound really strange, but I've got two ex–drug users working in my backyard right now."

"Huh?" Doogie's hand twitched spasmodically and coffee sloshed onto the counter. He scrambled to stand up. "Seriously? You're not just jerkin' my chain?"

Suzanne crooked an index finger at him. "Come on back and take a look."

Suzanne pushed through the swinging door into the kitchen with Doogie clumping along behind her in his uniform and heavy cop shoes. Petra looked up from where she was cutting lemon bars into perfect squares and said, "Nothing nefarious going on in here, Sheriff, unless you're trying to cadge one of my lemon bars."

"We're just passing through," Suzanne said. "Be out of your hair in a minute."

Doogie nodded politely at Petra. "Smells good in here though."

"Darn tootin' it does. We're serving chocolate chip cookies and lemon bars at the visitation tonight. You planning to show up? A lawman like you, it's good for your soul to be around some praying," Petra said.

"It's on my to-do list," Doogie promised.

"There. Out there." Suzanne tapped the back window with a fingernail.

Doogie peered out at the two men. "And you say they're ex-druggies?"

"No, Reverend Jakes says they're ex-druggies. Claims he rescued them from a court-ordered stint at the county workhouse. Says he's going to reform them." Suzanne was aware that her throat felt tight and her words sounded jangled.

Doogie stared at her. "But you don't believe Jakes?"

"I wish him luck with these two. But still . . ." Her eyes drifted back to the guys in the backyard. Brice was whacking at buckthorn with his knife, really going at it, while Redlin was raking the twisted branches into a large pile.

"Huh," Doogie said, mulling over the backyard scene.

"Can you go out there and demand to look at their wrists?"

"That's not exactly doing things by the book."

"When did you ever go by the book?" Suzanne asked.

"Suzanne, don't push me. And for gosh sakes, don't *you* go out there and start demanding they shove up their sleeves."

"I won't," she said. *In fact, I plan to keep a safe distance.*

Doogie continued to stare at the two men.

"You're scratching your head," Suzanne said. "Does that mean you're suspicious?"

"No, it means my head itches."

"You have to admit, two ex-druggies turning up in a small

town that just experienced a murder and two drug heists is a huge coincidence."

"And I don't much care for coincidences," Doogie said.

"What do you think? Could one of them be our guy?"

"You mean *my* guy. Yeah, I suppose it's possible. But I need more than the random suspicion of a jumpy neighbor." He favored her with a sad smile. "That'd be you. The jumpy neighbor and all."

Suzanne continued to stare out the window. "Drugs," she murmured.

"Stuff's all over the place now," Doogie said. "Bars, clubs, bowling alleys, even schools."

"It wasn't there when I was teaching," Suzanne said.

"Things are different now. Everything is rougher, meaner, a little more . . . out there."

Suzanne sighed. "What a depressing thought."

CHAPTER 13

SUZANNE and Toni cruised along Sparks Road, past Kindred's recently constructed industrial park.

"Isn't this where that stud muffin Robert Stryker was going to lease space?" Toni asked.

"He obviously did lease space," Suzanne said. She pointed to a temporary vinyl banner that said STRYKER TRANSPORT. It appeared that Stryker had leased eighty running yards of warehouse space that contained three truck bays. Next to his warehouse were self-storage lockers, a commercial printer, a scrapyard for reclaimed metal, and a truck terminal where Kenworth and Peterbilt trucks were pulling in, their air brakes hissing.

Sergeant Stan's Army Surplus was the next building over.

"Here we be," Toni said as they pulled into the parking lot.

Housed in an ugly, squared-off cinder block building, a red, white, and blue sign proudly announced SERGEANT STAN'S ARMY SURPLUS. Underneath, in small print, it said WORLD WAR II, KOREA, NAM, IRAQ.

"I hope they never have to add any more conflicts to their sign," Suzanne said as they pushed their way inside the shop.

Blaring fluorescent lights buzzed above tables mounded with dappled green uniforms, khaki packs, and lumpy-looking canvas bags. There were also tables full of desert camo as well as tents, folding shovels, canteens, and combat boots.

"I could outfit my own army here," Toni said.

"Help you find something, ladies?" asked a man who was standing behind a glass counter. He was slim, stood ramrod straight, and wore a navy blue T-shirt that said LAND OF THE FREE, HOME OF THE BRAVE. His camo pants were tucked neatly into lace-up boots.

Suzanne stepped closer to the counter. "What happened to Sergeant Stan?" She and Toni had been here last year, investigating possible murder weapons.

"Stan retired. Moved to Idaho. I guess he intends to hang out with all the survivalists."

At the word "survivalist," Suzanne lifted an eyebrow and gave Toni a look.

"So who are you?" Toni asked.

"I'm Colonel Fitzgerald—Colonel Fitz to my friends. This shop's under new management." He offered a self-satisfied smile. "My management."

"You gonna change the outside sign?" Toni asked.

"We're working on it," Colonel Fitz said. "Now, I should point out to you ladies that we're having a special on MREs this week." He'd moved flawlessly into his sales patter.

Toni bit. "M R whats?" she asked.

"Meals Ready to Eat," Colonel Fitz said. "Genuine military meals designed for maximum endurance and nutrition. Right now we have beef patty, shredded beef in barbeque sauce, chicken chunks, and maple sausage. All have a good-through date of twenty twenty-six."

"They last that long?" Suzanne asked.

"We're talking about the United States military," Colonel Fitz said. "They're not just excellent planners, they're smart little squirrels. Like to stash things away for later, just in case there's another . . ." He stopped abruptly and rubbed his hands together. "Now, what can I help you with?"

"We, uh . . ." For some reason, Suzanne had forgotten to come up with a plausible story.

As luck would have it, Toni stepped in to rescue her.

"My husband's birthday is next week and I was thinking of getting him a hunting knife," Toni said.

"What kind of hunting does he do?" Colonel Fitz asked.

Toni furrowed her brow, suddenly realizing that hunting wasn't exactly her forte. In fact, she didn't know ditz about hunting.

"Well, heh heh, now that you mention it, my husband's more of a . . . a trapper," Toni said. "Yeah, that's it. He sets out these little metal cages that he baits with stinky, week-old hamburger and tries to trap *wild* mink. Then he sells them to Heini Morlock over in Jessup." She glanced nervously at Suzanne. "You see, Heini's got his own established mink farm, but those are *ranched* mink as opposed to wild mink."

"Unless they were ranch mink that escaped," Suzanne said, trying to salvage the awkwardness of the conversation.

"Which I guess would then make 'em free-range ranch mink," Toni said.

Colonel Fitz's eyes were starting to glass over. "So a knife," he said.

"Right," they both said.

"What kind?"

"Big," Toni said.

"Back this way," Colonel Fitz said.

He led them past displays of jackets, webbed belts, tactical shatter-proof glasses, and field watches. He even had a rack of

Russian uniforms that looked like they'd seen better days. Sliding open a glass case, he reached in and pulled out a curved hunting knife with a serrated blade and rubberized handle.

"This is one of our finest knives," Colonel Fitz said. "The Grizzly."

"Nice," Toni said.

"The blade is high carbon stainless steel." The corners of Colonel Fitz's mouth twitched. "So there's never a dull moment."

"Clever," Suzanne said.

"Here," Colonel Fitz said, handing the knife to Toni. "Give it a heft. See how you like it."

While Toni hefted, Suzanne looked around the store and discovered a rack of jumpsuits.

"You carry jumpsuits?" she asked even though she was staring right at them.

"Are you looking for a gift for your husband, too?" Colonel Fitz asked. He didn't sound suspicious, more like resigned to waiting on two crazy women.

"Maybe," Suzanne said. "Do you carry any dark colors? Like black? These are all olive drab."

"What you see is what we got. Flight suits."

"And they look awfully small."

"Well, yeah," Colonel Fitz said. "These days a lot of pilots are somewhat smaller in stature. The boys in charge prefer it that way. Means they can pack a whole lot more tech and fire power inside a Tomcat or an F-16 fighter jet."

"There's a happy thought," Suzanne said.

ONCE they were outside, Toni clapped a hand to her forehead and said, "Did I sound like a babbling idiot in there or what?"

"Not any more than I did," Suzanne said.

"What a stupid story. About the mink, I mean."

"Actually, I think he pretty much bought it."

"And I bought myself a hunting knife. Which is good for what? Peeling potatoes? Whittling a stick?" Toni dug in her bag. "And the dude threw in a camo-colored Bic lighter as a thank-you gift. I don't even smoke."

"You're getting way too upset. You need to work at rebooting your emotions. Remember, we're attending a visitation tonight," Suzanne said. "The mood being *très* somber."

"Ugh. I hate going to funeral homes. I just can't get excited about looking at a dead guy's face covered in pancake makeup."

"I know, they never look real," Suzanne said.

"And what's with this *visitation* thing anyway? You sit there, but there's no way you can have a meaningful *visit* with a dead guy. I mean, it's kind of a waste of time."

"Toni, you really do need to reboot."

CHAPTER 14

THE Driesden and Draper Funeral Home wasn't exactly the most elegant building in town. In fact, with its turrets, finials, shabby gray paint, and blacked-out windows at the rear of the building (where they carried out the embalming process), the building looked ominous, a lot like the proverbial haunted house.

But that's where Suzanne, Toni, and Petra were at this exact moment. Fussing around in Slumber Room A—what George Draper called his Somnus Suite—hurrying to set up their coffee, cookies, and bars in anticipation of guests dropping by for the visitation.

Ah yes, the visitation. Harold Spooner, the deceased, was most definitely present and accounted for. In fact, he was lying in final repose at the opposite end of the room, spiffed up in a JCPenney charcoal three-piece suit and stretched out in an almost top-of-the-line walnut and brass executive-model casket. What George Draper called their Camelot Model.

"I wonder how many people will show up tonight?" Toni asked.

"A lot," Petra said as she unsnapped the lids of her plastic storage containers and carefully placed her lemon bars and chocolate chip cookies on silver trays they'd brought along. "And if these desserts aren't enough, I grabbed six dozen peanut butter cookies from out of the freezer. They should be thawed by now."

Suzanne knew that Petra always liked to be prepared. Maybe she should tell her about the MREs for sale?

"I think Harold Spooner was fairly well-liked," Petra mused.

"He was," Suzanne said. "I know for a fact that, besides his guard duties, the people at the hospital considered him a sort of goodwill ambassador."

Toni glanced toward the casket, gave a little shiver, and said, "Spooky in here."

The slumber room was dark and cool, with tall white candles and small red vigil lights flickering and throwing dancing shadows on the walls. Rows of black folding chairs looked like skeletal crows.

"Not to worry," Suzanne said. "In a few minutes there'll be crowds of . . ."

"Oh jeez," Toni said in a stage whisper. She was staring across the room, eyes wide in what was either shock or surprise. "I think that's Spooner's wife who just walked in. And his kids, though they're all grown up now." She pressed her arms across her chest and hugged herself tightly.

"His wife's name is Gloria," Petra said. She shook her head. "But I don't know anything about the kids."

"We should go up there and say a prayer," Suzanne suggested to Toni. "Then pay our respects. Be brave and beat the crowd."

Toni hunched her shoulders. "Do we have to?"

"I think we do."

Suzanne and Toni walked slowly up to the coffin and paused. Toni covered her face with her hands, but at the last moment, slowly spread her fingers open so she could peek at the body.

"You look like you're watching a horror film," Suzanne scolded. "Half scared out of your wits, but still anxious to see what happens."

"How's his makeup?"

"Pretty good considering the man is deceased."

Toni still had her face half covered. "Does he look sad?"

"No, he just looks like he's sleeping," Suzanne said.

"Yeah, but people generally don't take a snooze in a three-piece suit."

"Point taken."

Suzanne and Toni both mumbled short prayers and took a few moments to admire the many bouquets of flowers that formed a nice bower around the coffin.

"Pretty," Toni said. She wrinkled her nose. "Awfully heavy on the lilies though. I wonder why that is?"

"Tradition?"

Toni skittered away as soon as Suzanne turned to greet Spooner's widow and children.

When Suzanne introduced herself, Spooner's widow gently put a hand on her shoulder and said, "Mrs. Dietz? Thank you so much for coming." She was a soft-spoken woman with cottony white hair and sad eyes. She was wearing her best black dress and a tiny heart-shaped locket.

"Of course," Suzanne said. "You have my deepest sympathies, Mrs. Spooner."

"Gloria. Please call me Gloria."

"Gloria."

Gloria Spooner eyed Suzanne carefully. "You're the one who's got Sheriff Doogie's ear, aren't you?"

"I wouldn't go that far," Suzanne said.

"I've heard lots of nice things about you. That you're smart, that you have a good head on your shoulders." Now Gloria grasped Suzanne's hand.

"I don't know about that," Suzanne said, hoping this conversation wasn't going where she thought it was going.

Gloria's grip on Suzanne's hand increased. "Someone told me you're Kindred's own version of Miss Marple."

Suzanne was at a loss for words. "I don't . . ."

"Will you help me? Please?" Gloria's words poured out in a torrent. "I know you were there when Harold was shot. I know you saw the whole thing."

"Oh dear. Yes, I'm afraid I did."

"You were a witness, then. You saw the killer."

"But I didn't see . . ."

"Please," Gloria said. "I desperately need your help. I need . . . justice."

"I understand," Suzanne said.

"Just look at my poor Harold laying there. We were happily married for thirty-seven years."

Suzanne gazed at Harold Spooner lying in his bronze Camelot casket, then her eyes flicked to the doorway where a large group of people had just arrived. Among them was Ginny Harris, walking with a pronounced limp. *Damn,* Suzanne thought. *When the gunman shot Harold and Ginny he shattered a lot more than just those two lives.*

Suzanne turned back to the widow and said, "I can't promise anything, but I'll see what I can do. I'll try my best."

Tears sparkled in Gloria's eyes. "Bless you."

SUZANNE slipped between three rows of chairs to where Ginny Harris had settled herself.

"Ginny," Suzanne said, sitting down next to her.

Ginny's face cracked a sad smile as she leaned over and gave Suzanne a big hug.

"I'm so glad to see you," Ginny said. "I just knew you'd be here tonight."

"How are you feeling?" Suzanne asked.

"Well, as you can see, I'm out of the hospital. But my shoulder still hurts like crazy. Throbs as if somebody's beating a drum on it."

"I'm sorry."

"Ah, I expect I'll heal okay." Ginny paused. "I saw you talking to Gloria Spooner just now."

Suzanne nodded. "Paying my respects."

"She asked for your help, didn't she?"

"She . . . um . . . yes." There was no reason for Suzanne not to tell the truth.

"Good. That makes two of us."

"I told Mrs. Spooner I'm not sure what I can do."

"That's okay, I have faith in you," Ginny said. "I know you're nosing around behind the scenes and that you're doing your best."

They sat together for a few minutes, watching people stream in. It looked as if the entire town of Kindred was showing up for the visitation.

"Quite a crowd," Suzanne murmured.

"Lots of folks here from the hospital," Ginny said. "I expect there'll be even more of them at the funeral tomorrow morning."

"There's Birdie," Suzanne said, noting the woman's tentative movements as she walked in, the haunted look in her eyes.

"Poor Birdie," Ginny said. "She's, like, totally shell-shocked."

PETRA was gesturing frantically at Suzanne, so she bid goodbye to Ginny and hurried back to the goodie table.

"We need your help," Petra said in a panicked whisper. "We're starting to get overwhelmed. Toni's good with the coffee, but we need to keep things moving along. There's so many people here."

"Don't worry about a thing," Suzanne said. "I'll take over the serving."

"Okay. Oh, I've got those extra cookies in a plastic container under the table."

"Got it. Why don't you run along and join your prayer group, let me take care of everything," Suzanne said.

And Petra did just that.

Suzanne served cookies to Jenny and Bill Probst from the Kindred Bakery, Brett and Gregg from Root 66 Hair Salon, a whole bunch of hospital people, and almost the entire city council. Even Sheriff Doogie and his two deputies made their way over.

Suzanne stood poised with a pair of silver tongs. "What can I get you, Sheriff? Lemon bar, chocolate chip cookie, or peanut butter cookie?"

"I haven't had a lick of dinner yet, so I wouldn't mind one of each."

"You got it," Suzanne said.

Ten minutes later, Jimmy John Floyd smiled at her and gave a hopeful glance at a lemon bar.

"Here you go," Suzanne said, putting his bar on a small pink paper plate. She glanced around. Most of the guests had taken a seat and were waiting to be led in prayer. Toni was futzing with the valve on the coffee maker. Suzanne decided it was a good time to talk to Floyd.

"I understand you saw a gray pickup truck go flying out of town right after the Blue-Aid robbery," Suzanne said.

Floyd looked at her, a little frightened. "I did. And I told Sheriff Doogie all about it. As much as I could possibly remember that is."

"Were you able to catch a glimpse of the driver's face?"

Floyd shook his head. "Unfortunately, no."

"License plate?"

"No," Floyd said. He looked mournful, as if he knew he'd somehow screwed up or could have saved the day with a little more effort. "Unfortunately, I thought it was just kids hot-rodding. I didn't know there'd been another *robbery*. If only . . ." He sighed and shook his head again.

"That's okay," Suzanne said. "Remembering the truck is still a good lead. You did the best you could."

Things calmed down once Reverend Strait showed up and led everyone in prayer. He breezed through a couple of Bible verses, led them in a heartfelt rendition of the Lord's Prayer, and then asked everyone to join together in singing "The Lord is my Shepherd."

Suzanne was moved. The prayers, and especially the song, felt peaceful and personally meaningful, as if the whole town was united in their sorrow. Their voices rose and filled the room:

He restores my soul
Thank you, Lord

When the last note died, folks stirred in their seats for a few moments, then began heading for the exit.

Good, Suzanne thought. *I can pack up now and head home.*

But as she was transferring a lone lemon bar to a plastic container, Ed Noterman, the orderly that Doogie viewed as a possible suspect, walked up to the table.

Suzanne glanced at Noterman and thought, *Maybe, if I squinted a little, he could be the right guy. Or maybe not.*

"Suzanne," Noterman said. "A word?"

Suzanne gave him a pleasant smile. "Sure."

"Privately?"

"I guess," Suzanne said. Now she didn't feel quite so pleasant. She followed Noterman over to where a grouping of flowers created a small cul-de-sac. The whole time her mind was thinking, *Uh oh. What's this all about?*

When they were fairly sequestered from everyone else, Noterman glowered at her and didn't mince words.

"Are you pointing a finger at me?" he demanded in a harsh, ugly tone.

Suzanne was so taken aback by the resentment and rage he projected that she did the first thing that popped into her head. She lied.

"Of course not."

"Then why were you and Sheriff Doogie hanging around the hospital cafeteria yesterday? Goggling at everyone—particularly me."

Suzanne knew she needed a story and she needed it fast.

"I dropped by to visit Ginny Harris, then I ran into Sheriff Doogie and we had lunch."

"Why do I not believe you?" Noterman's face was growing so red it looked like the capillaries were about to burst.

Now it was Suzanne's turn to work up a head of steam. "What exactly are you implying?"

"Just that everyone's suddenly treating me like I'm a carrier for the Ebola virus. They're tiptoeing around me at work, basically ignoring me. And it makes me upset." His voice shook with anger.

"Maybe you're just being paranoid," Suzanne said. It came out sounding nasty, even though she hadn't meant it to.

"And maybe I really *am* under suspicion."

"Really," Suzanne said. "Shouldn't you take this issue up with Sheriff Doogie?"

"Don't worry, I intend to. But *you're* the one who was staring at me like I'm some kind of sideshow freak."

"I didn't mean to."

But Noterman kept battering away at her. "I feel like this is some kind of witch hunt. That you're accusing me of crimes I didn't commit."

"I'll tell you what. I promise to leave you alone no matter what. But I would like you to answer one simple question for me."

"What's that?"

"Do you own a motorbike?"

Noterman was taken aback for a moment. Then he snarled, "Yeah, I do. So what?"

"So that's all I need to know."

Suzanne spun lightly on her heels and walked away.

CHAPTER 15

"So that Noterman guy was giving you a hard time?" Toni asked.

They were standing in the dark next to Suzanne's car, ready to load up the leftovers.

"He's angry and scared," Suzanne said.

"Because he thinks he's a suspect?"

"Because he *is* a suspect."

"If Doogie was breathing down my neck with his hot doggy breath I'd be plenty worried, too," Toni said. She lifted the hatchback of Suzanne's Toyota and shoved in three plastic containers. "Done." She dusted her hands together and looked around. The night was black as pitch, trees shaking in a cool wind. No other cars were parked on the block. "Dark out," she said. "And spooky. With a crazy killer on the loose I don't really . . ."

WHAP. WHAP.

Something—or someone—was beating out a hollow, echoing sound.

Toni stiffened. "What's that weird noise?"

Suzanne cocked her head and listened carefully. There it was again, a faint *WHAP, WHAP, WHAPPING*. Drawing even closer this time.

"I don't know," Suzanne said. "It sounds like . . . something flapping."

"Like a giant bat?" Toni asked, hunching her shoulders and scanning the night sky. "Jeez, hurry up and get in the car. Lock all the doors." Toni rushed to the passenger side, grabbed the handle and pulled it open. Just as . . .

WHAP WHAP. WHIPPETY WHAP.

Louder now and practically on top of them.

Suzanne whirled around and was stunned to see a set of brightly flashing LED lights rapidly coming toward them. The lights strobed red, blue, white. Then the sequence repeated itself. Suzanne's brain improbably registered *UFO?* And then, thinking a little more clearly, *Noterman on his motorbike?* She was about to cry out for help, when a panting man whooshed by them. Running fast, checking his watch, not bothering to give them a passing glance.

Suzanne practically melted into the front seat with a sigh of relief.

"It was a jogger," she told Toni. "Wearing one of those new-fangled night vests. You know, to keep him safe."

"We need something to keep *us* safe," Toni responded. Then, "Did you see who it was?"

Suzanne shook her head. "No, but I gotta say, he had the same build as Noterman. Tall, kind of lanky. And the way he loped along . . ."

"That settles it," Toni said. "Noterman's our guy. I bet if we get in his face and brace him hard enough we can flip him like a pancake."

"Not so fast. What about those survivalists Smacky told us about? Don't you think there's an outside chance they're up to no good? Off in the woods by themselves. What do you think they're hiding?"

Toni shrugged. "Dunno. Maybe they're the ones who've been hijacking trucks. Or stealing drugs and gunning people down. If they're planning their own kind of extremist revolution, they might be desperate for money. Or maybe they're some rowdy outlaw motorcycle gang. We know for sure that some of them ride Harleys."

"Smacky didn't give us near enough information."

"What are you thinking?" Toni asked. "Maybe drive out there and take a look-see for ourselves? Do a hot prowl on the place?"

Suzanne thought for a few moments. "I think . . . possibly . . . yes. Maybe drive out there and take a look around. I mean, what could it hurt?"

It was a good twenty miles before they passed the bright neon lights of Shooting Star Casino and its crowded parking lot. The road was excellent until then, blacktopped, four-lane, and well maintained. After a few more miles, they crossed into Pope County and the road dwindled to a narrow, cracked, two-lane ribbon.

"You get out in the sticks like this," Toni said, "and everything gets kind of dreary."

"Not many houses around, either," Suzanne said. Every mile or so they'd see a twinkle of light from a distant window—maybe a farmhouse?—and then they'd be enveloped in darkness once again. She glanced left at a far-off radio tower with its blinking red lights. "Well, there's a radio tower at least."

"Reminds me of those things from *War of the Worlds*." Then, "I had no idea these guys lived so far off the grid. We could be lost out here forever."

"Let's hope not," Suzanne said as the road dipped and twisted and the woods closed in on them. Then the road abruptly dropped down and wound through a craggy ravine. When they emerged from that, the forest became increasingly dense, with oak trees almost forming a tunnel over the road. Could this road get any more forlorn? Suzanne reached down to flip on her brights and found they were already on.

"What's that?" Toni screeched as they swept around a turn. "Some horrible face that looks . . . ugh, like a gargoyle!"

Suzanne slowed her car to a crawl. A crumbling stone statue sat almost at the edge of the road. "It's a marker. For some kind of . . ."

Her lights picked out a number of strange hump-backed stones.

"Cemetery," Suzanne said. "Those are grave markers. A few tablets . . . and that stone thing you thought was a gargoyle is a kneeling, weeping angel."

"She looks awful sad."

"Probably because she's old as the hills and has been scoured for decades by snow, sleet, wind, and rain."

"Kind of like the postman," Toni said as she gazed out her side window. "Jeepers, this place looks abandoned."

"Needs some care, that's for sure," Suzanne said.

Toni continued to stare wide-eyed as they crawled past. "After a certain time cemeteries become the realm of ghosts and spirits, you know?"

"You don't really believe that, do you?"

"I do and I . . . Wait just a second. Slow down. I think I saw a mailbox."

"What?" Suzanne lifted her foot off the gas.

"Yeah. Back up."

Suzanne came to a stop and put her car in reverse.

"There. Over there. You see it tucked in among all those brambles?" Toni said. "It's a mailbox alright."

"Good catch," Suzanne said. "And there's a wooden sign. It reads . . ." She squinted at it. "CAMP DEFENDER."

"That's gotta be the survivalists!" Toni cried. "This has to be their hideout. See, there's even a road leading in."

"A pretty bad road at that," Suzanne said as she turned onto a dirt driveway that looked more like two parallel cow paths.

"Gotta check it out," Toni said.

They bumped along a deeply rutted road through stands of white oaks, poplars, and buckthorn, then twisted up a long, fairly steep incline.

"This land sure is humpty-bumpty," Toni said as trees crowded in closely and bare branches scrabbled against the car, sounding for all the world like sharp claws.

Suzanne slowed as they approached a narrow wooden bridge. "This part could be a little tricky."

Toni rolled down her window and the sound of roiling water filled the air. "That creek down there sounds deep and fast-moving. Better go careful," she said.

Suzanne crawled forward then slammed her foot on the brake.

"What?"

"Look at that," Suzanne said. "There's a gap in the bridge."

"Holy baloney!"

Suzanne put her car in park, got out, and walked to the edge of the bridge. There appeared to be a single plank missing. Other than that, the bridge seemed structurally sound. She walked back and slid behind the wheel.

"It's a missing slat that's only about six inches wide. My tires should go right over it," Suzanne said.

"Are you sure?"

"You want to walk in from here?" Suzanne asked as fat rain-drops began to plop down on her windshield.

Toni snuggled back in her seat. "I'd hate to get my hair wet, so no."

"Okay, then."

They rolled across the bridge, the wooden slats creaking and crackling beneath their tires. Toni held her breath the entire way. They drove on another quarter mile and when they saw a faint glimmer of light up ahead, Suzanne stopped the car and said, "We better walk from here. Are you still game?"

"I guess."

The ground felt soft and squishy underfoot for the first twenty yards, then turned to sticky mud. Rain continued to filter down.

"This is awful," Toni complained. She stopped and leaned against a tree to knock a few chunks of mud from her boots and nearly lost her balance when a nearby owl called *hoo hoo*. "You hear that?" She ran after Suzanne. "They got us surrounded. Those survivalists are scattered in the woods, signaling back and forth to each other."

"No," Suzanne said as she topped a rise and a cluster of buildings came into view. "I think they're tucked in tight for the night."

And they seemed to be.

Slowly, carefully, Suzanne and Toni crept along a rail fence made of peeling logs. They were moving through what had once been an apple orchard, the trees now gnarled and knobby. Stepping though knee-deep weeds, they closed in on the small cluster of buildings. There was a dilapidated old barn, two smaller buildings, a log cabin that looked half-finished, and an old farmhouse built in the American Gothic tradition. Restored, the farmhouse would have been a stunner, but the wood was silvered with age, the roof sunken in places, and the porch hung off one side of the house. There was a general air of neglect. None of the windows or doors looked level, which gave the house a curious lopsided look.

As Suzanne and Toni studied the old house, a bolt of lightning flashed across the sky and backlit the entire property. It looked like the opening scene in an old William Castle haunted house movie. All that was needed was blood dripping down the screen to highlight the credits.

Toni clutched Suzanne's arm. "Maybe we should forget about this?" Rain was starting to sluice down harder now.

"Just a few more minutes," Suzanne whispered. "I'd like to get . . . a little closer. Try to be brave."

"If I have to put on my big-girl panties one more time the elastic's going to snap," Toni said. "Besides, what if the survivalists grab us? What if they brainwash us and make us rob a bank like they did with Patty Hearst?"

"That's not going to happen," Suzanne said. She grabbed hold of Toni's arm, pulled her across a beaten-down patch of grass, and up onto the tumbled-down porch of the main house. Toni may have gotten cold feet, but Suzanne's curiosity was burning at a fever pitch. She couldn't help it, she had that curiosity gene embedded in her brain.

Together they tiptoed down the length of the porch, trying not to step on any broken or rotted boards, trying not to fall through. They stopped at a grimy window where a thin sliver of light shone through. Suzanne put an eye to the glass but couldn't see anything. The shade was drawn tight.

They moved past an old swing and tiptoed to the next window. Just as Suzanne leaned forward to peek in, Toni's foot hit one of the rotten boards. There was a *CREAK* and then a *CRACK* as it partly gave way and Toni's leg was plunged into squishy darkness up to her knee.

"Help!" Toni squeaked. "Help me."

Just as Suzanne turned to grab Toni and pull her to safety, the front door whapped open and a rectangle of light fell on the porch.

"Who's there?" a man's voice demanded. "Who sent you?"

Stunned by such a strange question, working fast, Suzanne quickly pulled Toni to safety and they both turned and bounded off the porch.

The man at the door was still shouting at them and waving his fist. His rumpled khaki T-shirt barely covered his stomach and he kept yanking up camo pants that threatened to slide down over his hips. To Suzanne he looked like a POW who'd been released after a long and arduous captivity.

"You heard me, what are you doing here?" the man shouted again.

He grabbed the waistband of his pants and started running after them. That's when Toni decided she'd had enough. She pulled out a couple of firecrackers from her purse, lit them with her Bic lighter, and tossed the firecrackers in the direction of the angry man.

The firecrackers sizzled and burned as sparks flew through the air like so many angry insects. Then they exploded—*BOOM!*— in a burst of noise, sulfur, and scraps of flimsy red paper.

The man who'd been chasing them suddenly flung himself down on the ground and covered his head with his hands. "No!" he sobbed. "Make it stop, please make it stop!"

Toni took a step back in sudden alarm. "Jeez, buddy, don't go all postal on us. They're only Black Cat firecrackers."

Suzanne was both stunned and fascinated. "You scared the beejeebers out of him," she cried.

The man continued to scream and moan like crazy, his pitiful cries starting to wake up the rest of the survivalists. Lights were going on in the main house's second floor and in a nearby cabin.

"We better split!" Toni cried. "Before we get blamed for starting World War III."

Suddenly an older white-haired guy came flying out of the barn. He shook a hand at them and yelled something, but Suzanne and Toni were already well out of earshot and headed for the hills.

That didn't stop the old man. He ran in little stutter steps, as though something was wrong with his leg, and jumped into a nearby Jeep. He fired up the engine and the lights blazed on.

"Holy cats!" Suzanne yelled as she heard the Jeep start up. "Somebody's coming after us."

They ran up the hill, flew over the mud, and hurled themselves into Suzanne's car. Out of breath and scared out of her wits, Suzanne turned on the ignition, negotiated a reckless turn, and took off in a flurry of leaves and mud. Behind them the Jeep's headlights flooded Suzanne's rearview mirror.

"Faster!" Toni yelled. "That guy is right behind us."

Suzanne punched it. She was flying through the woods, out-driving her headlights, her vehicle jerking to and fro in the terrible ruts. She prayed she wouldn't rip out the undercarriage of her car. Then, when she saw the bridge coming up, she cried, "Hang on!" as they blasted across it.

Toni had her hands over her eyes, screaming. "Is he still behind us? Is he still chasing us?"

Suzanne gunned her engine even harder and slalomed down the last hill. When she spotted the paved road up ahead, she slewed into a wide turn, tires gripping with all their might, and then, thankfully, they were back on terra firma.

"Go, go, go," Toni prodded.

And Suzanne did, fishtailing down the narrow highway, speedometer tracking up to fifty, sixty, and then seventy miles an hour.

"Be careful you don't hit something," Toni warned. "And please don't go all *Thelma and Louise* on me."

When Toni finally looked back and didn't see any headlights chasing after them, she did a faux wipe of her brow and said, "Whew. That left me shaken but not stirred. Who were those weirdos anyway? And why'd that one guy go apeshit over a few lousy firecrackers? I mean, they're like left over from Fourth of July."

"And that white-haired guy chasing after us in his Jeep," Suzanne said as she gradually showed down. "It was like something out of *Smokey and the Bandit*."

"Or *Dukes of Hazzard*," Toni said. "Who'd have guessed they'd freak out so badly?"

"Well, we were trespassing on their property." Suzanne punched on her heater and they were hit with a cozy wave of warmth.

Toni shrugged. "What's a little trespassing anyway? A misdemeanor at most?" She was starting to chill out and kick back, when her cell phone tinkled.

"Whoa. I hope those dingbats we just invaded back there don't have my number." Toni held her phone up, waggled it in the air, and said, "Just in case, I'm gonna put this on speaker, okay?"

"Sure," Suzanne said.

"Hello?" Toni said a bit stiffly.

"Toni? This is Deputy Robertson. I'm filling in for the night dispatcher at the Law Enforcement Center and . . ."

Toni relaxed. "How ya doin' there, Ralph?"

Deputy Robertson's voice was suddenly all business.

"Toni, you gotta come quick! Something's happened to Junior."

"What did he do now?" Toni asked. "Get caught fishing for muskies without a fishing license? Or did he jump up on the bar at Schmitt's and do a strip tease?"

"Toni, no," Robertson cried. "Somebody . . . they beat Junior up!"

CHAPTER 16

IT was like déjà vu all over again for Suzanne. Driving to the hospital, pulling up outside the Emergency Room, rushing in, feeling frantic and discombobulated.

"Where is he?" Toni cried as she sprinted through the doors and accosted the woman sitting at the reception desk. "Where's Junior?"

Suzanne put a hand on Toni's shoulder. "Take it easy," she cautioned. "If he's here you know he's probably okay. He's being taken care of, getting medical attention." As much as Toni complained bitterly about Junior's stupid antics, she was still crazed with worry and fear.

"I'm sorry," the receptionist said. "What's the patient's name again?"

"Junior!" Toni screeched.

"It's Junior Garrett," Suzanne said in a much calmer tone of voice. "We understand he was brought here by ambulance?"

The woman tapped a few keys and consulted her computer screen.

"Here it is, the assault and battery case. Mr. Garrett is in Exam Three and one of the doctors is with him right now. Then he's scheduled for X-ray."

"He *broke* something?" Toni wailed.

"That's what the doctor needs to determine," the receptionist said.

"Which doctor is handling this case?" Suzanne asked. She was pretty certain Sam hadn't been called in, but wanted to make sure.

"It's Doctor Reynolds," the receptionist said. "One of our residents."

"A resident?" Toni said. "Does that mean he's not really a doctor?"

"He's a doctor," Suzanne said.

"Please can I see Junior?" Toni begged. "Even if it's only for a second?"

"Best to wait," the receptionist said in a kindly voice. She obviously had experience dealing with frantic family members.

So they sat in the waiting room. Toni fidgeted while Suzanne glanced around. She noted that the chili con carne mess from Sunday night had long since been mopped up, though she saw that a different couch had been moved in. A green vinyl couch. One that was easily washable.

"This waiting, not knowing, is killing me," Toni said. She fidgeted nervously, grabbed a copy of *Hospital Today*, fanned the pages, and tossed it aside. She stood up and started walking in tight circles, like a caged animal.

"I'm sure it won't be long before they let you see him."

Toni flopped back down into her chair. "What a crappy night. First we gotta hang out at a creepy visitation. Then we invade a bunch of ex-military guys who turn out to be scaredy-cats—lots of luck if this country ever goes to war again. And now this. I could be home eating popcorn and watching hot reruns of *Temptation Island*."

"Come on," Suzanne said, trying to be upbeat. "I thought you lived for excitement. That you craved it."

"Well, sometimes. I mean . . . a good car chase is kinda fun."

THIRTY minutes later, they got the nod that they were allowed to see Junior. He'd already been moved upstairs to a room, so they took the elevator to the third floor, stepped out, and looked around. There was nobody sitting at the nurse's station and the hospital corridor was hushed and dim as they walked along, trying to locate Room 310.

"Couldn't they afford to turn on some lights?" Toni asked.

"Shh, it's late," Suzanne said. "People are asleep. Besides, I think . . . yes, this is Junior's room right here." There were voices coming from inside—maybe the TV?—so she knocked softly on the door.

Toni, on the other hand, kicked the door open with her metal-capped boots and barged right in.

Junior was sitting up in bed, bolstered by a half dozen fluffy white pillows and sipping a can of 7Up through a straw. The TV was on and an old James Bond movie was playing. Ursula Andress was rising from the ocean like some kind of exotic water nymph.

"Huh?" Junior said when he saw them. With a white bandage wrapped around his head, he looked like a lounging pasha.

"Junior!" Toni shouted as she ran to his bedside. "What were you *doing*? What were you *thinking*?" Then, "I was so worried about you!"

Junior looked happily surprised. "You was?"

"Of course," Toni said, even though she looked like she wanted to smack him.

"We were both worried," Suzanne said.

"Your head's all swaddled up like you're wearing a diaper," Toni said. "Are you hurt bad?"

"Ah, there's no concussion or anything. But the doc said I sustained a few contusions. That's doctor talk for cuts and scuffs."

"You had *stitches*?" Toni asked.

Junior motioned with his thumb and forefinger. "Just three or four teeny ones. They numbed me up good so I didn't really feel it when the needle went in."

Toni made a fist and shook it in his face. "I'd like to numb you up. You're always getting into trouble."

Junior pulled back from her. "Whoa, babe. Easy there. The *good* news is there's nothin' broken. No major organs damaged or gone kaput. Don't need a kidney transplant."

"More like a brain transplant," Toni said.

"Junior, what exactly happened?" Suzanne asked. "How did you get beat up? *Why* did you get beat up?"

"That's kind of a long story," Junior said.

"We've got time," Toni said. She sat down in the chair next to Junior's bed, plunked her purse on the floor, and stared at him.

"Well, I was minding my own business, reading a Marvel comic book and eating a Snickers, when I got to thinking about what I told you guys about long haul truckers," Junior said. "About how a lot of them are super speed freaks. And then I thought about the drugs that were stolen. So I went over to the office park where that new trucking outfit is . . ."

"Stryker Transport?" Suzanne said.

"That's the one," Junior said. "And I kind of prowled around. You know, nice and sneaky, like . . . like . . ." He glanced at the TV. "Like James Bond. Like a suave, international spy."

"But that place must have security," Toni said. "There must have been cameras."

"I never thought about that," Junior said in a rueful tone. "But you're right, they must have seen me on a closed-circuit setup. Because I wasn't tippy-toeing around for more than two or three minutes when a couple of tough guys, really big bruisers, came steaming out and started wailing on me with their fists. No questions asked."

"You *never* think things through, do you?" Toni cried. "You went sneaking around where you didn't belong and got the stuffin' beat out of you."

Junior squirmed uncomfortably in his bed. "You know me, babe. I can take a licking and keep on ticking."

"Wrong!" Toni cried. "Case in point, you got your clock cleaned."

Toni's voice was so loud and shrill that a nurse poked her head in the door and asked, "Everything okay in here?"

"Peachy," Toni said in a sour tone.

"So let me get this straight," Suzanne said. "You were creeping around outside Stryker Transport's warehouse?"

"Yup. Trying to figure a way in . . . until those guys came out and started punching me, hitting me with sticks, swearing at me. Somehow I managed to get away, staggered over to the Pixie Quick down the road and had the night manager call 911 'cause I was bleeding like a stuck pig." Junior touched a hand to the side of his face and said, "Jeez, now somethin' inside my mouth is starting to hurt. I think they might have knocked a tooth loose."

"That's the least of your problems," Toni said.

"I know," Junior agreed. "I was working on that wooden Eiffel Tower that you guys wanted me to build. Now I'm not so sure I can finish it."

There was a soft knock on the door and then Toni yelled, "What?"

A woman peeked in and said, "Is this a bad time?"

"For what?" Toni asked.

"I'm Mrs. Mickelson from Admitting. There's a small matter of some paperwork I need to finish up with Mr. Garrett?"

Mrs. Mickelson smiled tentatively, nervously. She was a short, plump woman wearing a purple floral dress. Her glasses were the size of pie plates and she held a clipboard in her hand. She looked tired, as if she'd been hard at it all day.

"It seems Mr. Garrett was admitted in quite a rush and the people in the ER didn't get all the details when it comes to health insurance. But it's my job to dot the i's and cross the t's." Mrs. Mickelson bobbed her head. "It's my job to see the hospital gets paid."

"Please come in," Suzanne said.

"Thank you," Mrs. Mickelson said. She advanced toward Junior, who was suddenly playing with the controls for his bed. He hit a button and raised the head of the bed, hit another button and the lower part lifted, folding the bed like an accordion.

"Look at me," Junior said. "I'm a human taco."

Toni whacked Junior on the shoulder. "Pay attention."

"I believe you and I met once before," Mrs. Mickelson said to Junior. She cleared her throat nervously. "You sustained a broken leg, I seem to remember?"

Junior reached down and rubbed his leg. "It still gets wonky when there's a storm brewing. I could probably go on TV and predict the weather."

"You couldn't predict breakfast," Toni muttered.

"Again, I'm sorry to bother you," Mrs. Mickelson said. "Especially at this late hour. But do you have your health insurance card handy?"

Junior's head lolled toward her. "Insurance? You bet." He waved at Toni. "Sweet cheeks, dig in the back pocket of my jeans and grab my wallet, will you?"

Toni pulled Junior's jeans from a nearby cupboard and dug around. "Here it is." She handed over a black plastic wallet laced with brown lanyard.

Junior fumbled around in his wallet, picking his way through dozens of cards, expired lottery tickets, and coupons. Every once in a while he'd pull something out, look at it, and chortle.

"How you doing there?" Suzanne asked. "Need any help?"

"I'm good. Workin' on it," Junior said. "Okay, this might do the trick." He handed a card to Mrs. Mickelson.

"Sir," she said. "This is a coupon good for six dollars off an oil change at The Grease Pit."

"Sorry," Junior said. "Try this."

Mrs. Mickelson shook her head as she studied the second card he handed her. "A frequent games reward card for something called World of Warcraft? No. Sorry."

"I think we're out of luck," Junior said. "Unless you'd accept this ticket for a meat raffle at Grumpy's Saloon. Who knows, you could win yourself a nice porketta package."

"Sir," Mrs. Mickelson said, "do you even *have* health insurance?"

Junior looked at Toni. "Do I?"

Toni shook her head.

Junior took another hit of 7Up, burped loudly, and said, "Oops."

IN the end Toni put one hundred and seventy-five dollars on her Mastercard and listed her apartment address as Junior's permanent home.

"But that's just to get you off the hook," Toni told him once Mrs. Mickelson had toddled off. "Don't get any romantic notions about us getting together again."

"I sure wish we could," Junior said. He grabbed Toni's hand and tried to pull her close. "You can even stay the night if you want. That plastic sofa over there folds down into a bed." He gave a quick wink. "Or you can jump in here with me, sweet cakes."

Toni shook her head. "Not on your life." Then to Suzanne, "I hope there's a *Divorce for Dummies* book out there somewhere 'cause I sure need it."

* * *

Suzanne dropped off a tired Toni at her apartment and then headed home. As she drove down curving streets past maples, oaks, and cottonwoods that were beginning to leaf out, she wondered why Junior had been targeted like that.

If he was snooping around Stryker Transport, then the guys that beat on him must have been Stryker's hired men. But why wail on Junior? What were they being so secretive about? What were they protecting? Or were they just extra jumpy because a truck had been hijacked last week?

When Suzanne pulled into her driveway and saw the lights glowing in the upstairs bedroom, she was flooded with a sense of relief.

Home at last.

She walked in, hung up her jacket, then knelt down to greet the dogs and let herself be showered with a dozen wet, sloppy kisses.

"Come on, guys, let's go find Sam."

Sam was lying in bed reading a book. Of course Baxter and Scruff immediately piled on top of the bed before Suzanne had a chance to stake a claim.

"Off, off," Suzanne ordered, clapping her hands together. "You've both got overpriced orthopedic dog beds. Kindly make use of them for once." Grudgingly, the dogs slunk away and she hopped on the bed and snuggled next to Sam.

As Sam put an arm around her, he glanced at his watch. "You're late. The visitation must have lasted a long time."

Suzanne nodded. "A lot of people showed up. Almost the whole town. And then Toni got an emergency call about Junior so we had to . . . deal with that." She decided to conveniently leave out their survivalist camp fiasco for now. TMI. Too much information . . . especially at bedtime.

"What happened to Junior?" Sam asked.

"He got beat up."

Sam wasn't a bit surprised. "Again? Was it bad?"

"Not really."

"Where's he now?"

"Overnighting at the hospital." Suzanne paused. "Aren't you going to ask *why* Junior got beat up? The circumstances?"

Sam shook his head. "Nope. All I want to do is finish these last two pages, then snuggle under the covers with you."

"That's the best offer I've had all day," Suzanne said. She sighed and slipped off the bed. "Two minutes, give me two minutes and I'll be right back."

"Forget about the book," Sam said, setting it aside. "And please try to cut your time down to one minute."

CHAPTER 17

IT was the morning of Harold Spooner's funeral at First Methodist Church and the day had dawned cloudy.

"Such a gloomy day," Toni said as she, Petra, and Suzanne walked into the church and took a seat toward the back.

"But so lovely in here," Petra murmured. Candles glowed on the simple wooden altar, scenes of Christ's life were depicted in lovely stained glass windows, and tiny Agnes Bennet, an octogenarian who'd played the organ for countless decades, was upstairs, pumping out the strains to "How Great Thou Art."

"I think this is going to be a standing-room-only crowd," Suzanne whispered to Toni as people continued to stream in and fill the pews. "Everybody in town seems to be showing up."

"Do you think the killer is here, too?" Toni whispered back.

Toni's words gave Suzanne a sudden jolt and she glanced around again, this time with a more speculative eye. "Maybe. I know the police sometimes watch for the killer to show up at the victim's funeral."

"They do that on TV," Toni said. "But here, in real life, who knows?"

The church continued to fill with mourners. All the pews ahead of them and behind them were now packed, and Suzanne noted that two of the ushers were straining to add three rows of folding chairs at the back of the church. Definitely a full house.

"Did you talk to Junior today?" Suzanne asked Toni.

"Just a quick phone call before we got here."

"How's he doing?"

Toni rolled her eyes. "Some better today. But he's begging like a little puppy to come stay with me while he recuperates."

"Are you open to that idea?"

"Frankly, I'd rather stick my head in a bear trap."

Petra looked up from her prayer book and gave a little shake of her head. Suzanne guessed they were probably talking a little too much for Petra's churchly sensibilities.

Okay, fine. But Suzanne's curiosity was warming and starting to build. Would the killer show up here? Was he one of them? Would he turn out to be a Kindred resident who worked as a mild-mannered banker or school teacher by day, but was a rabid drug thief and killer by night?

And then Suzanne remembered—the Blue-Aid Pharmacy had been robbed right smack in the middle of the day.

So maybe this guy's a part-time banker or school teacher. Or just a rabid drug thief. There's always that.

Suzanne squirmed in her seat, scanning the crowd even more carefully. When she looked three rows ahead of her, she spied Ed Noterman. He looked crabby and uncomfortable as he fidgeted in his wear-it-to-church-on-Sunday too-shiny blue suit.

Birdie Simmons was in the row just ahead of Noterman. Suzanne wondered how Birdie was faring. From what she'd seen so far, Birdie appeared fragile and nervous. Almost twitchy. But maybe, after getting beaten up like that, it would be difficult not to jump at every little noise and shadow.

Ginny Harris and several other people from the hospital were sitting toward the front of the church on the far left. They formed a good-sized contingent that had come to show their respect. Suzanne wondered why Noterman wasn't sitting with them. Unless the hospital people really were treating him as persona non grata. That's why Noterman had barked at her last night, that was his beef, but Suzanne wasn't sure if she'd believed him or not. But now . . . maybe she did. She stared at Noterman again. If some of the hospital people thought he might be guilty, maybe there was something there. After all, where there's smoke, there's fire.

There was a clatter at the back of the church and then a high-pitched squeaking of wheels.

The coffin had arrived.

The organ started up again—some kind of processional hymn—and then feet scraped and pews creaked as everyone in the church clambered to their feet.

Suzanne recognized George Draper, the funeral director, in his somber black funeral suit. He walked backward down the aisle, gesturing with his hands like the ground personnel who guided airplanes to the gate. Except in this instance Draper was supervising the transport of the coffin.

And then, slowly, very slowly, the coffin appeared, gliding down the aisle. A large spray of white roses and a tangle of baby's breath was draped on top. Tucked into the flowers was a white envelope that said HAROLD in spidery handwriting.

Four men that Suzanne didn't recognize—must be relatives—served as pallbearers. Following closely behind the coffin was Gloria Spooner, the newly minted widow, and Spooner's two adult children.

As everyone followed the progress of the coffin with their eyes,

Suzanne turned slightly and noticed that Sheriff Doogie had snuck in the side door at the very last minute.

Here to pay his respects? Suzanne wondered. *Or hoping to catch a glimpse of a killer?*

Reverend Strait stood at the front of the church, gripping the podium as he waited for the coffin to arrive. He was a distinguished-looking man with silver-white hair and an aura of kindness about him. When the coffin was finally seesawed into place, and the relatives had taken their seats, the rest of the congregation sat down and the prayers began.

Halfway through the service Spooner's daughter was invited to the podium, where she delivered a sad, stirring eulogy for her father. Then the director of the hospital took his turn. He praised Spooner for his friendly demeanor and can-do attitude. Talked about how the hospital was working in concert with law enforcement to bring this unfortunate incident to a close.

At that Toni turned to Suzanne and whispered, "Unfortunate incident? You notice how bureaucrats and politicians never man up and call it the way it really is? It's never a murder or a drug heist or a bloody assault. It's always an unfortunate incident. Sheesh."

There were a few more prayers then, and as a final tribute, Harold Spooner's thirteen-year-old granddaughter tiptoed hesitantly to the front of the church to play a violin solo for him. It was the song, "Shenandoah." The notes rose, haunting and pure, then fell among the congregation like gentle rain. Suzanne could almost hear the words in her head:

> Oh, Shenandoah, I long to hear you
> Look away, we're bound away
> Across the wide Missouri.

By the time the girl had finished, there wasn't a dry eye in the house.

* * *

WITH the funeral concluded, everyone milled about on the steps and broad sidewalk outside of church. Folks greeted each other, sentiments were whispered to Gloria Spooner, a few people had to dash off to work.

Ginny Harris saw Suzanne, waved at her, then scurried over to say hello.

"Suzanne." Ginny flashed a sad smile at her. "I figured I'd see you here."

"How are you doing, Ginny?" Suzanne asked. The bandage was gone, and Ginny's color had started to return to normal.

Ginny reached up and touched her wounded shoulder almost unconsciously. "Getting better every day." She dropped her voice. "How are *you* doing?"

Suzanne knew darn well that Ginny wasn't referring to the bottom line at the Cackleberry Club. She was asking about the investigation. The shadow investigation that Ginny hoped Suzanne was running.

"There are suspects," Suzanne said. "Just not a whole lot of evidence."

"But you're not going to give up on this, are you? All these people . . ." She gestured at the crowd around them. "All of us . . . I mean, we just laid poor Harold to rest."

Suzanne thought about the two guys from the Journey's End Church, the survivalists, Robert Stryker, and Ed Noterman. All of them seemed to harbor secrets, all of them felt a little hinky to her, a little suspicious.

"No," Suzanne said. "I'm not going to quit. Not yet anyway."

"Does Sheriff Doogie know that you're investigating?"

"Let me put it this way, if I start to push Doogie in a certain direction it's not exactly going to knock him for a loop."

"Good. Thank you, Suzanne," Ginny said. She looked back at

the church. "Harold getting murdered, me getting shot, the pharmacy in Jessup getting robbed . . . it's just been awful."

"It sure has." Suzanne held up a finger. "Ginny, will you excuse me? I see Birdie over there and I need a quick word with her."

"Of course. Oh dear, I hope the poor woman is some better," Ginny said, stepping aside. "She seems so traumatized."

Suzanne saw Birdie walking down the middle of the street as she headed toward a slightly rusted Ford Fiesta.

"Birdie," Suzanne said, a little breathlessly, picking up the pace as she tried to catch up. "I didn't get a chance to talk to you last night, but I . . ."

"Apologies, Suzanne, but I have to hurry home," Birdie said, still heading for her car. She got there, put a hand on the door handle, and turned back reluctantly. "I don't mean to be rude . . ."

"Of course not," Suzanne said.

". . . But my husband is waiting."

Suzanne could see that Birdie was shaking like a leaf. Was this what trauma did to a person? Kept them perpetually rattled and on edge? Is this what PTSD looked like? Or was it something else?

"I'm sorry, Birdie, I just wanted to see how you were getting along," Suzanne said.

"I'm holding my own," Birdie said. She pursed her lips, then said, "I'm trying hard to work my way past that awful night, really I am."

"Okay, then, apologies for taking up your time."

Suzanne glanced past Birdie and saw Sheriff Doogie talking to Ed Noterman. Doogie was doing the lion's share of the talking and his demeanor looked fairly intense. Noterman was frowning back at him and shaking his head.

"Bye, Suzanne," Birdie said as she climbed into her car.

Suzanne stepped away from her and gave a little wave. But something hadn't felt right to her. Was she mistaken, or had Birdie been doing her best to avoid her?

Suzanne didn't have a chance to mull that notion over for very long, because Sheriff Doogie suddenly broke away from Noterman and strode purposefully down the street in her general direction. He was heading toward his maroon and tan cruiser.

"Sheriff!" Suzanne called out to him.

Doogie hesitated and turned as a slow, reluctant smile spread across his face. "I was inches from a clean getaway."

"We need to talk," Suzanne said.

"Ya think?"

Suzanne did her best to project serious. "You do know that Junior got beat up last night, don't you?"

Doogie managed a faint nod. "I heard about it, yeah."

Suzanne spread her arms wide. "Anything? Are you going to do anything about it?"

"Doubtful. Fact is, Junior was probably the one who broke the law with his trespassing."

"But he was beat up. By some of Robert Stryker's people."

"We don't know that for a fact. It was dark, it could have been anybody. You can try to fancy up that area and call it an office park, but it's still a dicey neighborhood. There's a pawn shop down the block, plus a liquor store, and any number of junk car dealers. And what about Stenkie's Bar?" He shook his head. "Rough trade hang out there."

Suzanne decided to change the subject since she wasn't getting anywhere.

"What about the investigation?" she asked.

"Which one?"

"Both of them, all of them."

"I'm pushing every button I got." Doogie gazed past her toward the crowd that still hovered outside the church. "There are a few things I'm working on."

"Like what?"

"Like none of your business. I've probably said too much already."

"But what if . . ."

Suzanne's words were suddenly drowned out by a tremendously loud roar.

They both turned to see an honor guard of a dozen motorcycles lining up in front of George Draper's black hearse. A few of the riders were dressed in black leather motorcycle jackets, some were wearing Army-type clothing. All had American flags affixed to the fronts of their bikes.

"Spooner was a veteran," Doogie said, trying hard to make himself heard above the throaty roar of the engines. "Served at the tail end in Nam. He was just a kid when Saigon fell."

"I didn't know that," Suzanne said.

"I heard a rumor that these guys were going to escort his body to the cemetery."

As if someone had issued a silent command, the motorcycles began to roll forward. Suzanne and Doogie stepped to the side of the street so the bikes could pass.

Suzanne studied the men as they thundered by, picking up speed. *These men wearing Army clothing—could they be from the survivalist compound?*

And then she saw a familiar face. Smacky! Junior's friend from Hoobly's Roadhouse.

Taken aback, Suzanne wondered if Smacky was some sort of spy? After she and Toni had talked to Smacky at Hoobly's Roadhouse, had he gone back and told the survivalist guys all about her? Told them about this crazy lady who owned a little café? That she was beating her brains out, trying to solve a robbery-homicide? Had they popped a few brewskis and had a good laugh about it?

On the other hand, if she'd been made out to be such a comical figure, why had those survivalist guys gone apeshit last night over a lousy firecracker?

CHAPTER 18

"THERE'S so much to do," Petra said. "People will be banging on our door before we know it." She wound the strings of her chef's white apron around her waist and tied it securely. Then she turned on the industrial oven and set the temperature to 350 degrees.

The clock was already reading ten-thirty as Suzanne, Petra, and Toni bustled about the Cackleberry Club kitchen, cracking eggs, chopping veggies, getting out the pre-diced chicken chunks. Because it was already mid-morning, Petra had come up with what she termed a brunchy-lunchy menu. In this case, chicken hash, stuffed green peppers, mini pizzas, bird's nests, and cinnamon cake for dessert.

"What's a bird's nest?" Toni asked.

"A hollowed out mini loaf of crusty artisan bread stuffed with a poached egg, cheese, and veggies."

"Seems like you've got a lot going on. What can I do to help?" Toni asked.

"Buy me another hour?" Petra said.

"Sorry, no can do."

"Then grab the cinnamon cake out of the cooler and cut it into individual servings," Petra said.

"Generous servings?"

"Is there any other size?"

"These green peppers are all washed and cored," Suzanne said. "You want me to start stuffing them?"

"Naw, I can do that," Petra said. "You just line up a few plates." Petra sprinkled a generous amount of pepper into her lentil soup and said, "Suzanne, did you remember that I have my knitting group tonight?"

"Absolutely. And I plan to stay and help out."

"Thank goodness for that." Petra was already looking frazzled.

Suzanne hurried out into the café, turned the sign on the door from CLOSED to OPEN, and picked up a copy of the *Bugle* that had been delivered that morning.

"I'd stay, too," Toni said to Petra. "Except I gotta go see Junior."

"How is the little hell-raiser?" Petra asked. Right before the funeral began this morning, Suzanne and Toni broke the news to her that Junior had been beaten, spindled, mutilated, and ended up in the hospital.

"I talked to Junior on the phone and he said he's sore but a little better. Hey," Toni said as Suzanne walked back into the kitchen, carrying the newspaper. "The *Bugle* came. Anything interesting? Anything about the murder? The robberies?"

Suzanne raised her brows and placed the newspaper face down on the butcher block table. "I wouldn't know."

"Come on," Toni wheedled. She grabbed the paper, unfolded it, and let out a low whistle.

"What?" Petra said.

"Look at this headline," Toni crowed. "'Grisly Murder and Two Robberies!' Not only that, it's splashed across the front page in super humongous type! And get a load of this lead-in: 'After the masked gunman murdered Harold Spooner and wounded Ginny Harris, he escaped from the hospital and all but disappeared into thin air according to eyewitness Suzanne Dietz, owner of the Cackleberry Club. Ms. Dietz was not injured in the robbery.'" Toni lowered the paper. "Suzanne, you're famous! And what great publicity, huh?" She thunked the back of her hand against the paper. "A big fat mention on page one."

"It's terrible," Petra said.

"Wait, it gets better," Toni said, her nose in the paper again.

"It can only get worse," Suzanne said.

"There's just a few more paragraphs," Toni said. "Don't you want me to read 'em?"

But Petra had heard enough. "Toni, in a matter of minutes we're going to be feeding a hungry horde. So kindly put down that paper, get the garlic bread from the cooler, and wrap it in foil."

"Okay, okay, I'm motorvatin'," Toni said. But not before she snuck another look at the big story.

CUSTOMERS arrived just as Petra had predicted. All were hungry, most were curious. They'd either attended the funeral this morning, heard about it, or they'd read the sensational story in the *Bugle*. And it was clear that people were still worried. After all, there'd been no arrests.

Suzanne took orders, hustled them to Petra, and doggedly adhered to her strict "no comment" policy. And, for the most part, it worked.

The chicken hash and the stuffed peppers turned out to be the stars of the show. The small pizzas not so much.

"It's because they need more spice," Toni said to Petra when she dashed into the kitchen to grab an order. "You gotta toss on some garlic, jalapenos, and red pepper flakes. Call it something fun like the hot lips pizza."

Petra wrinkled her nose and said, "You think?"

Suzanne ducked her head in and asked, "How many stuffed peppers do we have left?"

"Not many," Petra said. "How many do you need?"

"I got orders for three."

"We got three. But that's it. That's all she wrote."

"That's all she cooked," Toni muttered.

Just as Suzanne was wiping down one of the tables, Robert Stryker strolled in. He still looked good. A sharp suit, something designer. Definitely not from Men's Wearhouse.

Suzanne threw a hasty glance at Toni and mouthed, "You or me?"

"Me," Toni mouthed back. "Let me take care of Jimmy Hoffa over there."

Toni made sure her shirt was primly buttoned, then walked over to Stryker and pointed to a vacant table. Her face betrayed no emotion, she was as mechanical as a robot.

Stryker flashed a flirtatious but slightly questioning smile at her. "Is it my imagination or is it a bit frigid in here today?"

"Gotta be you," Toni said.

"So what's good?" Stryker asked as he sprawled at his table.

"We got a special today that's not written on the chalkboard," Toni said.

"Oh yeah?"

"We call it the Cackleberry Club Cleanse. It's a triple patty butter burger topped with six slices of extra-thick bacon that comes with a side of cheese curds, deep-fried jalapeños, and *pico de gallo* sauce."

Stryker's eyes almost crossed. "Are you serious? Are you trying to give me a heart attack? Or indigestion? Or both?"

"Goodness no," Toni said.

Stryker ended up ordering the chicken hash and when it was ready, Suzanne delivered it to him along with a cup of coffee.

"Here you go," Suzanne said.

Stryker eyed his chicken hash and then he eyed Suzanne. "At least someone around here is in a good mood. The other waitress— Toni, is it?—nearly took my head off. I was expecting a little collegiality here today."

Suzanne jumped at the opening. "I'm afraid Toni's awfully upset. It seems her estranged husband was beaten rather badly last night."

"That so?"

"Interestingly enough, it happened right near your warehouse."

Stryker shook his head. "Tough area, I guess. Hope the guy's okay."

"So none of your employees reported seeing a prowler last night? Or mentioned that they started wailing on some scrawny little guy for no reason at all?"

A muscle next to Stryker's right eye twitched. "Haven't heard much of anything—except that another truck got hijacked over near Mankato. But hey, I'll be sure to ask around."

Suzanne stalked into the kitchen and said to Petra, "He darn well knows what happened."

"Who knows? What happened?" Petra asked as Suzanne brushed past her.

"With Junior. That guy Stryker probably beat him up. He or his men did." Suzanne gritted her teeth and shook her head. "Man, am I ever steamed." She stalked to the back door and ripped it open. A breath of fresh air was suddenly topmost on her agenda.

"You think those trucking people are covering something up?" Petra called to her. "Or were involved in the shooting and robberies?"

Suzanne heard Petra's voice in the background, but only faintly, because she was suddenly focused on something else. A long-stemmed red rose was lying on the top step. Underneath it was a white envelope with her name on it. She bent down and picked up both items gingerly. Sniffed the rose—it was luxurious—and opened the envelope. It was empty.

Strange.

Suzanne walked back into the kitchen and closed the door. "Petra, did you notice anybody making a delivery? Or see somebody hanging around out back?"

"No. Why?" Petra asked.

Suzanne held up the red rose.

"Oh pretty. Is that from Sam?"

"Doesn't say."

Petra's eyes twinkled. "Looks like you've got a secret admirer."

Or someone who went out of his way to flirt with me, Suzanne thought.

Yes, Suzanne suspected the rose might be from Billy Brice from next door. And she wasn't one bit thrilled.

AFTERNOON tea was underway, the air perfumed with the aroma of Indian Darjeeling and a mellow black tea from Ceylon. Petra had baked coconut-cherry scones today and made chicken salad tea sandwiches as well as traditional cucumber and butter sandwiches.

Suzanne had just poured a cup of tea for Sarah Jenkins and her two guests when Sheriff Doogie walked in. He was followed by a grim-looking man with a slightly florid complexion, thin brush mustache, and white close-cropped hair.

And he walks with a military bearing. Interesting.

Doogie cast a peevish glance at Suzanne, then his eyes lit on Toni. He lifted a hand and beckoned to both of them.

"Who, us?" Toni said.

"What?" Suzanne said, hurrying over. "What's wrong?"

"Is there someplace private where we can talk?" Doogie asked. He looked serious, a lot more serious than he usually was around a café full of scones, brownies, and glazed donuts.

"Let's go in the Knitting Nest," Suzanne said. She cast a quick glance around and decided they could let things ride for a few minutes. Then she walked in with Toni, Doogie, and the grim-looking man, and shut the door behind them.

Doogie didn't beat around the bush.

"Tell me straight," Doogie said to the man. "Are these the two crazy women who trespassed on your property last night?"

"They certainly are," the man said without hesitation.

Toni gave a long, drawn out, "Whaaaat?"

"Don't look so puzzled, ladies," Doogie said. "This is retired Major Allan Winston."

"Uh-oh," Suzanne said. She felt a sinking feeling deep in the pit of her stomach, and pretty much knew what was coming.

"The good major here runs a halfway house for vets with PTSD," Doogie said.

"Aw jeez." Toni slumped down into a nearby chair.

"And what you did last night, firing the gun or whatever it was . . ." Doogie said.

"Firecrackers," Suzanne said.

"Okay, the firecrackers that you ladies so wantonly tossed out . . . might have set some of Major Winston's guys back months in their treatment." Doogie jabbed at the air with his index finger for added emphasis.

"We thought they were crazy survivalists," Toni said.

Doogie placed his hands on his ample hips. "Where did you ever get *that* idea?"

Suzanne thought about mentioning Smacky by way of Junior, but figured the story would sound too preposterous. Instead she said, "We were operating under the theory that they could have been the ones who shot Harold Spooner and robbed the pharmacies. Look, you can't blame us for being suspicious. Those guys were hiding out in the woods, hunkered away from everyone. Who knew what they were up to?"

"I'll tell you what they're up to," Major Winston said. He could barely control his anger. "They're trying to heal. Do you have any idea what these men, men who valiantly served our country, are going through?"

Suzanne and Toni remained silent. It felt like the safe thing to do.

"I'll tell you," Major Winston continued. "These men have seen battle, they've endured hardships. They did it willingly for their country—for citizens like you—and they deserve to heal in peace." Winston peered at Suzanne and then Toni, the frustration evident on his face. "How would you like to live with constant anxiety, flashbacks, nightmares, and even a heightened response to ordinary things—like loud noises?"

"You see what you ladies did?" Doogie said, jumping in. "You went off half-cocked without any real information at all. You acted like a couple of crazies. That's why you should let *me* handle any and all investigating!"

"Hey," Suzanne said, pushing back now. "We got chased. We were scared." There was an edge of impatience in her voice.

Major Winston shook his head. "That was Ted in the Jeep. He tends to go rogue on us now and then. But you were perfectly safe. Ted never leaves the property."

"We're good now, right?" Doogie said to Suzanne and Toni. "I can assure Major Winston that you and your firecrackers will never go near his camp again? In return, he's agreed not to press charges."

"Right," Suzanne said.

"Okey-dokey," Toni said.

They watched as Doogie and Major Winston trooped out the door. Then Suzanne turned to Toni and said, "We might have jumped the shark on that one."

Toni shrugged. "Yeah, maybe." Then, "Military guys, huh? Good thing it wasn't an armed response."

"You got that right."

Suzanne scanned the café to see if her tea drinkers needed anything. Probably refills.

"So. You're still going to bug out early?"

Toni nodded. "Gotta bounce. Go visit Junior and see what he managed to screw up today."

"Good luck with that."

CHAPTER 19

THE Cackleberry Club was empty now, with scattered rays of late afternoon sun streaming in through the windows. Petra fussed about in the Knitting Nest, arranging skeins of yarn just so, while Suzanne answered a knock at the front door. And discovered that a surprise guest had come calling.

"Carmen," Suzanne said, pulling the door open. The CLOSED sign was hung, but that hadn't stopped Carmen.

Carmen Copeland, local romance author and first-class pain in the butt, flashed a thousand-megawatt smile at Suzanne and said, "I was in the neighborhood and thought to myself, wouldn't it be *fabulous* if I dropped by the Cackleberry Club and signed all the new copies of *Rapturous Rendezvous*!" Her eyes glinted hard as obsidian as she added, "You *did* order them, didn't you?"

"Two dozen copies."

"I can always get more, you know," Carmen said as she followed Suzanne into the Book Nook, clacking along on four-inch-high stiletto heels.

"Good to know," Suzanne said with an almost, but not quite, sigh.

Carmen tossed her Gucci bag on the counter, shrugged out of her leopard-print coat that had to be this year's Dior, and fixed Suzanne with an intense stare. She was raven-haired with a heart-shaped face and drop-dead figure, but her beauty was marred by her overbearing personality. Carmen always projected the air of an entitled, wealthy duchess waiting for court buglers to announce her arrival and roll out the red carpet. Unfortunately for her, there were no red carpets at the Cackleberry Club. Not unless you were willing to settle for one of Petra's colorful, handmade rag rugs.

"Carmen," Suzanne said again, determined to be friendly even if it killed her. "It really is nice to see you."

Carmen grabbed a stack of books, produced a Mont Blanc pen, and started signing her name in big swooshy flourishes. "I'm going to sign all your stock. Do what I call a phantom signing. That way I don't have to come back and waste time interacting with actual readers."

Or you could look at them as buyers who help keep you in designer duds, Suzanne thought. Then decided not to argue the point. What good would it do? She wasn't about to change Carmen for the better.

"Okay, and I'll put stickers that say SIGNED BY THE AUTHOR on all the books."

"Do that. But kindly don't cover up the title. Or my name. Or my photo."

Carmen finished signing her books, then buzzed about the shop, checking out other romance authors, mumbling to herself, and shuffling books around. She bent down, frowned, and grabbed a book.

"What's this?" A blood red fingernail tapped against the book's cover. "My *Tempting Trust* doesn't belong down there."

No matter that it was released four years ago and she's lucky I still carry it, Suzanne thought.

Carmen was all atwitter as she busily arranged face outs of her books, humming tunelessly and talking to herself. "Face outs, I like my books to always do a face out."

"You're in a good mood," Suzanne said. She had to say something to put an end to all the fussing and rearranging.

Carmen stopped humming and fixed Suzanne with a slightly superior gaze.

"If you must know, I've been dating someone new, someone very special."

Suzanne decided to take the high road. "That's wonderful, Carmen. Anyone I know?"

Carmen remained her haughty self. "Probably not, dear. He's new in town and soon to make his mark as a very prominent businessman. Robert Stryker?"

"Actually I *have* met him."

Carmen lifted a single eyebrow in displeasure. "You've met? Really? May I ask under what circumstances?" Carmen sounded suspiciously suspicious.

"Mayor Mobley brought him in for lunch a few days ago."

At that Carmen seemed to visibly relax. "Oh, just business."

"And then he came in again today."

"With Mayor Mobley, yes?" Carmen asked quickly.

"No, he was all by himself."

"Then he must certainly enjoy Petra's cooking," Carmen said through gritted teeth. She tossed her coat over her shoulders and made a hasty exit.

As Suzanne finished arranging books in the Book Nook, Petra wandered in.

"You know what, Suzanne? I feel awful about not attending Spooner's graveside service this morning."

"Couldn't be helped. We had to dash back here and open the café," Suzanne said.

"I know, I know, but I still feel bad. So I went ahead and called Starbright Florists and had them deliver a lovely funeral bouquet. I've got it back in the kitchen. But . . ."

"Yes?" Suzanne knew Petra had something important on her mind.

"But I'm absolutely crazed about getting things ready for my knitters tonight."

"So you'd like me to . . ."

Petra was practically squirming. "To deliver my flowers to the cemetery? And place them on Harold Spooner's grave? Would you do that for me? Would you really?"

Suzanne glanced out a window. It was getting dark and the cemetery would be a little spooky. But she saw the pleading look on Petra's face and simply couldn't refuse her.

"Of course, I'll take them," Suzanne said. "You focus on getting ready for your knitters and I'll be back in no time to help prep the food."

"Suzanne, you're an angel."

THE black wrought-iron gates of Memorial Cemetery loomed up like disapproving sentinels as Suzanne's Toyota labored up the narrow, rocky road.

"There it is," she said aloud. "Dead ahead." Then shivered slightly at her own choice of words. She remembered when, a few years ago, the cemetery had staged a sesquicentennial celebration and a candlelight tour had gone way off the rails.

That's not gonna happen today, Suzanne told herself.

She decided that her mission was to get in and get out fast, because . . . well, she was also under a time crunch. And because the overly fragrant aroma of the flowers in her back seat was starting to get to her. It was a little too cloying, a little too reminiscent of a funeral home.

Suzanne crunched along the gravel road through the oldest part of the cemetery, the part where settlers and Civil War veterans lay in quiet repose. Here were enormous first-growth oaks and cottonwoods, trees that had been shooting skyward ever since covered wagons had pushed across the prairies into what had been called the Big Woods. Now, spread out under these trees were ancient grave tablets, battered and bruised by the elements.

"I wonder where I should drop the bouquet?" Suzanne mused. She'd forgotten to ask Petra if she knew where Spooner's grave site was located. Now she had to wing it, in the dark, with nobody around. Not even a grave digger in sight.

Stop that, she chided herself. *Stop trying to scare yourself silly.*

Suzanne peered out her side window as she drove along, hoping to find a clue or landmark of some sort. And, a few moments later, rolled to a cautious stop. Some fifty yards off in the distance, down a grassy slope and flapping in the breeze, was a black canopy held up by four spindly poles.

That's gotta be it. The place where they held this morning's graveside service.

She stopped her car, grabbed the bouquet, and headed across the grass. The ground was slightly soggy underfoot and wind whooshed through nearby trees, making a strangely mournful sound.

A moan? No. Get a grip, girl.

Tiptoeing up to what was a newly dug—and now newly filled-in—grave, Suzanne saw a simple gray marble tablet. And there was Harold Spooner's name, birthdate, and date of death carved into the stone. She shook her head sadly. It was heartbreaking because Gloria had had her own name carved into the tablet as well. With only her birthdate inscribed—but her death date left blank.

Suzanne hated the idea that a tablet was standing there, just waiting to be filled in.

Placing the bouquet next to the headstone, she whispered a quick prayer and hurried back to her car.

It was full-on dark now as Suzanne drove back down the narrow lane. She switched her lights on and, a few moments later, noticed a vehicle following behind her.

That's strange, I didn't see any cars when I was looking around in the cemetery.

But she knew it could be another late mourner from a different part of the cemetery. Or even a caretaker heading home for the night.

She drove down the hill, past a deserted lot where a cinder-block foundation had been half built, then the project abandoned, and turned left on Grove Street. The car behind her made the same turn.

Suzanne's brow furrowed. She drove two blocks, then hung a quick right, watching in her rearview mirror as the vehicle behind her did the same. She felt a blip of adrenaline touch her heart. Then decided, no, she was probably overreacting.

She negotiated another random turn into an area of older homes—large Tudors and Colonials—where streets curved and twisted to accommodate a small meandering stream, and got the shock of her life when she glanced in her side mirror.

The vehicle was still following her!

Was it the truck that had been spotted racing away from the Blue-Aid Pharmacy holdup?

Maybe.

Was it following her because the driver knew she'd been investigating?

Possibly. In any case, this is so not good.

Suzanne floored it, completely ignoring the 20 MILES PER HOUR sign, the DRIVE LIKE YOUR KIDS LIVE HERE sign, and the NEIGHBORHOOD WATCH sign.

She zigged, zagged, and spun around curves, watching the truck in her wing mirror as it fought to keep up with her. She spun around a sharp turn and backtracked, always keeping an eye on her pursuer. Finally, when she'd pulled ahead and gained some much-needed distance, she skidded around a turn and darted down a narrow alley. She turned off her lights and hunkered next to a black SUV, hoping, praying, that she'd finally lost the pickup truck.

And, finally, she had.

Whew.

THE Cackleberry Club was warm and welcoming as Suzanne hurried in and slammed the door.

Petra looked up from a basket of colorful yarns. "How'd it go at the cemetery?"

"Okay, I guess. Fine." Suzanne decided not to tell Petra about the pickup truck that had laid chase. It would only cause her to worry.

"Thank you *so* much," Petra said, touching a hand to her heart. "Now I feel right with the world."

"Okay," Suzanne said, still feeling a little discombobulated. "You already baked cookies and bars, I just have to make the sandwiches?"

"Yes, and bless you for that."

Suzanne drew a deep breath. "What's your knitting project for tonight?"

Petra picked up a skein of yarn and handed it to Suzanne.

"We're using this banana fiber yarn to make tea cozies for the Methodist Church. They're going to sell them as a fundraiser."

Suzanne fingered the yarn. It felt satiny and lush. "Seriously? This is made from banana fiber?"

"The fibers are initially harvested from the trunks of banana trees. The special softening process makes them similar to silk. Soft and strong, very eco-friendly."

"It's the Green New Deal for knitting," Suzanne said.

"Exactly. And next week . . . this is really exciting . . . we launch our Pink Slipper Project."

"Cute name. But what is it exactly?"

"We're using MillaMia Merino wool to knit slippers for all the women and kids who are living at the women's shelter over in Jessup."

"It sounds like I'm going to have to learn to knit one of these days," Suzanne said.

Petra fingered a copy of *Knitting Pretty Magazine*. "Honey, I could teach you everything you need to know in about fifteen minutes."

"Somehow I doubt that." Suzanne's cell phone vibrated in her pocket. "Excuse me."

She pulled her phone out and saw the caller was Ginny Harris. *Is she going to push me some more about trying to solve Harold Spooner's murder?* Suzanne hoped not.

"Hi, Ginny."

"Suzanne, have you heard?" Ginny burbled excitedly. "I think Sheriff Doogie might have solved the case!"

"What? How?" Suzanne felt both flustered and mystified. Doogie had been here a little more than two hours ago and never said a word.

Ginny pressed on. "I heard via the grapevine that Birdie Simmons was just arrested!"

CHAPTER 20

"GINNY, no! You can't be serious!" Although Birdie had crossed Suzanne's mind as a possible suspect, she was more like a wild speculation, nowhere near the top of her list.

"Apparently Deputy Robertson looked in Birdie's trash can this morning and found . . ."

"Looked into it?"

"I guess more like confiscated it. The actual process doesn't matter. What matters is he found hypodermic needles and some drug packaging. Lots of it."

"I don't know what to say." Suzanne's head was spinning. Could the case be solved just like that? Maybe it could. "Where's Birdie now?"

"At the Law Enforcement Center. Locked up in one of their cells."

"I'm . . . I'm speechless," Suzanne said.

"But this is a good thing, don't you think?" Ginny asked. "It means we can put this terrible nightmare behind us."

"I suppose it's possible. Maybe it is."

But Suzanne knew darned well that Birdie hadn't been the one who shot Harold Spooner. Yes, there was a slim chance that Birdie could be *in* on the robbery, but she wasn't any kind of killer. Still, any active role she played would make her a co-conspirator.

"Maybe I can finally get a decent night's sleep now," Ginny said. "I'm sick of waking up drenched in sweat from flashbacks and nightmares about being shot. And once Birdie gives up the name of her co-conspirator, that should be it. Case closed."

"Maybe," Suzanne said for about the forty-seventh time.

SUZANNE was still staring at her phone, looking befuddled when Petra emerged from the Knitting Nest, carrying two stacks of quilt squares.

"Honey, which of these stacks do you like best? The red and pink florals or the more contemporary blue and green ones?"

"Um . . . what?" Suzanne said.

Petra's brows creased together. "Earth to Suzanne. You look a little flustered. Are you okay?"

"Yes. No. I'm not sure."

"What's up? What was that call about?"

"Doogie just arrested Birdie Simmons," Suzanne said. "Hauled her off to jail."

"He *what*?" Petra cried. She looked almost defeated for a moment, then drew a deep breath and said, "So what's the story on *that*?"

"According to Ginny Harris, Deputy Robertson found needles and drug packaging stuffed in Birdie's trash."

Petra's eyes got big and she put a hand to her mouth. "Oh my Lord! I can hardly believe it."

"Please don't tell anyone about this, okay? Keep this under your hat."

"Yes, of course. But, Suzanne, that can't be right. Birdie isn't any kind of criminal, she's churchgoing folk!" Petra fretted for a few more moments then said, "What are you going to do about this?"

"Call Sheriff Doogie for one thing. Something smells fishy to me."

"Good. You do that, Suzanne." All of a sudden, Petra looked like she was ready to cry. "Lord have mercy. What strange surprises will befall us next? Some kind of plague? Frogs dropping out of the sky?"

SUZANNE called the Law Enforcement Center and got Wilbur French, the night dispatcher, on the line. She vaguely knew him, had a memory of a tall, skinny guy with a friendly smile and a bad comb-over.

"This is Suzanne Dietz at the Cackleberry Club," Suzanne said to French. "Is Sheriff Doogie around? It's critical that I speak with him."

"I'm sorry," French said, "but the sheriff's gone for the day."

"Gone home?"

"He didn't say."

"Is Deputy Robertson there?" He was Suzanne's next best contact.

"He's out on patrol," French said. "In fact, I just radioed him about a fender bender out on Highway Two Twenty-Two, so he's going to be tied up for a while."

"Here's the thing," Suzanne said. "It's very important that I speak to Birdie Simmons. So can you please put me through to her? I promise to make it quick."

"Sorry. No can do. Mrs. Simmons is in lockup. I'm strictly forbidden to remove a prisoner from the lockup facility for a phone call unless it's a bail bondsman or their attorney."

"What if I came over there—?"

But French hastened to cut her off. "Absolutely not. Besides . . ." He sounded embarrassed now. "I don't have the authority."

"Okay. Well . . . okay."

Disgruntled, Suzanne hung up and dialed Doogie's home number. It rang almost a dozen times until a gruff voice came on the answering machine and said, "Not home, leave a number." And that was that.

Feeling dejected, Suzanne clicked off her phone.

"No luck?" Petra asked. She'd been hovering nearby, arranging a basket of colorful nubby yarns.

"None whatsoever." Suzanne felt frustrated and a little morose. She wanted—needed—a report on Birdie. And she was anxious to tell Doogie about the truck that had followed her from the cemetery.

"Will you try again later?"

Suzanne nodded. "Count on it."

TWENTY minutes later, Petra's knitters came pouring through the door. There were more than a dozen women, all carrying knitting bags bursting with skeins of colored yarn and different-sized needles.

That was Suzanne's cue to head into the kitchen. She bustled about, laying out slices of bread, buttering them, then generously spreading on different fillings. Tonight she was doing chicken salad, goat cheese with pesto, and smoked salmon spread topped with thin slices of cucumber. She assembled the sandwiches, sliced off the crusts, then diagonally cut some of the sandwiches into quarters and made straight cuts on some so they ended up as finger sandwiches. She arranged all the sandwiches on three-tiered trays, then placed chocolate chip and peanut butter cookies on a large, white ceramic platter. Finally, she frosted the small mocha cakes that Petra had made earlier and arranged them on an octagonal-shaped silver tray.

Suzanne carried all the food into the café and placed it on a large table. Then she went behind the counter and brewed a pot of coffee as well as two pots of Earl Grey tea.

When Suzanne finally gave Petra the high sign, Petra and her knitters stopped their clack-clacking of needles and emerged for their refreshment break.

"This was so great of you to help out," Petra whispered to Suzanne as the group happily helped themselves to all the goodies.

"No problem," Suzanne said.

"Did you get hold of Doogie?"

"Not yet. When I get home I'm going to talk to Sam about this. See if he has any brilliant ideas."

"Good idea," Petra said. "Why not take him some leftovers, too."

As laughter and good feelings continued to swirl in the Knitting Nest, Suzanne went home to Sam. The second she opened the front door Baxter was nuzzling her foot, one ear tickling her leg. Not to be outdone, Scruff started jumping up and down, vying for her attention. Suzanne knew they were glad to see her but suspected the eau de pesto chicken was a major draw as well.

Then Sam got into the act, leaning in to give her a kiss and casting a longing gaze at the white bakery box she held in her hands.

"Umm. I smell basil. And garlic?" he asked.

Suzanne opened her mouth to tell him it was pesto chicken, but a completely different set of words came tumbling out.

"Birdie Simmons has just been arrested. Can you believe it?"

Sam's eyes widened. "Birdie the nurse? The one who got smacked around during the robbery?"

"That's the one."

"What's going on?" Sam wondered.

"Apparently one of Doogie's deputies searched Birdie's trash and found hypodermic needles and drug packaging."

"That came from the hospital?"

"That's the scuttlebutt." Suzanne walked into the kitchen, took a plate out of the cupboard, and arranged a half dozen tea sandwiches for Sam.

Sam pulled up a seat at the breakfast bar, took a sandwich, and said, "Aren't you going to eat?"

"Already did. These are all for you."

"Thanks but . . . wow, you must really be upset."

"I am. Because none of this makes any sense," Suzanne said.

Sam frowned as if he were lost in thought. Then he shook his head. "Well . . . it actually does in a way."

Suzanne pounced on his words. "What do you mean? Do you think that Birdie is guilty? That she was the inside man . . . woman . . . working in concert with the shooter?"

Sam nibbled at his sandwich. "No, I don't believe that at all."

"Then why are you giving me a spooky, half-baked non-answer?" Suzanne asked.

"It's just that . . . well, truth be told, Birdie's husband, Carl, is a diabetic. He takes daily insulin injections."

"Are you serious?"

A mental *ping* sounded in Suzanne's brain. She knew she'd been handed a critical piece of information. She just wasn't sure how it all fit together.

She leaned closer to Sam and said, "Tell me more."

He shook his head. "I really can't. I shouldn't have divulged anything at all about Carl Simmons's medical history. You know as well as I do that every patient's medical record is covered by doctor-patient confidentiality. So that's it. Period. Full stop." Sam slowly folded his arms across his chest in an "end of discussion" pose that Suzanne had seen before.

Suzanne gave him a look of pure astonishment. "You're telling me I can't use that information?"

"That's exactly what I'm telling you."

Suzanne was almost stammering. "But . . . but there's a good chance that Birdie has been falsely arrested!"

"I imagine that's a strong possibility, but it has nothing to do with me or with her husband's patient confidentiality rights."

"Stop being a stickler for protocol and think like a warm-blooded human being," Suzanne chided. "We really do have to tell Doogie about this."

Sam thought for another few moments. "Maybe."

"No maybes. I'm going to call him right now." Suzanne picked up her cell phone and punched a few buttons. As it rang she said, "Probably you're going to have to talk to him, too. You'll lend a lot more . . . authority."

But Doogie still wasn't home. And Suzanne got the exact same runaround when she called the Law Enforcement Center again.

"Can't get hold of him?" Sam asked.

"No."

"Have a sandwich, it'll make you feel better."

"No it won't. You finish them up. I'm going to . . ." Suzanne stopped. What *was* she going to do? "I think I'll take the rambunctious canines outside for some fresh air and exercise."

"Sure, why not?" Sam said. "It's only been five minutes since Baxter and Scruff dug yet another hole in the backyard." He gave her a meaningful look.

"I'll check it out, see if I can fill it in."

"Good luck with that. The place looks like it's been overrun by a legion of gophers."

*   *   *

SUZANNE opened the kitchen door, then stepped aside as the dogs thundered past her. She grabbed two rope dog toys off the counter and followed them out.

Immediately, the dogs circled around her, anxious to play. Suzanne tossed the toys onto the lawn as Baxter and Scruff lunged after them. Baxter brought his back to her, Scruff just grabbed the toy, shook it like mad, then dropped it and wandered off to sniff. He was more interested in completing their current excavations.

Suzanne stood on the damp grass and looked at the moon as it cast a silvery shadow on a powder puff of low-hanging clouds. She tried to admire the evening, tried to relax. Baxter ghosted past her and she ran a hand along his soft, furry back.

Problem was, she couldn't quiet her mind. It was still spinning in circles and making her heart feel heavier than ever. Harold Spooner's killer remained on the loose, no matter that Birdie was sleeping in a jail cell tonight. And if Sam was right about Birdie's husband— and of course he was—then Birdie probably wasn't involved at all.

The survivalist guys, who really weren't survivalists at all, were now pretty much out of the picture. So who was left?

Well, Reverend Jakes had brought in those scraggly druggies to take up residence in the church basement. So it was possible that they might be involved. And Robert Stryker, whose guys had beat up Junior, wasn't exactly a picture of innocence, either.

But who was desperate enough to kill for drugs? That was the million-dollar question.

Suzanne contemplated all of this as she stood shivering in the cool night air, her backyard iced in moonlight as the clouds parted. Her eyes sought out the Big Dipper and the ubiquitous North Star. And she wished for a meteor shower—always a harbinger of good luck. But that was still months away.

CHAPTER 21

SUZANNE was dreaming. Not the floaty, warm, snuggle-in-and-enjoy-it kind of dream. More like a stress dream. A dream where she was trying to locate something, but the plot kept shifting and she was suddenly fleeing from some sort of terrible danger. And then, the dream morphed again, and she was struggling with a faceless man. A man who was trying to put a pair of manacles on her and drag her into some deep, dark pit.

The dream blew Suzanne sky high right out of her REM sleep. Which is why she clambered out of bed at five o'clock this Friday morning, dressed quietly in her walk-in closet, and went downstairs to fix herself a cup of coffee. She sat in her kitchen, sipping slowly, thinking about all that had gone on in the past week, waiting for daybreak. Baxter kept her company, his graying muzzle soft against her knee.

When the sun finally burned orange over the horizon, Suzanne figured Sam would be getting up in another five or ten minutes. So she left him a banana muffin and a glass of orange juice with a note that said, EAT ME, DRINK ME. Then, getting her courage up, Suzanne headed out to the Law Enforcement Center.

Suzanne knew she was taking a chance as she walked down the long corridor, her heels clicking loudly on the highly polished linoleum floor. Colorful posters on the walls warned about the evils of drugs, urged care in building campfires, and cautioned school children to beware of strangers. No kidding.

"Sheriff Doogie isn't in yet," Deputy Robertson said as Suzanne slipped through the door into the Sheriff's Department. Robertson was sitting behind the front counter, unwrapping a granola bar.

"That's what you're having for breakfast?" Suzanne asked.

Robertson shrugged. He was young and skinny—maybe twenty-six, with an earnest expression, watery blue eyes, and sandy brown hair.

"It tastes like cardboard," he said.

"I'm sorry I didn't bring along a box of Petra's pecan sticky rolls."

"Oh yeah?" Robertson suddenly looked interested. "I sure wish you would have."

"Can I see Birdie?" Suzanne asked.

"Umm . . . I'm not sure."

"She's here, isn't she? All snug and secure."

"Yeah." He drew the word out slowly.

"Then I'd like to see her." Suzanne favored him with a confident smile.

Deputy Robertson was clearly conflicted. "But you're not a lawyer."

"I'm better than a lawyer," Suzanne said. "I'm a friend."

It took another minute or so of coaxing, but Deputy Robertson finally led Suzanne through a heavy door, down a short hallway, and then unlocked the door to a sparse but surprisingly spotless cell.

Birdie was sitting on the bed, her back against the wall. She looked tiny and frightened, like a dissident awaiting her fate in a Soviet prison.

"Birdie," Suzanne said as the door swung closed behind her with a jarring *clank*.

Birdie looked over at Suzanne and a single tear rolled down her cheek. "Hi," she said in a small voice.

"Have you spoken to a lawyer yet?"

Birdie shook her head no. She was wearing a blue shirt, light brown slacks, and tennis shoes without the laces.

"Are you planning to call one?"

This time Birdie just shrugged.

"May I sit down next to you?" Suzanne asked.

Birdie scooted over a few inches.

Suzanne sat down and took one of Birdie's hands in her own. She knew the woman was feeling scared and vulnerable, so she spoke to her in her softest, gentlest voice.

"Sam shared some information with me last night," Suzanne said.

Birdie turned to stare at her. "Doctor Hazelet?"

"Yes. As you probably know, we're engaged to be married. So, as you might expect, we're very close."

Birdie nodded.

"Anyway, Sam told me that your husband, Carl, is a diabetic."

"Carl is diabetic," Birdie said to her in an almost robotic voice.

"That's right. Which means he needs to receive his insulin shot every day."

Birdie gazed at Suzanne, as if she knew what was coming.

"I'd guess that making sure Carl gets his daily supply of insulin is very hard on you," Suzanne said. "So I can understand that, if the opportunity presented itself, you might . . ."

"How did you know?" Birdie asked, choking out her words.

"I didn't until just now," Suzanne said.

Birdie dropped her head as a torrent of tears streamed down her cheeks. Suzanne reached in her bag, grabbed a tissue, and passed it to Birdie. Finally, Birdie managed to stem her tears.

"Right after the robbery, after I got beat up, there were all these packages and vials just lying around on the floor," Birdie said. "Most of them were damaged or smashed so I figured that nobody would ever miss them. That nobody would *want* them."

"How many did you take?" Suzanne asked.

Birdie blinked. "Six?"

"Are you asking or telling?"

"Telling," Birdie said. "I knew it was wrong. But it was kind of a bizarre . . . opportunity." Birdie dropped her head a notch in shame. "That robbery was the perfect cover-up for my own petty crime. I *knew* it was wrong. I hated myself for taking them. It's just that Carl needs his insulin every darned day . . . and it's so expensive. We try to keep up, but everything costs so much. And . . . and the medicine was just lying there."

"You didn't explain any of this to Sheriff Doogie?"

Birdie dropped her head again. "I was too embarrassed. And if people found out that I took drugs . . . *stole* drugs . . . I knew I'd never get another job again. Ever. And then where would I be? What would happen to Carl? No, I'd rather just stay quiet and go to prison."

"Honey, you were under duress and you made a mistake," Suzanne said. "But nothing that's impossible to correct." Suzanne patted Birdie's arm. "So I want you to remain calm and try to make peace with yourself while I do my best to straighten out this mess with Sheriff Doogie."

"You'd do that for me?" Birdie brushed away tears, suddenly looking hopeful.

"Of course I would."

* * *

BACK in the reception area, Doogie had long since arrived and was waiting for Suzanne. He stood there, arms folded tightly across his chest, his meaty face a veritable thundercloud. His complexion was so mottled with anger, his jaw clenched so tightly, that Suzanne wondered if steam might start pouring out of his ears.

"We need to talk," Suzanne said to him, trying to keep her voice steady.

"No, *you* need to talk," Doogie said in a low growl. He dropped his arms, but his hands remained tightly clenched. He looked like a grizzly bear on the verge of attacking. "You have broken . . . I don't know how many different laws and protocols. So, Suzanne, you have some serious explaining to do."

"And I will," Suzanne said.

Doogie spun around and thrust a finger at a cowering Deputy Robertson. "And you, you little twerp, I'll deal with you later."

Ears burning bright crimson, Robertson ducked as if fearing that Doogie would reach out and swat him like a bug.

"Please can we go in your office?" Suzanne asked. She was trying to maintain her cool and hang on to her confidence.

Doogie stomped into his office ahead of Suzanne, waited until she came in, then kicked the door shut with his foot.

BLAM!

The door rattled in its frame. A document—some city citation in a plastic case—popped off the wall and hit the floor.

Doogie paid no notice.

He circled his desk, plopped his bulk down hard in his chair, leaned back, and said, "What the Sam Hill Jones is going on here? How dare you march into my Law Enforcement Center and sweet talk one of my deputies just so you can *parlez-vous* with a prisoner!"

"There are extenuating circumstances in Birdie's case."

Doogie's chair snapped forward and his feet hit the floor. "I don't like the sound of that."

"Birdie didn't tell you anything at all?" Suzanne asked.

"She didn't say one single word to me when I showed up at her house. Just nodded yes when I asked her if she took the insulin. To me, that constitutes a confession."

"Okay, I need to explain a few things."

Doogie twirled a finger. "Make it snappy."

Suzanne laid it all out for Doogie as simply and straightforward as she possibly could. Birdie's paralyzing fear during the robbery, the scattering of drugs all over the floor, her admitted lapse in judgment, her husband Carl's very real medical need.

"What?" Doogie muttered. "Huh?" He hunched forward as Suzanne spoke and propped his elbows on his desk. "Carl's a diabetic?" He raked a chubby hand through his sparse hair.

By the time Suzanne had finished, Doogie's attitude had softened markedly. He touched two fingers to the side of his face and said, "Why didn't Birdie tell me about this herself?" He wasn't just stunned by Suzanne's explanation, he was genuinely amazed that Birdie hadn't stood up for herself.

"Because Birdie was ashamed of what she'd done," Suzanne told him. "She knew it was wrong and she was scared to death of the consequences. Right now the poor woman thinks she's going to be convicted and sent to prison for stealing."

Doogie stood up abruptly. "Well, damn it, she's not! Contrary to popular opinion, I ain't no ogre or heartless jerk. I didn't know diddly about her circumstances when I brought her in."

"Okay, explain that. Tell me *why* she was brought in?"

"We got a tip. Thought it was credible."

"A tip," Suzanne said. She didn't like the sound of that. It was as if some outside force—really a person—was trying to direct the investigation. Steer it off course.

Doogie rambled on. "Picking up that insulin wasn't exactly

right, but it wasn't completely wrong, either, considering the sky-high cost of drugs these days." He thumped a hand against his chest. "It's criminal what I have to pay just for my own blood pressure medication."

"So just to be clear, you'll drop the charges?"

"I can do that."

"And I'm assuming this whole episode can remain confidential and maybe even be wiped clean from the books?" Suzanne asked.

Doogie gave a slow nod. "I won't say nothin' if you won't."

"Good," Suzanne said. "Thank you. And I don't believe Birdie will want this issue, this . . . miscommunication . . . to be spread around town, either." She reached a hand out, tapped an index finger on Doogie's desk. "A couple more things."

"Oh for cripes sake . . . what now?"

"Just out of curiosity, have you taken a look at the two guys who are staying at the Journey's End Church?"

"Are they the fellas who drive around town in that souped-up Mustang? I've been trying to catch them so I can give them a speeding ticket."

"You must be under your monthly quota," Suzanne said.

Doogie shook his head. "It's not a quota, I got to uphold departmental metrics. Besides, I got nothin' to suspect those fellas of and I hate to hassle Reverend Jakes. I know he's got some sort of program going on." Doogie sighed. "Is that it? Are we done? Can I please get on with my day now?"

But Suzanne wasn't finished.

"I think I saw that gray pickup truck last night. The one with the tinted windows."

Doogie wrinkled his forehead, feigning interest, and said, "Problem is, Suzanne, there are about a million gray trucks out there."

"This particular one followed me out of the cemetery until I lost him over near Oxford and Madrid, that tangle-town area."

"What were you doing in the cemetery?" Doogie asked.

"Placing flowers on Harold Spooner's grave. But that's beside the point."

This time Doogie actually looked interested. "You think it was our shooter? That he might have been shadowing you?"

"That would be my biggest fear, yes," Suzanne said.

Doogie rocked back on his heels and said, "Then stop investigating!"

SHERIFF Doogie brought Birdie into his office and gave her a stern talking-to that morphed into more of an apology. Then he released her on what he termed "her own recognizance."

Suzanne volunteered to give Birdie a ride home.

Birdie was subdued as she rode along in the car. Until they turned into her driveway and she saw Carl standing on the front porch, waiting for her. Carl was in his seventies, rail thin and frail looking, wearing a threadbare Minnesota Vikings sweatshirt. But his lined face lit up like a Christmas tree when he caught sight of Birdie.

That's when Birdie really broke down. When she flew from the car, tears streaming down her face, and was finally reunited with her beloved husband, Carl.

CHAPTER 22

SUZANNE came bustling through the kitchen door, shimmying out of her camel-colored suede jacket as she offered an apology to Petra. "Sorry to be so late. You won't believe my crazy morning." She paused. "Well, maybe you would."

Petra pulled a fry pan off the stove, slid a cheese omelet onto a white plate, added two sizzled strips of bacon and a garnish of red pepper, and set it in the pass-through. "We were beginning to worry when it got late and we didn't hear from you. Toni tried to call you . . . twice."

"Oh, my phone." Suzanne pulled it from her pocket. "I turned it off at the jail and forgot to turn it back on again."

"So what happened with Birdie?" Petra asked. "Please tell me you worked your magic and she's not still sitting in jail."

Toni's head appeared in the pass-through, her eyes blinking in surprise.

"*That's* where you were? Hanging out at the jail? Wait, say no more. Let me deliver this order and I'll be right back."

Seconds later, Toni whipped through the door and skidded into the kitchen.

"What's goin' on?" Toni asked. "Something happened with Birdie?"

"You didn't tell her?" Suzanne asked Petra.

Petra shook her head. "I was waiting to see how it all turned out." She started cracking eggs into a large speckled bowl.

"How *what* turned out?" Toni asked.

"Birdie was a conspiracy suspect for about ten minutes," Petra told her.

"Actually, it was more like overnight," Suzanne said.

"Huh?" Toni said.

"Long story short," Suzanne said, "Birdie was semi-arrested by Sheriff Doogie and held in jail. But, in the end, she was only guilty of poor judgment."

"What do you mean?" Toni asked.

"Turns out, when the gunman robbed the hospital pharmacy, some drugs, namely insulin, got dropped and scattered on the floor. And in a moment of reckless opportunity, Birdie scooped them up," Suzanne said.

"Why'd she go and do that?" Toni asked.

"Because Birdie's husband is a diabetic," Suzanne explained.

"Really," Petra said in amazement. She added a froth of cream to her bowl and continued to whip her eggs. "I had no idea."

"Hoo boy," Toni said. "So Carl needs the expensive stuff just to keep on truckin'."

"Was Doogie terribly upset with Birdie?" Petra asked.

"At first he was, yes. But when I explained the circumstances and everything, he gradually settled down. And when Birdie admitted her own bad judgment, Doogie ended up apologizing to her," Suzanne said.

"So now what happens?" Petra asked.

"Now we pinky swear with each other and vow never to breathe a word of this to any living soul," Suzanne said.

"That's for sure," Toni said. "If somebody found out about this, Birdie's career would be ruined. A nurse has to be trusted around medicine."

"Mum's the word," Petra agreed.

"But . . ." Toni said.

"No, Toni, this matter is settled," Petra said. There was a *tone* in her voice.

Toni shook her head. "No it's not, because we still have a stone-cold killer walking around in our midst."

Toni's words gave them all pause and took them from a brief respite of relief into a state of consternation once again.

Suzanne went out into the café with Toni, welcomed a few guests, seated them, and took orders. When she came back into the kitchen, she said to Petra, "People are really loving your French toast sticks."

"Good," Petra said. "Because I made, like, a jillion of them. We can keep them on the menu for lunch."

Suzanne cocked her head. "French toast sticks with . . . ?"

"Fried chicken. We'll serve 'em just like they do chicken and waffles in the South. With syrup and everything."

"Inventive," Suzanne said.

"Hey, it's what I got. Especially after being so rattled about Birdie."

Suzanne grabbed Petra's hastily sketched-out luncheon menu—yes, she'd been that late—and went back into the café to update the blackboard. For lunch they'd be serving chicken with French toast, shrimp fajitas, and pulled pork with cornbread. With apple pie and banana bars for dessert.

Done with her chalkboard scribbling, she grabbed the plastic bag from the trash bin behind the counter and carried it into the kitchen. "Got anything to . . . ?"

"Yes," Petra said. She aimed one Croc-shod foot toward an overflowing trash can. "You can take that stuff, too. And those empty cartons."

"I'm on it."

When Suzanne opened the back door, the first thing she saw was a long-stemmed red rose sitting on the steps.

Oh no, this is becoming too much.

Balancing her bags and a couple of cardboard boxes she'd picked up, Suzanne carried everything to the trash and recycling bins. Then she came back, picked up the rose, and stared at it. There was no note this time, but she was pretty sure who it came from.

This has to end. Once and for all, I am going to nip things in the bud, so to speak, with Billy Brice.

Arms pumping, Suzanne crossed the back parking lot with a determined stride. She was building an edge as she thought about the shootings and the robberies—and all the people who'd been affected by them. And wondered if Billy was behind this. Was he a modern day Billy the Kid or was he exactly what Reverend Jakes had said he was—a young man who deserved a second chance?

Slipping though the small woodland that separated the Cackleberry Club from the Journey's End Church, Suzanne crunched along, noticing that all the buckthorn had been pulled out and a few branches trimmed from low-hanging trees. The larger pieces had been cut and neatly stacked for use as firewood.

Suzanne ended up at the heavy wooden back door of the church. It was an old-fashioned Gothic peaked door with a small stained glass window covered with a brass cross. She stood there for a minute, trying to figure out where Billy and Loren were living. Downstairs. All she knew was downstairs. Okay, she knocked on the heavy door. And waited. And waited. When nothing happened, Suzanne drew a breath and pulled open the door.

Cement steps yawned toward the basement.

Suzanne went down a dozen steep steps and ended up in a long hallway with doors on both sides. Like a contestant on *Let's Make a Deal*, she chose Door Number One. The first door on her right. She knocked with a firm *rat-a-tat-tat* and, seconds later, was rewarded with the sound of hissing and whispering, which eventually turned into actual voices. Then there was a mumbled, "Yeah?" directly on the other side of the door.

"It's Suzanne Dietz from next door." She tried to sound pleasant but authoritative.

"Just a sec." The muffled voice was stronger now.

A lock clicked and there was Billy Brice, looking a little sleepy and extremely puzzled. His denim shirt was mis-buttoned and untucked over gray sweatpants, his hair stuck up all over his head.

He blinked sleepily, recognized her, and grinned. "Hey."

"It's ten o'clock in the morning," Suzanne said, getting right on top of him. She felt a little outraged that she'd spent such a tortured night while Brice had so obviously slept in. "If this was the Army you'd be in the stockade."

"I've been up." Brice stretched and smiled sheepishly. "I just went back for a quick catnap."

Suzanne waved the rose in front of his face. "Is this from you?"

Brice blushed and gave her a shy smile. "Could be. Depends. Do you like it?"

"No. Well, yes, it's actually quite beautiful. But, Billy, you have to stop doing this."

"Why?"

"Because it's inappropriate. I'm not only twice your age, I'm engaged to be married."

"But we could be friends."

"I have an idea that your idea of friendship might be categorically different from mine."

There was a twinkle in Brice's eye now. "Maybe we could explore that difference . . ."

"Nooo, I don't think so."

". . . 'Cause you seem like a really nice lady."

Suzanne stared at Billy Brice with his cocky manner, good looks, and obvious physical prowess. And wondered if he could be the shooter. If this guy, standing right in front of her, looking youthful and a little goofy, was the one who'd killed Harold Spooner and robbed those two pharmacies.

Could he be that heartless? Better yet, does Billy know I've been investigating? Could he know he's high on my list of suspects?

And just maybe, if Brice thought that she suspected him, might he be trying to change her opinion by gifting her with red roses?

Suzanne thought of something else. Doogie had mentioned something about the Blue-Aid robber having a tattoo. Could she straight out ask Brice if he had a tattoo? Why not? He'd been forward with her, she could be forward with him.

Suzanne took a step toward him. "There's one thing I'm curious about. A young, hipster guy like you, I bet you have a tattoo."

Brice puffed out his chest. "Sure I do. I'm not one of those wimps who's afraid of a needle."

"Maybe on your forearm?"

"You guessed right."

"May I see it?"

"Wait a minute." A shadow crossed behind Brice's eyes. He knew something wasn't quite right here. "Am I being investigated?"

"Maybe," Suzanne said, half flirtatious, half serious.

Brice rolled up the sleeve of his denim shirt, revealing ropy muscles and . . . a cartoon of a small yellow bird with an oversized head.

You could have knocked Suzanne over with a feather. "Tweety Bird," she said. "That's not a prison tattoo."

"Probably because I've never been to prison," Brice said.

Feeling a flood of relief, Suzanne poked a finger into his chest. "Good. Let's see that you keep it that way."

SUZANNE walked back to the Cackleberry Club feeling a lot calmer than she had when she first saw the rose. The sun was high in the sky, lasering down its spring warmth, while a light breeze ruffled the treetops. She stood in the sunshine for a few minutes savoring the fresh air. Enough with drugs and murder! She decided that if she could carve out a few free hours later in the day she'd stop by the farm and go for a long ride on her horse Mocha Gent. Too many weeks had gone by since she'd made time for a good trail ride.

She walked back into the Cackleberry Club, her step a touch lighter. Inside, Petra was humming away and rattling pans, the kitchen smelling like grilled shrimp, roasted red peppers, and fresh chives. Getting ready for lunch.

Petra glanced over her shoulder, saw Suzanne, and said, "Did you remember that the Kindred Garden Club is coming in today for afternoon tea?"

"Sure did," Suzanne said.

"Okay, so right after our last luncheon guest departs, you and Toni get the tables all gussied up. Use the good white linens because Annie Bishop, the club president, said they'd be sending over several rather elaborate floral centerpieces and I want to show them off to perfection."

"Got it. Anything else?"

"Um, there was a call for you."

"Who was it?"

"A man who said his name was Ed Noterman." Petra's gaze wavered for a few seconds, then she set down her spatula. "Wait a minute." She frowned, as if trying to recover a lost memory. "Isn't that the guy . . . ?

"Yes, it is."

CHAPTER 23

"ED Noterman was the guy Doogie especially wanted me to take a look at," Suzanne said. "That day he picked me up and drove me to the hospital."

"Noterman is still a serious suspect?" Petra asked. Now she sounded a little apprehensive.

"As far as I know he is. When you talked to Noterman, did he want me to call him back? Did he leave a number?"

Petra just shook her head. "No. Nothing."

Suzanne thought about Noterman's call as she walked into the café. What was going on? Did Noterman want to yell at her again? Or was something else going on? Either way, it felt creepy and a little ominous.

"Where did you run off to?" Toni asked Suzanne as she brushed past her.

"I had to run over and have a talk with one of the guys at the Journey's End Church."

"The cute one, I bet. Billy something?"

"Billy Brice. He left me another red rose," Suzanne said.

"Play your cards right and you might get a ride in that classic Mustang of his. Fun to have a young admirer like that."

"Yeah . . . fun."

A few minutes later, the Cackleberry Club was super busy for lunch. But as Suzanne waited on customers, took orders, and poured coffee, Ed Noterman was never far from her mind. Had he really called the Cackleberry Club and asked for her? If so, why? Or had *someone else* called in an attempt to make her nervous and stir up trouble? If an anonymous tip had been called in about Birdie, couldn't the same person call her? A person who was trying to manipulate things? Suzanne gave a shiver. She hoped not.

As Suzanne served two orders of shrimp fajitas, Toni tapped her on the shoulder.

"You got a phone call," Toni said.

Suzanne set down two ramekins of salsa and made sure her customers had everything they needed. Then she slid behind the counter and lifted the receiver off the hook. She felt jittery. But as it turned out she had nothing to worry about.

It was Sam calling.

"I wanted to know if you stormed the Bastille first thing this morning and set Birdie free."

"I did exactly that."

"I figured you would, sweetheart." There was a fair amount of mirth evident in Sam's voice.

"Thanks for trusting me. For sharing the information about Birdie's husband."

"Uh-huh," he said. "So . . ."

Suzanne gave him a quick recap of how it all went down.

When she finished Sam said, "That's my Suzanne. Champion of underdogs, stray dogs, old dogs, and turtles crossing the road."

"Well, maybe not so much if they're snapping turtles," Suzanne told him.

* * *

AT one-thirty Junior came stumping in. He was dressed in his usual jeans, T-shirt, and boots, his hair all mussed up. He also looked unsteady on his feet and more than a little unfocused. Then again, Junior had always been a little unfocused.

Junior glanced around, saw Suzanne, gave her a V for victory sign, and said, "I've been released. I'm a free man."

"That's great. But how are you feeling?" Suzanne asked. She noticed that his head was still bandaged, but now it was a smaller bandage.

Junior seesawed a hand back and forth. "Okay, I guess. I started a GoFundMe page to aid in my recovery."

Suzanne stared at him. "That's a joke, right?"

"I kid you not. My page is already up and running on the World Wide Web. One of those cute little student nurses showed me how to do it."

From behind the counter, Toni noticed Junior's sudden presence, made a face, then came running over. "Junior," she said. She was obviously surprised to see him up and walking. "You're ambulatory."

"Nah, I didn't need no ambulance," Junior said. "I caught a ride over here with Teddy Butters."

"Tell Toni what you just told me," Suzanne said. "About your GoFundMe page."

Junior earnestly repeated his pitch for Toni.

Toni's response was hysterical laughter that rose up and echoed throughout the café. She shrieked and guffawed until the ceramic chickens started to rattle on their perches, until her laughter turned into a series of choking spasms. Finally, after flapping a hand in front of her mouth to try and suck in some air, Toni said, "Junior, have you lost your freaking mind? A GoFundMe page is for people who are in desperate need of help. Like orphans and widows, and people suffering from horrible diseases."

Junior put a hand to his wounded head and, in his best quavering voice, said, "I'm suffering, too."

"You could've gotten just as roughed up in a fistfight at Schmitt's Bar. In fact, you *have* gotten roughed up in fistfights at Schmitt's Bar. Besides, Junior, I can't believe anyone would donate a single red cent to your page," Toni said.

Junior flashed her a smug smile. "They already have. Somebody chipped in a buck."

"That's it?"

"It's still early. Later on, the donations will probably roll in. Then I'm gonna start investing in that crypto-cyber stuff."

"You mean cryptocurrency?" Suzanne asked.

Junior shrugged. "Yeah. I guess."

"Junior, you better watch yourself," Toni warned. "I put your hospital stay on my Mastercard, so I don't want any crazy stuff that'll trigger a relapse. You better toe the line. If not, I'm gonna be on you like a hot sweat."

"You don't have to be so mean and crabby," Junior said. "Because I'm not a well man."

"We knew that," Toni said.

"No, I think I might've picked up a fungus in the hospital. Or some kind of virus." Junior scratched at his head. "My brain feels all hot and bothered."

"Maybe go slap an icepack on your head?" Toni suggested.

Rather than let Junior and Toni duke it out for a full ten rounds, Suzanne decided to intercede by way of offering Junior something to eat. That brought him up short.

"You mean you'd give me free food?" Junior asked.

"Complimentary, yes," Suzanne said.

"Hot dog, that's the best offer I've had in weeks." Junior headed for the counter, catching Toni's hand on the way. " 'Cept for you, sweet cheeks."

Toni ripped her hand away. "Forget it, bub. Keep your sticky mitts to yourself."

Petra leaned down and peered through the pass-through at Junior. She'd overheard the conversation. "Whatcha want, Junior?"

"Do you have any of that beer and pork goulash?" Junior asked.

Petra shook her head. "Sorry. Not today."

"Then can you fix me a plate of scrambled eggs with hot sauce?" he asked.

"You want toast or hash browns to go along with that?" Petra asked.

"Toast please." For some reason, Junior was always polite to Petra. Maybe because she was keeper of the foodstuff?

"Coming right up, kiddo." She cracked three eggs into a bowl. "You still gonna build us that Eiffel Tower for our big event tomorrow?"

"I'm workin' on it. Already got a bunch of wood scraps and I looked up a historic picture and everything."

"Atta boy."

Junior was quiet (except for an occasional burp or belch) as he worked his way through his eggs and toast. Finally, when Suzanne placed a brownie on a plate for him, Junior spoke up.

"I got a new theory on the hospital murder and those two robberies," Junior said.

"Oh yeah?" Toni said from a nearby table. She was half listening while she folded a pile of freshly laundered linen napkins.

"I think it was done by one of those guys who are staying at the Journey's End Church," Junior said. He picked up his brownie and took a bite out of it.

"Why would you say that?" Suzanne asked.

"Because they act all pious and sanctimonious, like they're

sweet little choir boys or something. But I saw 'em going into Schmitt's Bar last night."

"Wait a minute," Toni said. She stood up, walked behind the counter, and picked up a glass pot filled with fresh, hot coffee. She turned to face Junior. "I thought you were still in the hospital last night. I mean, you were when I came to visit."

A foolish grin spread across Junior's face. "I mighta got an early release." He set his brownie down, dusted his hands together.

"Junior, do you know how difficult it is for me *not* to pour this pot of boiling-hot coffee over your head right now?" Toni said. "Do you see how badly my hand is shaking? I am truly itching to douse you in Blue Mountain dark roast."

Junior cowered from her. "That'd mean third-degree burns. Maybe even another trip to the hospital."

"God willing," Toni said. "Better than you staying at my place."

"Toni," Suzanne said, a warning in her voice.

"What?" Toni snapped. "You want me to work on my inter-office communication skills?"

Junior held up a hand. "Hold everything. I just remembered something else. Something really important that pertains to the hospital robbery."

"This better be good," Toni said. She lowered the coffee pot a notch.

"It is. In fact, it has to do with something Suzanne mentioned a few days ago," Junior said.

Suzanne gave him an encouraging nod. "What's that, Junior?"

"Suzanne, you know how you said you didn't hear nothin' after you went running out after the gunman? Like no getaway car, no motorcycle, just nothin'?" Junior asked.

"Yes. Go on," Suzanne said.

Junior scrunched up his face. "I just heard that Kuyper's Hardware is carrying those new 'lectric bikes."

"What do you mean?" Toni asked.

"Just what I said. They got these spiffy regular-looking bicycles, only they have an electric motor attached," Junior said. "I think maybe you pedal them to get the motor started and then it kicks in. They can whiz around like little go-carts, cruise up to twenty miles an hour, but they don't make hardly any sound at all."

"No sound," Suzanne said, almost to herself.

Toni studied Junior for a few moments. "Actually, that's not such a terrible theory."

Junior shrugged. "Yeah, it's a theory alright. 'Course, you never know." He picked up his brownie again and took a huge bite. While he was chewing he said, "Speaking of bikes, Teddy Butters was telling me about this beach bar down in Jamaica where you can whip up your own banana daiquiri by peddling a bike. They got a blender attached to this old-fashioned stationary bike, so you just stick in your rum and fruit and stuff, hop on, and start pedaling. Whip up a nice refreshing beverage. Pretty cool, huh?"

"Cool," Suzanne said. But she was still thinking about the electric bikes at Kuyper's Hardware.

CHAPTER 24

PETRA came out of the kitchen, wiped her hands on her apron, and looked around at the nearly empty dining room. "Looks like we can start setting up for tea in another ten minutes or so."

"That should work just fine," Suzanne said. She'd been perusing her fairly extensive collection of loose leaf teas, trying to decide between an oolong, a Darjeeling, and the rooibos. She studied the shiny little tins. So many teas, so little time.

"This sure has been a busy week," Toni said. "Between a couple of tea parties, tomorrow night's Petit Paris Gourmet Dinner . . ."

"Plus a murder, two robberies, a shooting, and Junior getting beat up," Suzanne added.

Petra touched a hand to her forehead. "You had to go and bring all that up, didn't you?"

"Can't pretend it didn't happen," Toni said.

"Well, call it tunnel vision, but I'm focused only on today's tea and tomorrow's big dinner," Petra said. "In fact, I've got it all worked out. The steaks are in the cooler, but everything else—the cheeses, the produce, and especially the caviar—will be delivered tomorrow afternoon. I even made Mr. Floyd juggle his route around so everything will be as fresh as possible."

"Petra rules," Toni said, holding up a fist as she headed for the cash register to ring up their last customer.

"Okay, so I'm thinking our set of Royal Doulton china in the Arcadia pattern, the cut crystal glasses with the pinwheel designs, and white linen tablecloths," Suzanne said to Petra.

"Plain white?" Toni had finished with her customer and was back to add her two cents worth. "That sounds kind of boring. Me, I like a pop of color for table linens."

"Toni, you like a pop of color for everything," Petra said. "Your shirts, your boots, probably even your undies."

"Especially my undies," Toni said. She pulled her cowboy shirt open a tiny bit. "Wanna see my blush pink bra?"

"Not especially," Petra said. She tapped a foot, looking a little impatient. "So the tablecloths and then keep an eye out for the floral bouquets. They should be arriving any minute."

"Got it," Suzanne said as Petra disappeared back into the kitchen.

Toni knelt down in front of their antique cupboard and started pulling out the tablecloths. "Okay, here we go. Blech."

"If you're so unhappy, why don't we add a little more punch to our tables," Suzanne said.

"I suppose we could use these pink candles." She reached into the cupboard and pulled out an armload of pillar candles.

"They're lovely."

"And maybe put some smaller candles in the hurricane lamps we scored at the flea market last year?"

"Now you've got the hang of it," Suzanne said.

There was a knock on the front door and then it popped wide open. A delivery man wearing a jaunty blue cap and jacket walked in carrying an extra-long light green–colored box. "Is there someone named Suzanne here?" he asked.

Suzanne raised a hand. "That's me."

The delivery man set the box down on the nearest table and said, "Hold on, I got another box in the truck." He grinned. "Somebody must really like you."

"Looks like our floral centerpieces have arrived," Suzanne said to Toni.

"Excellent," Toni said.

The delivery man came back in, dumped another box, and said, "Wait one, looks like I got a third box."

"These must be some super fancy arrangements," Toni said.

By the time the third box arrived, Suzanne was starting to get worried. "These boxes look awfully flat," she said.

Toni grabbed a pair of scissors and started cutting the strings that held the first box closed. "Chill," she said as she worked. "They're probably, like, floral table runners or something super elegant like you see in fancy magazines."

"Hurry up and pop that box open so we can see how well they match up to our china and candles and . . . What!"

They both stared into the first box. Instead of artfully put together floral arrangements, the box was filled with dozens of flowers. Some were banded together, some were lying loose, many were tangled in each other's leaves and stems.

"There must be some mistake, Toni!"

Toni ran for the door and ripped it open just in time to see . . . the back of the delivery truck disappearing down the road. "Too late, Suzanne. He's gone."

Suzanne gazed at the labels on the boxes. "No, I guess it's not a mistake. These boxes are all addressed to me from the Kindred Garden Club." Her brows knit together. "What were they thinking?"

"Maybe the fancy arrangements are in these other two boxes," Toni said, fumbling with the unopened green boxes. "Maybe we haven't, um, dug deep enough." Then, after she'd opened the second box, "Oops. Nope. Just a whole lot more loose flowers. They're real pretty but . . . what are we supposed to do with them?"

"I don't know. We better come up with something fast."

"Vases," Toni said.

"Vases would be good."

They pulled out every vase, pot, crock, and bucket that they could find.

"These glads should look great in our tall pots," Toni said. She was trimming madly, sticking yellow and orange gladiolas into a homey-looking brown ceramic crock.

"And the roses and carnations look very classy in our crystal vases," Suzanne said. She was also cutting, trimming, and arranging as fast as she could.

"You think it's like this in floristry school?"

"I didn't know there was such a thing as floristry school."

"Oh yeah," Toni said. "Over at the Vo-Tech in Jessup. I had to drive Junior over there once for his welding lessons 'cause he'd lost his driver's license. And I saw they had floristry classes going on." She popped a few daisies into a blue vase and said, "Could be fun."

They worked with nimble fingers for another twenty minutes, then Suzanne said, "Think we've got enough arrangements?"

"Maybe. Tell you what, I'll keep going while you start setting out the plates and stuff."

"I gotta get the crystal out of my office."

"Then you go do that," Toni said.

Suzanne hurried into the Book Nook, went on through to her office, and grabbed a large cardboard box from a cupboard that was filled with crystal stemware nestled in an individual section. She carried the box into the café and stopped short. "Oh my, that's gorgeous!"

Toni was standing on a step stool tying tiny mixed bunches of flowers to the brass curves of the ceiling chandeliers. "I thought you might like this."

"I would never have thought of it myself, but, yes, I love it. Maybe the flowers will even keep until tomorrow's dinner?"

"They will if I take them down afterwards and stick them in water," Toni said. She climbed down from the ladder, looked around, and said, with an affected English accent, "By Jeeves, I think we did it."

THREE o'clock was witching hour at the Cackleberry Club. The garden club ladies all seemed to arrive en masse, with Annie Bishop, the president, leading the charge.

"Suzanne," Annie gushed as she came through the front door and saw flowers and floral bouquets literally everywhere—on tables, the highboy, the marble counter, even on the shelves sprinkled among the ceramic chickens. "This all looks smashing. Oh, and even little nosegays hanging from the chandeliers. Aren't you the creative ones!"

"You gave us a lot to work with," Suzanne said. She wasn't about to tell Annie about the leftover flowers they'd stashed in the cooler. Or the mad rush it had taken to transform the Cackleberry Club from a homey café into a veritable English garden.

"And I brought along seed packets for favors," Annie said, as everyone spread out around them and began to take their seats.

"Perfect," Suzanne breathed. Now if the tea and food could match their floral artistry, she was sure all their guests would be very happy indeed.

As it turned out, they were.

Suzanne and Toni poured cups of luscious amber oolong tea along with cups of rose-colored rooibos tea. But it was the food service that literally took their guests' breath away.

When Suzanne, Toni, and Petra carried out three-tiered tea trays, the guests went wild.

"Scones!" they cried. "And tea sandwiches!"

"Today's scones are pistachio cream scones," Suzanne told their guests as they set the tea trays on the tables. "Served with strawberry jam and Devonshire cream. They're basically your first course."

"But the sandwiches!" they all cried.

"That's your lovely little second course," Suzanne explained. "And we've prepared three different kinds of tea sandwiches today. One with avocado egg salad, a tea sandwich with prosciutto, sliced apple, and brie cheese, and a crab salad tea sandwich accented with cranberries and walnuts."

A contented hum rose up as the ladies sipped, helped themselves to the wonderful sweets and savories, and congratulated themselves on their choice of venue.

"We did good, huh?" Toni said to Suzanne as they stood behind the counter, brewing more tea and refilling teapots.

"I think it's all going smashingly well," Suzanne said.

When everyone was sated, when there were only crumbs left, Annie Bishop stood up and clinked a spoon against her glass to attract everyone's attention. She launched into her "what a successful year we're going to have," speech, then segued into a big thank-you for the staff of the Cackleberry Club.

"Suzanne," Annie said, spreading her arms, obviously feeling magnanimous. "Thank you for hosting such a wonderful tea."

Suzanne held up a finger. "Ah, but it's not quite over yet."

Annie looked mystified. "It isn't?"

"We have a surprise for you ladies." Suzanne clapped her hands together. "Toni? Petra?"

The door from the kitchen flew open and Toni and Petra marched out carrying trays of what looked like ice cream cones.

"Ice cream cones," Annie said. "How delightful."

"Ice cream cone *cakes*," Suzanne said to the group.

"Cakes? What? How? Really?" came the cries.

Toni and Petra passed out the ice cream cone cakes as Suzanne explained the secret behind the dessert.

"What you're enjoying right now is a mixture of crumbled chocolate cake and chocolate ganache made to look like ice cream. We blended the ingredients together until they were nice and creamy, scooped it into balls, just like ice cream, and placed them atop cake cones. Then the faux 'ice cream' was topped with colored sprinkles and chilled for twenty minutes."

By four-thirty, the party was pretty much over. A few women shopped in the Book Nook and Knitting Nest, which was always a nice lucky strike extra for the bottom line. But by five o'clock the Cackleberry Club was empty.

Except for Suzanne, Toni, and Petra.

"Woof," Petra said. They were sitting in the dining room at one of the tables. "Maybe I'm getting too old for this."

"Come on," Toni said. "You love it. I know you do."

"Gotta make the magic happen again tomorrow night," Petra said. "That's not always so easy."

"But you said yourself that you've got everything all planned out. The steaks are chilling, the cheeses and veggies will be delivered fresh . . ."

"What are you thinking, Petra?" Suzanne asked. "Is there something we can help with?"

"Well, I've been going over my recipes and I wouldn't mind adding some fresh morels to my wine sauce," Petra said.

"Mmn," Suzanne said. "Morels would be delicious."

"But Mr. Floyd doesn't have any. I just checked with him," Petra said.

"Morels are in season right now. We could probably hunt around and pick some in the wild," Suzanne said. "Do a little local foraging."

"Foraging is very big right now," Toni said. "There are even books about urban foraging. How you can find salad greens and seeds and stuff in your own backyard or in parks."

"Seriously?" Petra didn't quite believe them.

"Come on, Toni. Let's take a ride," Suzanne suggested.

"Yeah? Where to?"

"I'm thinking Cottonwood Park. That's where I found a nice big patch of morels growing wild last year," Suzanne said.

"Wouldn't that make them property of the city?" Petra asked.

"You want to call Mayor Mobley and ask his permission?" Suzanne asked with a wry smile.

Petra thought for a moment. "I guess I'd rather have the boot-legged mushrooms."

CHAPTER 25

SUZANNE and Toni helped Petra clean up, then took off on their morel hunting expedition.

Suzanne drove while Toni gave a running commentary as they wound their way through Kindred, heading for Cottonwood Park.

"And here they are, two of the nation's most renowned woodland foragers. Wearing their pith helmets and safari jackets, armed with their trusty trowels, they've cast aside all doubt and are ready to embark on a lifetime adventure that other foragers only dream about . . ."

"Stop it," Suzanne said. She was laughing so hard she could barely drive.

"What?" Toni said. "I should be on TV, right? I should have my own comedy show and change my name to Toni Spumoni?"

"More like Toni Baloney."

"I like that," Toni said, looking out the window. "Boy howdy. Look at the monster size of some of these homes."

They were driving through the oldest part of Kindred, where Victorian homes, many with wraparound porches and old-fashioned turrets, sat on large lots with miniature forests of pine and oak surrounding them.

"Imagine living in one of those fine old homes," Toni said. "You'd feel like somebody out of *Lifestyles of the Rich and Famous*."

"Imagine having to clean it."

"Good point. I have enough trouble keeping a one-bedroom apartment spick and span." She paused. "Well at least span."

Two blocks later, they left the Victorian homes behind and drove through a more modest section. When they came to a double set of railroad tracks, the gate was down and a train had just entered the crossing. The BNSF engine blasted its air horn and steamed past them, pulling a long string of refrigerated cars—reefers—that were covered in colorful graffiti.

Toni began to get fascinated. "Every car . . . it's like a traveling art show. Look at that one. All purple squiggles. And look at the funky cat cartoons. And that car with the graffiti heart and 'Marf loves Zig.' I wonder if Zig knows how lucky she is?"

But two seconds later Toni was bored and squirming around in her seat.

"You know what? If we turn left here and follow along Powell Street, we'll be able to cut across the tracks and zip around the end of the train. It'll be a whole lot faster."

"Okay." Suzanne thought Toni's plan sounded better than simply sitting alongside the train tracks.

They turned left and bumped along for seven or eight blocks. At the next railroad crossing, they sat and watched the tail end of the train pass by. And finally crossed the tracks.

"The Morningside neighborhood," Toni said. "Some pretty decent homes in this part of town, too."

"Smaller Cape Cods with a few newer ranch-style homes thrown in for good measure," Suzanne said.

"What's going on up there?" Toni was staring straight ahead.

"I can't imagine," Suzanne said. As she approached a gaggle of cars and people, she slowed to see what was happening.

And then—pandemonium hit!

"Holy buckets, will you look at what's coming at us!" Toni shouted.

They both stared as two cruisers, light bars pulsing red and blue, came tearing down the block directly toward them. Then the cruisers swerved hard into a driveway that was partially blocked from view by a line of cedar trees.

"It's like something you'd see on TV," Suzanne said.

"One of those cop reality shows."

"Let's find out what all the fuss is about. Do a little rubber-necking."

"Oh yeah," Toni said.

Suzanne hit the brakes, pulled to the side of the street, and cut the engine. Then they both jumped out and ran toward the scrum of activity up ahead. As they ran across a lawn, a voice on a bull-horn warned, *"PLEASE GET BACK. MOVE ALL THE WAY BACK, PEOPLE."*

As they jostled through the herd of onlookers that were stand-ing on someone's front lawn, they were just in time to see Sheriff Doogie and two of his deputies go storming into a house, guns drawn.

"Whose house is that?" Toni asked a man who was cradling a gray schnauzer in his arms.

The schnauzer's owner shrugged, but a woman standing next to him said, "That place belongs to Ed Noterman."

Suzanne and Toni exchanged a quick glance. The schnauzer just looked bored.

"Oh holy hiccups," Toni said.

Suzanne stood on tiptoe, trying to peer over the crowd. "What do you think is going on in there?" Noterman's house was an ordinary-looking bungalow, yellow with white trim. A bird feeder hung from one of the eaves.

"Is Noterman being arrested?" Toni asked in a low voice. "Could he be the pharmacy killer?"

Suzanne and Toni stood with the growing crowd, but nobody came to the door, and, after five minutes, there still was no indication of what was happening inside.

"Maybe Noterman's in there pouring out a tearful confession to Doogie and company," Toni suggested.

But Suzanne shook her head. Out of the corner of her eye she saw an ambulance approaching from down the street. The crowd quieted as the ambulance's horn gave a quick *blip-bloop* and then Deputy Robertson came running out of the house. He looked harried and a little green around the gills.

"Stand back, stand back," Robertson cried.

The crowd moved aside as the ambulance backed up over the lawn and bumped to a stop right at the front door.

Curiosity burning, Suzanne said, "Something big just went down. We need to get a better view."

"Yeah, but where?" Toni asked. "How?"

Suzanne did a quick jerk of her head. "Sneak around back?"

"What if somebody sees us? What if we get caught?"

"Try not to."

Suzanne and Toni eased away from the crowd and crept slowly around the side of Noterman's house. They followed a flagstone path past well-tended flower beds of crocus and iris that were snugged right up against the foundation. As they passed under a half-open window they could hear loud voices coming from inside. An argument of some sort.

"Somebody's hot under the collar," Toni said.

"I'd know that voice anywhere," Suzanne said. "It's Doogie and it's his angry voice. Believe me, I ought to know."

"Can't see in, though," Toni said, taking a little jump but getting nowhere. "Windows's too high."

"Seems like something serious is going on, so I'd sure like to get a look inside. Maybe I could boost you up and you could grab a look-see?"

"That window is still awful high. Maybe we could find something to stand on?"

Suzanne glanced around. All she could see was a rusty old wheelbarrow sitting next to the detached garage.

Toni followed Suzanne's gaze. "Might work," she said.

Together they pushed and half dragged the rickety wheelbarrow, got hung up over a twisted green hose, then finally muscled it over to the window.

"This sucker is heavier than it looks," Toni grunted. "Give it one more—that's it—good shove."

When they'd finally jockeyed the wheelbarrow to a spot beneath the window, Suzanne looked around and said, "Has anybody got eyeballs on us?"

"I don't think so. Better go now!"

Suzanne put one hand on Toni's shoulder and stepped into the wheelbarrow. It tipped slightly and let loose a rough creak, but it didn't spill over. That got Suzanne up another couple of feet. She grasped the edges of the window frame, stood on tippy-toes, and pulled herself up as high as she possibly could. Then she leaned forward and put her face against the window.

"What do you see?" Toni asked.

Heart banging against her ribs, the little hairs on the back of her neck standing up straight, Suzanne took in the scene. She let loose a sharp gasp and darned near lost her footing.

Hyped up and frantically curious now, Toni jumped into the

wheelbarrow alongside Suzanne, stretched up, and pressed her nose flat against the window.

Toni's eyes searched the interior, then landed on . . .

"Oh no," Toni groaned.

Ed Noterman was slumped over like a discarded rag doll, face down on his kitchen table, surrounded by a glistening pool of blood.

CHAPTER 26

It felt like an emotional gut punch for Suzanne, but she continued to cling to the window ledge, listening to the furor that was raging inside.

Doogie was yelling while one of his deputies—probably Driscoll—shouted right back at him. As their voices rose in a high-pitched frenzy, they sounded like a couple of chattering squirrels.

"He could have been cleaning his gun," Driscoll argued. His voice conveyed both fury and anxiety.

"No, man, he ate it," Doogie barked back. "Sat down at his kitchen table cool as you please and pulled the trigger."

"But it doesn't make any sense."

"It does if he's the guy we've been looking for all along," Doogie said.

"You mean the robber? The killer?" Driscoll asked.

"Maybe Noterman couldn't live with a pile of guilt on his conscience so he shot himself," Doogie said.

Another deputy—maybe Robertson this time—said, "What kind of gun?"

"Don't touch it!" Driscoll warned.

Doogie: "It's a 9mm. Same as the weapon used in the hospital shooting."

"Possibly the same," Robertson said. "We gotta do some serious ballistics testing."

"And call the county coroner," Doogie said. "Right away."

Outside, still huddled on their perch, Toni said, "So Noterman *shot* himself?"

Suzanne looked grim. "Could have. Or maybe—and this is a big maybe—someone broke into his house and executed him?"

More mumbling from inside the house: "Doesn't appear to have gunpowder residue on his hands." Then, "Well, we gotta bag his hands anyway and send that weapon in."

"This is just awful," Suzanne whispered.

Suddenly . . .

"Get away from there!" Doogie bellowed. His voice was a terrible, walloping blow that rolled across Suzanne and Toni like clashing waves of sound. Then his angry face appeared in the window, his expression that of a twisted, melted Halloween pumpkin.

Toni bailed over the side of the wheelbarrow like she was an elite paratrooper. Suzanne scrambled down, too, but not before she took another glimpse and saw the pistol lying on the kitchen table, just inches from Noterman's fingertips.

Clutching each other, Suzanne and Toni ran around the side of the house, got tangled up in the crowd of looky-loos, and collided—smack!—with Deputy Robertson.

Robertson dropped a hand on Toni's shoulder and pinched hard. "You," he said.

"Ouch," Toni squealed, struggling to get away. "Stop it. What's with the Vulcan death grip anyway?"

"Sheriff wants to talk to you two ladies," Robertson said.

"Run away, save yourself," Toni cried to Suzanne.

"He wants to talk to you, too," Robertson said to Suzanne as he gradually released his grip on Toni.

Suzanne nodded. "Okay." She *wanted* to talk to Doogie. Was willing to worm her way into this investigation any way she possibly could.

Robertson held up a finger. "Wait here," he cautioned. "Don't go running away on me."

Twenty minutes later, Doogie came outside. He was sweating heavily and had lost much of his usual swagger. He lifted both arms above his head and waved at the crowd, ordering them to disperse. Told them there was nothing to worry about and that law enforcement was handling everything.

"No, it's not," Suzanne murmured to herself. To her, Doogie looked utterly lost and shell-shocked. His usual ruddy complexion was sallow, his shoulders sagged, and he seemed dispirited.

Suzanne got right in his face. "What happened?" she asked, as Toni muscled in next to her. The crowd that had been ordered to move back didn't.

Doogie stared at the two women as if he barely recognized them. His eyes remained glazed.

"We can probably cross Ed Noterman off our suspect list," Doogie finally said in a dry, croaky voice.

"Why is that?" Suzanne gazed past him at an EMT who was writing something on a clipboard. He looked detached and efficient, as if he'd seen death hundreds of times before. Which he probably had.

"Because Noterman's dead." Doogie's eyes finally focused directly on Suzanne. "But you already know that. You snuck a look in the window and saw his body."

"I want to hear the story from you," Suzanne said. "I want you to tell us what happened."

Doogie sighed. "It would appear that Noterman shot himself."

"You're saying it was suicide?"

"Well, there's no note. Nothin' that we've found so far anyway. Just . . . boom. Looks like the guy decided to blow his brains out."

"That's awful," Toni said.

"On the other hand, he could have been cleaning his gun. There was a can of Hoppe's sitting on the kitchen counter," Doogie said.

"Is that what you think happened, Sheriff?" Suzanne asked. "That maybe Noterman had a bullet in the chamber and didn't realize it?"

Doogie shook his head. "Dunno for sure. We need to investigate the circumstances a whole lot more and I don't need you two doofuses getting in my face."

"Hey!" Toni said.

But Suzanne was unfazed. "How about this scenario," she said. "Somebody set this up, all nice and convenient. Just like they tried to set up Birdie Simmons." In the back of her mind she wondered if Noterman was already dead when she got that call at noon. *Was his killer calling to poke at me?*

"You think somebody else killed him?" Toni asked.

"Maybe they wanted to make it look like Noterman was overwhelmed with guilt and couldn't face living anymore," Suzanne said.

But Doogie was shaking his head like he didn't quite buy into Suzanne's story. "There's no sign of anyone else being there. Probably no prints anywhere," he said.

"There weren't at the hospital, either," Suzanne said. "Or the Blue-Aid Pharmacy."

"Except this time we got some evidence," Doogie said. "Evidence that would probably have convicted Noterman if he'd been arrested and gone to trial. Only now he'll be . . . I guess the legal term would be tried *in abscentia*."

"What evidence are you talking about?" Suzanne asked.

"We recovered a backpack with drugs in it," Doogie said.

"All the stolen drugs?" Toni asked.

"*Some* of the stolen drugs," Doogie hedged.

Just enough to cast blame? Suzanne wondered.

"And how exactly did you know to come screaming over here like a big city SWAT team?" Suzanne asked.

Doogie put both hands on the sides of his gun belt, gripped it hard, and said, "We got a tip."

"Let me guess," Suzanne said. "Another anonymous tip?"

Doogie nodded. "That's right."

"And you believed it?"

"The caller said he was a neighbor. That he'd heard a gunshot and was worried, but didn't want to get involved."

"And just like that you rushed in and found Ed Noterman shot to death in his own kitchen," Suzanne said. It sounded way too perfect, way too staged.

"Yeah, he was there along with some of the drugs," Doogie said.

"Can I see this cache of recovered drugs?" For Suzanne, seeing was believing. It was important she take a look at this so-called evidence.

Doogie gestured for Deputy Robertson to bring him the backpack. When Robertson came outside he was carrying a green nylon pack and leading a basset hound on a leash. Doogie grabbed the pack, held it up, and said, "Isn't this the backpack you saw the gunman run out of the hospital with?"

"Duffel bag. I saw a duffel bag."

Doogie's brows knit together. "Isn't that pretty much the same thing?"

"Not at all. This is all wrong. This is a setup. Sheriff, someone's trying to set you up big time."

Doogie looked shaken. "Well . . ."

"Think," Suzanne said. "If someone murdered Noterman, it's someone he must have known. Someone he felt comfortable letting into his house."

"Ah jeez," Doogie said.

"Do me a favor," Suzanne said.

"I don't owe you any favors," Doogie said. He sounded irritable and a little frantic. "I'm the duly elected sheriff sworn to do my job. And right now my job is to deal with a suspicious death."

"Will you please stop being a curmudgeon and listen to me?" Suzanne asked.

Doogie closed his eyes and pinched the bridge of his nose as if he was experiencing the worst migraine of his life. He opened his eyes. "Okay, I'm listening."

"Is there any way you can keep the circumstances surrounding Noterman's death under wraps?"

"I was planning to do that anyway."

"Good. Because you know and I know that there's a chance Noterman might have been murdered."

Doogie took a step backward. "But maybe . . ."

"You know it's possible," Suzanne said, pressing him harder. "And you know there's a high probability that the killer—Harold Spooner's killer and now Noterman's killer—is still out there. He may even be planning to make some kind of move."

"Like what?" Doogie asked.

"Like I don't know," Suzanne said. "But whoever this maniac is, he's been leading us on a merry chase. And he seems to be enjoying it enormously."

"This thing has totally gone off the rails," Doogie said.

"Absolutely it has," Suzanne said as Toni nodded in agreement.

Doogie looked dejected. "And now what am I gonna do with Banjo?"

"Who's Banjo?" Toni asked.

"Noterman's dog."

They all gazed down at the sad-looking basset hound that stood at Doogie's feet.

"Oh no," Suzanne said.

BUT the fireworks weren't over yet. A few minutes later Gene Gandle, the pushy, nosey, intrepid reporter for the *Bugle,* showed up. He wore a navy jacket over his yellow golf shirt with a computer-printed sign that said PRESS stuck in the lapel pocket.

"Sheriff, Sheriff," Gandle yelled. "I need to talk you."

Doogie pursed his lips and said, as an aside to Suzanne, "I don't need this."

"Then don't talk to him," Suzanne said. "Tell him you can't release a statement yet. That it's way too early."

"Sheriff!" Gandle yelped again. He'd forced himself through a small crowd that refused to leave, slithered around the ambulance, and was now jumping up and down in Doogie's face. "Was it murder? Suicide? There are all sorts of wild rumors flying around. What can you tell me?"

Doogie held up both hands, palms facing out. "I can't tell you anything, Gene. Because I don't know anything yet."

"It's Ed Noterman, right? Noterman's dead? Just sketch out the general circumstances for me," Gandle begged. "Let me write *something* up."

"Sorry, no can do," Doogie said.

Gene Gandle glanced at Suzanne and his eyes went hard. "Then how come she's standing here with you?" He switched his glance to Toni. "And that other one?"

"Hey!" Toni yelled. "I got a name, you numbskull."

"I don't have to explain anything to you, Gene," Doogie said.

"But there's a body," Gandle said. "A dead body."

"Which we can't even move until we secure the scene, take photos, and run several forensic tests," Doogie said.

"Can you at least give me the cause of death?"

"I can't speak to that. Not until the county coroner arrives."

Gandle tapped his pen against his spiral notebook. "Well, when do you think that'll be?"

Toni, who'd been looking out toward the street, suddenly jerked an elbow sideways into Suzanne's ribs.

"What?" Suzanne asked.

"County coroner," Toni whispered.

Gandle overheard Toni's remark and gazed toward the street, where a dark blue BMW had just pulled up.

All eyes were focused on the vehicle as a tall man climbed out, then reached back in to grab his medical bag.

"Uh-oh," Toni said.

"Sam," Suzanne breathed. "And he's not going to like my being here one bit."

CHAPTER 27

Dr. Sam Hazelet was all business. He walked quickly toward the front door, head down, looking neither right nor left. When he finally lifted his head, he nodded to Sheriff Doogie and Deputy Driscoll. Then his eyes skittered across to Suzanne and widened in surprise.

"What are you doing here?" Sam asked. He looked suddenly suspicious.

"Honestly, Sam, we had no idea," Suzanne blurted out. "We were just passing by and saw all the commotion, all the people standing around and sheriffs' cars. So we stopped to rubberneck just like everybody else."

She pointed to the spectators still gathered in front of the house, feeling frustrated. Wandering into Ed Noterman's death had been a complete accident—an unserendipitous moment if there was such a word. How could she make Sam believe her?

Completely ignoring Suzanne and Sam's exchange, Gene Gandle pushed his way in between them. "I'll be standing by to take a statement for the *Bugle* as soon as you finish, Doc. Just let me know when's good."

Sam ignored Gandle.

Suzanne knew she had to diffuse the situation—and fast. She motioned for Sam to walk a few steps away with her, so they could hopefully leave the so-called press and Sheriff Doogie out of their conversation. Sam followed her, with Toni tagging along behind, dying to know how the conversation would go.

But instead of Suzanne controlling the conversation, Sam spoke up immediately.

"Suzanne, do you know how worried I get when I find you nosing around something dangerous like this? Have you forgotten how we met? How battered you were when I first saw you in the Emergency Room?"

"Sam, listen to me," Suzanne said. "We were just . . ." She saw the intensity in his eyes and foundered a bit.

"We were on our way to pick mushrooms!" Toni cried out.

"Mushrooms," Sam said. The word rolled off his tongue as though it were foreign to him.

"Morels," Suzanne said.

"Tasty wild morels," Toni said.

"Nice try," Sam said. "For the life of me I can't imagine how you two ended up here. But . . . that's what you do."

"You mean investigate?" Suzanne asked.

Sam shook his head. "I meant meddle. But now . . . now it's time for you to pack it in and leave. Let the sheriff and I puzzle this thing out. Okay?"

"Okay," Suzanne and Toni said, their voices chiming in together.

"Whew," Toni said once they'd climbed into Suzanne's car. "That was one close call."

"Tell me about it," Suzanne said. "I have to live with him."

"You think there'll be repercussions?"

"Mmn . . . more like intense discussions," Suzanne said as she pulled away from the curb.

"You know, maybe this is some kind of poetic justice. Maybe Ed Noterman is the right person after all," Toni said. "The killer-slash-drug thief."

"And maybe he's not."

"What makes you think he isn't?" Toni asked.

"For one thing he barely had any drugs."

"Is there a second thing?"

"Because this suicide—if that's what it really is—feels too easy," Suzanne said. "Too slick."

"Does everything have to be complicated?" Toni asked.

"Generally, yes. That's pretty much the way the world is today."

"Not for me. I'm willing to have Noterman nailed as the killer if it means this whole nasty episode is over." Toni pulled herself into a ball and pressed her hands into her eye sockets. "I gotta tell you, I'm feeling awfully stressed from seeing that dead body covered in blood. It made me totally sick."

"I'm sorry, Toni. I did kind of drag you into this."

"Aw, it's really my fault."

"Of course it's not," Suzanne said.

"No, I'm the one who got all agitated when we were stuck at that railroad crossing. We should have just sat there calmly and waited for the train to pass." Toni was talking fast, her words almost getting tangled. "Then we never would have driven down that street and we wouldn't have been caught at a crime scene and then Sam wouldn't be hopping mad at you."

"He isn't that mad," Suzanne said. "At least I hope he's not."

Toni patted her stomach. "And now I've got another crummy case of the whim-whams."

"If your stomach's upset, maybe I should drop you at your apartment."

"But we were going to . . ." Toni cocked an eye at her. "Are you sure about that?"

"Positive. You curl up on the couch and watch TV or something. Feel better."

Suzanne drove across town, taking care not to make any fast turns, then slowed to a stop in front of Toni's apartment.

"There you go," Suzanne said. "Be sure to call me if you need anything."

"I will." Toni was halfway out of the car when she paused and said, "Don't worry so much."

"The only thing that concerns me right now is Sheriff Doogie."

Toni gave a questioning look. "What do you mean?"

"Noterman's death is one more blow to his law enforcement ego. He's stumbling through this investigation, worried sick, and looking like he's not getting much sleep, either."

"Maybe we could drag him to the hospital and put him in a medically induced coma," Toni said.

"Now, there's an idea."

Toni turned her gaze to the blue car that was parked just ahead of Suzanne.

"Jeez, that's the Blue Beater. Junior's car. It means he's sitting upstairs with his clodhoppers on my sofa, chowing down on Cheetos and getting orange gunk all over everything." She sighed. "Now I gotta contend with that meathead."

"You'll be fine," Suzanne said.

WHEN Suzanne finally got to Cottonwood Park, out on the eastern edge of town, it was almost dusk, so she wasn't surprised that the parking lot was deserted. She cut her engine, glanced around, and thought, *Gotta hurry up before it's full-on dark.*

She climbed out, rummaged around in her trunk, and came

up with a woven basket—technically a French market basket—with a curved leather handle. Perfect for gathering mushrooms.

Suzanne walked down a gray flagstone path with sturdy iron railings on both sides. The limbs and branches of the poplars and willows on either side of the path were just starting to bloom. Some had tiny buds and others had mid-sized leaves that would be lush and full in a week's time.

The path led Suzanne deep into the lower level of the park where a designated picnic area offered picnic tables, barbecue pits, hand-hewn benches, and an old swing set. Nearby, Catawba Creek slapped up against neatly mown banks, the pristine water swirling in eddies and rushing over boulders as it burbled along.

The entire valley here was surrounded by high bluffs lush with spring greenery.

It reminded Suzanne of Brigadoon, that wonderful, mythical Scottish village that disappeared into the Highland mist only to emerge every hundred years.

Suzanne crossed the picnic area and ducked into a grove of quaking aspens. It was a tree that grew well in moist soil, so it just might be a fertile spot for morels. She spotted a sloping trail and followed it, then crossed a narrow wooden footbridge that was basically two railroad ties laid across a boggy spot.

The second she stepped off the bridge she could feel the texture of the land change beneath her feet. Now the ground was swampy and spongy.

Maybe . . . perfect for morels?

Suzanne scoured the ground for a few minutes, but there wasn't a morel to be found. She looked around—a dozen feet away two oaks stood fairly close together.

Ah, that could be a treasure trove.

Morels had such a distinctive look, that Suzanne knew they'd be easy to spot. She squatted on the ground near the trees and hunted around, finally seeing what looked like an oblong cone with a jagged honeycomb appearance of pits and ridges. She reached for it, then tossed it back. No good. Only a piece of tree bark.

She wandered around the swampy area scanning the ground as if her eyes were a Geiger counter and morels were made of precious metal. Still nothing.

Suzanne straightened up and continued looking. There was a chill in the air and the towering bluffs that seemed so charming a few minutes ago were now giving her a caged-in feeling. A musty, almost rotten-egg smell permeated the air. Swamp gas nearby. Which made her expedition somewhat less enticing.

Checking around the base of another tree, Suzanne heard the sharp snap of a twig. And then another. And yet another. She stood up abruptly, acutely conscious of being totally alone in the woods.

Careful now . . .

She glanced around, her eyes frantically seeking out the creature (Animal? Human?) that had made that sound. And was relieved when she spotted the white-tipped tail of a red fox disappearing into a grove of ferns.

Suzanne shivered as a chilly breeze swept around her. While she was searching for morels, the park seemed to have gotten much darker.

Five more minutes and then I'm out of here.

Even the prospect of facing Sam at dinner was preferable to wandering around in the dark woods all by her lonesome.

Suzanne moved on to a slightly more open spot, inspected the ground, and sighed. She was about to give up when a nubbin of brown caught her eye. Yes! There was a group of morels clustered around the base of a white oak tree.

Unconcerned with the mud underfoot, Suzanne dropped to her hands and knees. She picked the morels, snapping them off at the stem and gently brushing any dirt off. Then she placed them carefully in her basket.

As Suzanne pushed away a stand of weeds, hoping to find more, she felt a faint gust of wind and shivered. Then some sort of shadow hovered overhead for a few seconds and then disappeared. Startled, Suzanne jumped to her feet and looked skyward.

What was that?

It seemed as if something overhead had cast a momentary shadow. Some kind of large bird? An eagle perhaps?

She knew there were quite a few eagles living in the nearby bluffs. One of the local colleges had even set up some sort of raptor cam that you could view on the Internet.

Glancing around again, Suzanne felt a ripple of worry work its way up her spine. What was the old expression when you suddenly felt spooked? Like someone was walking across your grave?

Working furiously, she plucked the remaining morels and tossed them into her basket. Then it was back down the squishy trail and over the footbridge. By the time she reached the parking lot, she was running and nearly out of breath.

She felt a whole lot safer once she'd jumped into her car and clicked the locks. And that's when it struck her. Had the shadow been an eagle . . . or something else?

CHAPTER 28

Suzanne hurried into her house carrying her basket full of morels. She set the basket down on the hall table, slipped off her jacket and muddy shoes, and turned to find Sam standing there. Baxter and Scruff were lined up right behind him, muzzles quivering, ears pitched forward, looking like a backup posse.

"Hi," Suzanne said. She wasn't sure what kind of greeting to expect.

"Hi, yourself," Sam said. Then, "Do you mind explaining to me exactly why you were hanging out with Sheriff Doogie at a murder scene today?"

Okay, now she knew.

Suzanne picked up her basket and hugged it to herself as if for protection. "I told you. Toni and I were driving by and saw all the commotion, so we stopped to investigate. We didn't even know it was Ed Noterman's house until one of the neighbors told us."

"Shocking," Sam said.

"It sure was."

"No, I mean it's shocking that you seem to have an absolute genius for showing up at the scene of a crime. I mean, it happens like clockwork."

"Well, ever since the hospital robbery I've been kind of involved in this whole thing."

"No, it's more than that. You're like some sort of angel of death."

Suzanne peered at Sam. She wasn't sure if he was kidding or not. If that was a half smile or half frown on his face. Maybe this would be a good time to change the subject? To try to pivot the conversation? And she knew exactly how to wrangle it.

"Are you hungry?" Suzanne asked.

"Famished." Sam suddenly looked a lot less serious. Then his nose twitched. "Whatcha got in there anyway? Something good to eat?" He took a step forward, peered into her basket, and smiled. "Oh boy, are those what I think they are?" His mood had suddenly shifted for the better. "You really *did* go out and pick wild morels." He sounded pleased.

"I told you that's what I was up to."

But Sam was already thinking of the next step. "So are we having grilled steak with morels in butter sauce for dinner tonight?"

"Not exactly. These babies are reserved for the red wine sauce Petra's serving at tomorrow's gourmet dinner. So you'd better keep your mitts off them."

"Not even a few slices, gently sautéed?"

"I can barely spare one."

"Would you prefer we continue arguing about your ridiculous *faux pas* this afternoon?"

"Okay, I guess I could spare one morel." Suzanne definitely did not want to continue their argument.

Sam poked a finger in her basket. "I'd like that big fat one right there."

"Sure, why not." Suzanne hadn't realized what a good negotiator Sam was. Tricky.

"So you're going to grill our steaks in a cast iron fry pan on top of the stove, right?" Sam asked. "With butter and sliced morels and then a splash of red wine at the end?"

"If that's what you want, okay." Suzanne was relieved that Sam had decided to drop the subject of her snooping. Good thing, too, because she might not be finished.

SUZANNE fed the dogs, sliced one of the larger morels, and then grilled it in butter sauce along with two petite fillets. She whipped up a side salad of romaine lettuce, croutons, raisins, and walnuts, then added a splash of poppy seed dressing. She toasted two slices of French bread, put plates and silverware on trays, and served up the food. They carried their trays into the living room and sat down companionably on the sofa, noshing away as they watched a rerun of *The Big Bang Theory*.

When there was a commercial break, Suzanne said, "What do you think? About Noterman, I mean. Did he screw up while cleaning his gun or was it . . . you know, a hit?"

"A hit?"

"Did someone shoot Noterman and try to make it look like an accident?"

"I don't know yet. Yes, I'm taking my turn as county coroner, but that only means I can pronounce death. We need a medical examiner to determine the actual cause of death."

"And that's happening right now?" Suzanne asked.

"Absolutely it is."

"But what do *you* think happened? You've seen accidental

deaths before and you've seen murders. What do you think happened?"

Sam turned to her, his eyes glowing with intensity. "If I give you my off-the-cuff opinion, you have to promise not to tell anyone."

"Cross my heart."

"The trajectory looked wrong to me," Sam said.

"So you're saying . . . ?"

"I think somebody shot him."

SUZANNE pondered Sam's theory throughout the rest of the show. Tried to figure out who might have sweet-talked their way past Noterman's front door, shot him, then set up a phony-looking suicide and/or accident. Could it be someone she saw every day? Someone who glad-handed their way into the Cackleberry Club for breakfast, slapping friends on the back while harboring a terrible secret? If so, who could that be?

Sam was in his office trying to catch up on paperwork and Suzanne was shoving dishes into the dishwasher when Toni called.

"Did you get your morels?" she asked.

"Got a basket full."

"Good." Toni paused. "Say, I've been sitting here, talking to Junior."

"Oh no, you're letting him stay over, aren't you?" Suzanne cried.

"The proverbial camel's nose is in the tent, yeah yeah, I know. But that's not the reason I called."

"Then why did you call? You must be feeling better."

"I had a jelly glass full of cheap rosé that seemed to fix me right up. Listen, I asked Junior about Wednesday night, kind of pumped him for details on what happened when he snooped around Stryker's warehouse and got clobbered. And Junior says there were shipments coming into the warehouse that night."

"So what? Shipments are supposed to come into a warehouse."

"Shipments are also supposed to go *out* of a warehouse," Toni said. "Junior doesn't think that's happening."

"What are you saying? What's the drift of this conversation?"

"Only that something seems fishy. Which I think warrants a quick look-see at Stryker's place."

"You mean we should do a creepy crawl?" Suzanne said. The idea intrigued her. Scared her half silly, too.

"Bingo."

"Do you remember what happened when we creepy crawled the survivalists' camp? Didn't work out so hot."

"We're just gonna take a good hard *look*," Toni said. "Not break in and rob the joint or steal a two-ton truck or anything like that. And we're especially not going to be clumsy and stupid like Junior was." Toni's voice drifted away. "Yeah, I know you can hear me. Big deal. Suck it up." Then she was back. "Come on, Suzanne, isn't that fat cat Stryker still on your suspect list? Where's your sense of adventure?"

"It's . . . Hold on a minute." Suzanne set the phone down, walked down the hallway, and peeked in at Sam. He was sitting at his desk, hip deep in paperwork, frowning.

"I have to run out for a little while," Suzanne said. "Do you mind?"

"Nope." Sam shook his head without looking up.

That was enough for Suzanne. She ran back to the phone and said, "Toni?"

"Yeah, I'm here."

"I'm game. You want me to come by and pick you up?"

"Naw, I'll swing by your place in, what, about ten minutes?" Toni said.

"Okay. Be sure to wear dark clothing."

Toni chuckled. "You mean like a cat burglar?"

"That's one way to look at it."

* * *

TONI pulled up to the curb outside Suzanne's house and gave a little toot of the horn. Suzanne grabbed her jacket, fought her way past a curious Baxter and Scruff who were dying to go with her, and ran out the door.

"Hey," she said as she pulled open the door of an aging Chevy Corsica, aka Blue Beater, and jumped into the passenger seat. "I see you're driving another one of Junior's rehabs." The car had been pimped out with a spoiler and turned into a lowrider.

"Yeah, it drives pretty good," Toni said. "As long as you don't feel the need to back up."

"Really?"

"It's something to do with the gears. Junior was fooling around, doing some kind of experimental repair, and it got all screwed up. So, no reverse."

"This from a boy who went to mechanic's school."

"From a boy who *flunked out* of mechanic's school," Toni corrected.

"Anything else I should worry about?" Suzanne looked around at the car's interior. Yellow foam stuffing oozed out of tears in the upholstery, red and green wires formed a tangle where the radio used to be.

"Naw, we're good. Except this steering wheel drives me bonkers."

Suzanne glanced at the steering wheel. Instead of a traditional wheel, Junior had swapped it out for a heavy chain that he'd welded into a circle.

"At least it's creative," Suzanne said. "You can't fault Junior on that."

"Hey, that sure was weird today, huh?" Toni asked. "Seeing Noterman like that?"

"It was crazy. And kind of heartbreaking, too."

"I don't get to see many dead bodies." Toni shuddered. "Don't *like* to see them."

Toni drove down Main Street through downtown Kindred, past a few blocks of older red and yellow brick buildings that housed Kuyper's Hardware, the Kindred Bakery, Root 66, Alchemy Boutique, and Schmitt's Bar, and then headed out Ridgeway Avenue. Ten blocks later they hit the more industrial part of town and turned on Sparks Road.

"Dark out here," Suzanne said. There were a few blue sodium vapor lights, but they were few and far between.

"That's good, yes?" Toni said.

"Maybe."

They drifted past the Econo-Wash, a discount used car lot (NO OFFER TOO CRAZY!), Justin's Tire Emporium, and a small meat processing plant (PARTY MEATS—WE PROCESS DEER). A block later they passed the part of the office park where Stryker Transport was located. There were no cars parked nearby, no lights on in the building.

"Looks deserted," Suzanne said.

"Excellent. I'm going to park over by that surplus store we visited the other day and then we can hoof it back, okay?"

They parked, climbed out of the car, and stood there listening. Not much of anything was going on. It was pitch black with barely any cars around. A few blocks over, on a more well-traveled street, they could hear the occasional car or truck chugging along. And there was a dog barking—*arp, arp, arp*—but that was several blocks away as well.

"I guess it's go time," Toni said. She suddenly didn't sound so sure of herself.

They walked silently out of the parking lot and crossed a street, heading for Stryker Transport. The closer they got, the more the pavement underfoot felt oddly slick. As though there was a general skim of oil.

They stopped in front of a huge metal roll-up door and stared. The temporary vinyl banner that said STRYKER TRANSPORT was still strung across the top of the building.

"What do you think?" Toni asked.

Suzanne made a low sound in the back of her throat. "We really can't see much of anything."

"Not really. But they still might be, um, cooking meth in there or something."

Feeling frustrated, knowing Toni could be right, Suzanne looked up at the building and studied it for a few moments. She backed up ten feet, then twenty feet.

"What's clicking in that brain of yours, Suzie Q?" Toni asked.

"I'm looking for . . . There . . . now I can see them. Skylights up on the roof."

"Okay, yeah, good idea. Maybe we could look inside that way." Toni scrunched up her face. "But how the heck are we gonna get up there?"

Suzanne glanced left, then right. At the far end of the building, in a pool of shadows, she spotted a hulking green Dumpster.

"Maybe . . ." Suzanne said, studying it. The metal contraption was a good six feet high and built like a Russian tank. But if they could get on top . . .

In a kind of unspoken agreement, Suzanne and Toni strolled casually toward the Dumpster.

"So you're thinking we could climb on top of that big honkin' trash bin and then scramble up the side of the building like a couple of squirrels?" Toni asked. She sounded a teeny bit skeptical.

But Suzanne had already wedged a toe in the Dumpster's crossbar and, in a move as agile and lithe as a Siamese cat, boosted herself up.

CHAPTER 29

"COME on up, you can do it," Suzanne said. "Just step onto that cross bar and kind of boost yourself up."

"I'm wearing cowboy boots," Toni said.

"That's even better, they're nice and sturdy. Come on. Take a little hop and give me your arm. I'll pull you up."

Toni stuck the toe of her boot on the crossbar while she held on to a corner of the Dumpster for dear life.

"That's the ticket," Suzanne said. "Now push yourself up." She reached down and grabbed Toni's flailing hand.

"Owww, it feels like you're yanking my arm out of its socket!"

"Use your feet, keep pushing." Suzanne sounded like a fitness trainer, supportive yet firm.

"I'm trying!" Toni was still five feet below Suzanne.

Suzanne peered into the darkness. "Let go! You've got to let go!" Toni's fingers were still curled tightly around a corner of the Dumpster.

Toni finally muttered a prayer, let go, and found herself being hauled up onto the lid of the Dumpster. She landed with a loud, hollow thunk, spread-eagled and panting.

"Boy, am I sorry I called you tonight," Toni gasped out.

"What are you talking about? This is working out great so far."

"Maybe for you," Toni said as she struggled to her feet. Then she wiggled her nose and said, "Eee-yu, it stinks up here." She looked down at the green monster they were standing on and gave a little bounce. "That greasy smell must be from a year's worth of discarded pizza."

"Either that or the meat processing plant down the block has been doing some clandestine dumping."

"Don't even start," Toni said. "You know how I feel about stuff like that." She scrubbed a hand across her nose and said, "Now what?"

Suzanne pointed toward the rooftop. "Now we still have to get up there."

Toni let out a long sigh. "How . . . ?"

Suzanne cupped her hands together. "I'm gonna give you a boost."

"Me? Never happen, my legs are too short and that roof is too high."

"Step into my hands and take a big bounce, then grab for the roof ledge and pull yourself up."

"What? You think I did an aerialist internship with Barnum & Bailey?"

"You can do it," Suzanne said. "I have faith."

"A lot more than I do." But Toni did as instructed. She drew a deep breath, bounded into Suzanne's clasped hands, and flew upward, flapping her arms wildly like a primitive bird. At the last second she managed to grab the edge of the roof. Now she was dangling in midair, feet kicking helplessly.

"Help!" Toni cried. "I'm barely hanging on by my acrylic nails."

"Go ahead and pull yourself up," Suzanne urged.

"Can't." Toni made a choking sound. "No upper body strength. I'm like a jellyfish."

Suzanne scanned the side of the building, then stood on tiptoes and stretched up a hand, managing to press it up underneath Toni's right boot. "Okay, do you feel me supporting you?"

"Yup."

"Just to your left is a kind of air vent. If you can get your other foot wedged in there, I think you can boost yourself up."

Toni's left foot flailed around, hit something metallic, and skidded slightly. Then, at the very last moment, she found purchase. "Got it!"

"Okay, go!" Suzanne cried.

And just like that Toni propelled herself up and over the lip of the roof. She disappeared, leaving only a fine mist of loose tar particles to filter down.

"You alright?" Suzanne called.

Toni's grinning face peered down at her. "It's kind of cool up here. You can see everything. A sky full of twinkling stars, the whole town . . . I think I see my apartment."

"That's peachy, now let's get me up there, too," Suzanne said.

"Hold on," Toni said. She was gone for a few seconds and then returned. "I found an old broom handle. Like from one of those industrial push brooms?"

"If you dangle it down maybe you can pull me up," Suzanne said.

"Lemme give it the old college try."

Toni extended the broom handle, watched as Suzanne grabbed on to it, then huffed and puffed and slowly pulled her friend up. Just like Toni, Suzanne wedged a toe in the air vent, which gave her the exact leverage she needed. Seconds later, Suzanne was on the roof, too.

Suzanne brushed herself off, glanced around, then headed for the nearest skylight. Toni followed, though she still seemed dazzled by the view.

Carefully inching her face over the skylight, Suzanne peered in. There was a faint light that revealed nothing but empty metal shelves and a bare concrete floor.

Toni looked, too. "Nobody home. But I think this skylight might be over a still-to-be-leased part of the building."

They tiptoed to the second skylight and looked in. There was nothing but darkness below.

"Third time's the charm?" Suzanne said. But that space proved to be dark as well.

They crept along, feeling nervous, scared, and a little exposed on their rooftop perch. After all, what if someone spotted them? This kind of trespassing wasn't exactly a minor infraction.

"And on to the next skylight," Suzanne said. Her voice was bright but her insides were a ball of tension. "This has to be it."

And, incredibly, it was.

A faint light glowed from down below.

"What do you see?" Toni asked as she crouched next to Suzanne.

"Maybe, um, boxes on shelves along one wall? But what is that platform thing directly below us?"

"Hard to tell," Toni said. "This skylight's so grimy.

"You think we could pry it open?"

"Uh . . . no."

Suzanne felt around at the base of the skylight. "But there's a hinge here. Hinges. So maybe . . . ?"

"It's hinged?" Now Toni sounded mildly interested. She rummaged around in her purse, found a metal comb, a couple of bobby pins, and, finally, a beer can opener. "Don't have any pry bars on me, but maybe my trusty church key will work just as well."

Suzanne took the church key and tapped along the edge of the skylight. When she found a part that felt slightly loose, she jammed the church key in and worked it along the edge of the skylight. Gunk came out. Paint, dirt, whatever. But working doggedly, she finally found a spot where she could slip her fingers in. From there it was a matter of grasping the skylight and tipping it back on two groaning hinges.

Toni grimaced. "Like opening a tomb. You think anybody heard that awful sound?"

Suzanne stuck her head in the gaping hole. "Don't know. But there doesn't seem to be anybody home down there."

"What do you see?"

"Not much. There's a faint light on somewhere so . . ." Suzanne's voice trailed off.

"What?" Toni said.

"And there happens to be a truck parked directly below us."

"Yeah?"

"I'm going to drop down and take a look around," Suzanne said. "You can wait up here if you want."

Toni was offended. "And let you have all the fun? Uh-uh, girl-friend. Remember whose idea it was to come here in the first place?"

"Okay, then, let's do it." Suzanne dropped down about five feet and landed with a soft thud on the roof of a truck cab. Toni followed suit.

"Shazam," Toni said.

They looked around, then carefully slid down the windshield onto the hood of the truck. Then they grabbed hand holds and swung down onto the running board.

"Nobody here, thank goodness," Suzanne said. But the dim light revealed what appeared to be a fully stocked warehouse.

"Will you look at all this stuff," Toni marveled. Strangely, the warehouse was stocked mostly with cases of liquor and cigarettes. "There's booze. And cigarettes galore. Kind of crazy."

"Where are the pickles?" Suzanne asked. Something about this felt wrong to her. "Where are the bottles of olive oil?"

Toni peered at a couple of the crates. "This is weird. Some of this stuff still has waybills on it to be shipped to liquor stores over in Rochester and Albert Lea. So why would it be stored here?" She shook her head. "That doesn't make much sense."

Suzanne leaned in for a closer look. "Toni, this paperwork is dated last month."

"Maybe Stryker's behind on his deliveries," Toni said. "Because he, um, moved his headquarters?"

But the answer clicked in suddenly for Suzanne, like a puzzle piece that had befuddled her, then finally found its rightful place.

"Holy cow," Suzanne said in a startled whisper. "Stryker's not a distributor, he's the hijacker!"

"Whaaat?" Toni said loudly.

"Those truck hijackings? He's got to be behind them."

"He's a crook?"

"And what if he's also into dealing drugs?" Suzanne asked. "What if Stryker or one of his gang is the hospital killer? What if they were the ones who went after poor Ed Noterman and made him . . ." Suzanne stopped suddenly and put a finger to her lips. She'd just heard a faint buzz of voices. Men's voices. And they were dangerously close. "Listen," she whispered to Toni.

They both stood motionless and strained their ears to hear.

"You want me to unload this stuff?" a faint voice called out.

"Tomorrow's soon enough, Cully."

"So just pull the truck in?" Now the voice sounded closer.

"And lock up tight. We don't want any prying eyes."

Toni hunched her shoulders. "I know that voice."

Suzanne nodded her head. "So do I. It's Robert Stryker!"

"We gotta bug out fast," Toni said.

"Back to the truck!" Suzanne whispered. Her heart was beating wildly. To get caught now, red-handed, would be a disaster.

They scrambled up onto the roof of the truck cab, clutching at each other, helping pull each other up. Suzanne bent down and bounded upward like a white-tailed deer clearing a creek. She grabbed on to the ledge where the skylight was and swung back and forth. As she gained leverage, she pulled her knees up, and managed to hoist herself onto the roof.

"I need some help here," Toni whispered from down below.

Suzanne lay flat on the roof, the upper part of her body extending over the open space. She reached down and locked hands with Toni. Slowly, she began lifting her from the roof of the truck.

Toni was halfway through the hole in the roof, looking like a jack-in-the-box, when the man someone had called Cully shouted, "Hey! What's going on up there!"

A look of terror flashed across Toni's face. "Help me!" She was almost gagging with fear.

There was a metallic tremor below, then a series of grunts and gasps. Cully was climbing up onto the cab.

"Hurry!" Toni called. "Haul me up!"

But as Suzanne renewed her struggle to hoist Toni up, Cully reached a big hand up and grabbed one of Toni's cowboy boots.

"Come down from there!" he yelled.

Seconds later, he wrapped both hands around her boot and tugged hard.

"He's pulling me down!" Toni screamed as she sank lower toward Cully.

Suzanne yanked harder, but Toni didn't seem to budge. The jerk below—Cully—was hanging on to Toni like some kind of snapping turtle!

Suzanne refused to let go as she and Cully pulled Toni back and forth in a ferocious tug-of-war. She was panting, pulling with all her might.

"Ouch! Ouch!" Toni cried at Cully. "Let me go, you tub of lard!"

"Kick him!" Suzanne screamed. "Kick him hard with your other leg!"

Toni's unfettered leg flailed hard at Cully, brushed against his forehead, hit his ear, and then . . .

THWOK!

She finally connected with Cully's head!

"Shit!" Cully yelped as Toni popped free and he tumbled down, a chunky, angry man who began swearing a blue streak.

"I conked him in the melon!" Toni cried as Suzanne hoisted her the rest of the way up until she was safely on the roof. But there was no time to waste.

"Quick!" Suzanne cried. "Try to muscle that skylight back in place while I call Doogie."

MOMENTS later Suzanne had Sheriff Doogie on the line.

"Help," she stuttered out. "Toni and I are stuck on the roof of Stryker's warehouse."

"Jeez, don't tell me that," Doogie said. "I'll have to arrest you for trespassing."

"Doogie, listen carefully. Stryker's warehouse is full of stolen goods. I think he's the one who's been running that truck hijack ring. For all we know he could've robbed those pharmacies, too."

Suzanne heard only breath sounds on the other end of the line.

"Are you there?" she asked.

"Yeah," Doogie said. "I'm thinkin'."

"Well, think real fast because we're trapped and need help bad."

From down below there was another barrage of shouting and swearing.

"What the Sam Hill is that?" Doogie asked.

"Stryker and some of his buddies. Listen." Suzanne dropped the phone down so Doogie could hear.

"Hey, Cinderella," Cully shouted up at them. "I got your shoe. Come and get it. And bring your friend."

"You hear that?" Suzanne asked Doogie.

"On my way," he said.

"Bring help. And lots of deputies. Lights and sirens all the way." But Doogie had already hung up.

Cully's voice bellowed again. "You got nowhere to go, girls. Better come down."

Toni finished dropping the skylight into place then turned and clutched Suzanne in a heartfelt embrace.

"Don't let them take me alive," Toni quavered.

"Doogie's on his way, try not to worry," Suzanne said.

"Yeah, but those jackholes are right here, right now."

Apprehensive now, picking up Toni's vibes, Suzanne stepped over to the edge of the building and looked down.

Oh no!

Cully was down in the parking lot with two other men. One Suzanne didn't recognize, one looked like Robert Stryker. Together they were muscling a tall metal ladder up against the front of the building.

"What's happening?" Toni asked.

"They're putting up a ladder," Suzanne said as her brain whirled feverishly. *What to do? What to do?*

"Toni," Suzanne said in an urgent tone. "We need some kind of weapon."

"We got the broom handle," Toni said.

"That's something. What else do you have in your bag of tricks? Any firecrackers by chance?"

"No, um . . ." Toni was rummaging through her oversized handbag. "I got a tin of Altoids, a rat tail comb, hairspray, bobby pins, chewing gum, a bunch of dimes and quarters, my favorite Candy Pink lip gloss . . ."

"Toni, focus. We need weapons."

"Got a couple crochet hooks that Petra gave me."

"Wait a minute," Suzanne said. "Have you still got that camo-colored lighter?"

Toni felt around some more and pulled out her Bic. "Yup."

"Give it to me. Along with the hairspray."

"You serious?" Toni said.

Suzanne grabbed the lighter and hairspray and stepped to the very edge of the building. Cully—she assumed the chubby guy was Cully—had his foot on the bottom rung of the ladder and was just starting up. The metal ladder made an ominous *clank* as it rattled against the building.

"Here I come, ready or not," Cully called out in a taunting singsong voice.

"You sure about that?" Suzanne called back. "Do you dirtbags really have the guts to take us on?"

"Wait'll I get my hands on you . . ."

"Was that a threat?" Suzanne called back in a bold voice.

Cully was halfway up the ladder now and still climbing. "That's a promise, smart mouth," he snarled.

"I don't think you're a match for us," Suzanne said as she flicked on Toni's lighter. The dancing flame flickered blue and yellow as Suzanne held out her hand. "See this?"

"What's the big . . ."

Before Cully could finish his words, Suzanne depressed the lever on the can of hairspray. The aerosol whooshed through the air, hit the flame, and created a six-foot-long incandescent string of fire that was worthy of a World War II flamethrower.

"Holy shit, lady! You just burned my . . ."

Suzanne kept the flame roaring even though her thumb was starting to feel hot and crispy.

Cully was screaming to high heaven as he scrambled down the ladder as fast as his chunky body could carry him.

Toni danced a little jig as she watched the flames die and Cully make his hasty retreat.

"Any other takers?" Suzanne asked as she held up the lighter.

"We still got a full can of hairspray," Toni yelled.

Cully stumbled on the bottom step, twisted awkwardly, and got his feet tangled up. Which brought the entire ladder crashing down on top of the other two men.

Toni giggled wildly at the sight of the three men sent sprawling. "Hot-cha, you did it, Suzanne, you corralled them."

Suddenly, the night air was filled with sirens and flashing lights.

"Here comes the cavalry!" Toni yelled as she tossed down the crochet hooks for good measure.

From their lofty vantage point, Suzanne and Toni watched the three cruisers swoop in. They approached from different directions, virtually trapping the three men at the front door. Car doors flew open, deputies wearing vests jumped out, guns were pointed.

"Give it up," Doogie yelled through his car's fuzzy PA system. "Get down on the ground and place your hands over your heads."

It was all over in a matter of minutes. Through a litany of protests, Stryker and Cully were handcuffed and stuffed inside the back of the cruisers. The other guy, who must have hit his head, kept walking in a circle going "Whada? Whada? Whada?" until he was finally captured, too.

Doogie went into the open warehouse, looked around, whistled, and said, "Holy shit." He walked back out and gazed up at Suzanne and Toni, who were still standing on the roof.

"You solved a major crime," he yelled up at them.

"No kidding," Suzanne said while Toni took a little bow.

Deputy Driscoll put a hand to his forehead, as if to shade his eyes from the flashing lights, and said, "Want me to put the ladder back up so's you can climb down?"

"That's okay," Toni said. "We'll just take the Dumpster express."

DOOGIE was standing next to the Dumpster, holding Toni's boot as they climbed down. His navy hoodie had the words OF COURSE I'M RIGHT, I'M THE SHERIFF emblazoned across the front in bold yellow type. As long as his baggy khakis were, they couldn't hide the fact that he was still wearing fluffy gray bedroom slippers.

"Nice outfit," Suzanne said.

"Well, you told me to come as fast as possible," Doogie said.

Suzanne suddenly felt a renewed surge of adrenaline. "Did you see any stolen drugs stashed in the warehouse?" she asked in a rush. "Have you had a chance to look at those guys' arms? Does one of them have a cocaine tattoo? Do you think you can tie them to Noterman's death?"

"All in good time," Doogie said. "I'm in charge from here on in."

"But one of them could be the pharmacy robber and killer," Suzanne cried.

"Calm down," Doogie said. "*Slow* down. We'll get there."

"There's so much that's still unsettled," Suzanne said.

"I *said* we'll get there," Doogie snapped.

"At least we brought down the truck hijack gang," Toni said as she snatched her boot from Doogie's hand. She jammed a stockinged foot into it, gave a little stomp, and said, "So who's the doofus now?"

CHAPTER 30

"SUZANNE?"

Suzanne cracked open an eye and saw a very handsome man standing over her. Sam.

She stretched her arms toward the headboard and aimed a drowsy smile at him. "Good morning."

Sam did not smile back.

"You had a big day yesterday," Sam said. "A double header. First you insinuated yourself into the Noterman death, and now Sheriff Doogie informs me that you and your compadre invaded a warehouse last night."

Doggone Doogie and his big mouth.

Suzanne shoved back the covers and hopped out of bed. Better to stand toe to toe for this conversation than have Sam looming over her.

Still unsure how to respond, Suzanne stammered out, "When did you see Doogie?"

"He called early this morning. Wanted to know how you were

doing after your grand adventure last night. Of course I had no idea what he was talking about." Sam crossed his arms and stared at her.

Tell the truth? Lie?

No, she couldn't lie to Sam. Not completely anyway.

"Toni and I wanted to take a look at that warehouse where Junior got beat up and we, um, kind of got caught up in a few things."

"Suzanne, Sheriff Doogie told me that you and Toni were accosted by three hijackers and got trapped on the roof. The roof! Even if those hijackers didn't hurt you—and I'm sure they would have if they'd caught you—you could have fallen to your death."

"It wasn't nearly as dangerous as it sounds." Suzanne tried to project an air of sincerity. "At the first sign of trouble I called Doogie. Toni and I were never *really* in jeopardy. And . . . and those truck hijackers were apprehended!"

But Sam wasn't buying it. "How do you expect me to go about my normal day when I have to worry about you and . . ." He threw up his hands. "I should have asked the sheriff if I could borrow a set of handcuffs. To lock you up and keep you at home."

Suzanne slipped into Sam's arms. "But I'm okay. Really I am."

Sam leaned forward and kissed her gently on the forehead. "I have to get to the clinic but, trust me, this conversation isn't over by a long shot."

"You're still coming to our Petit Paris dinner tonight, aren't you?"

Sam nodded. His eyes and mouth crinkled into the beginning of a smile, then he caught himself and turned serious again. "Yes. If only to keep a watchful eye on you."

ON the way to the Cackleberry Club, Suzanne was still trying to puzzle things out. It was hard to believe that Stryker had also been the shooter at the hospital. On the other hand, Doogie might find a pile of drugs stashed in his warehouse. Also, it was pretty obvious that Noterman wasn't the guy, either. So who was this mysterious killer and thief? Over the last few days, her suspects had been dropping like flies. So maybe she had to try a different angle?

Suzanne was sitting at a stop sign, waiting for two bicyclists to cross in front of her, when she remembered Junior's mention of an electric bike.

What had he said?

Oh yeah, he'd theorized that maybe the hospital shooter had made his stealthy escape on an electric bike that produced little to no sound.

And didn't Junior say that Kuyper's Hardware sold them?

Suzanne smiled as the two bikers rode away and decided to swing by Kuyper's to check it out. Couldn't hurt. And, as luck would have it, Kuyper's was right on the way.

Suzanne parked in front of the original 1930s red brick building on Main Street. Kuyper's large front display windows were sparkly clean and filled with antique hammers, shovels, and awls that sat side by side with today's counterparts.

Inside, the store was modern and well-lit, but with old-timey glass cases and cabinets.

When the bell over the door jingled, Roger Kuyper set down a can of green paint and came out from behind the counter.

"You're off to an early start, Suzanne. What can I help you with today?"

"I'm on a scouting expedition, Mr. Kuyper. I understand you sell electric bicycles."

Kuyper nodded. "E-bikes. Sure do. Want to see one? I got it parked over with the regular bikes."

Suzanne followed Kuyper and found herself gazing at a shiny silver tricked-out bike. "Nice. What can you tell me about it?"

"Electric bikes are just like regular bikes, but with an electric boost. You pedal and the bike's motor engages, adding power to your ride. Makes it easy to zip up hills and cruise over rough terrain."

"So you have to charge the bike?"

"Nope." Kuyper pointed to a flat box encased in a cage over the rear tire. "That's a 36-volt battery pack. It's sleek and stable. Lasts forever."

"And what about noise?" Suzanne asked.

"They're totally silent. You could ride away from the house at three in the morning and Dr. Sam would never hear you leave."

After this morning's go-round, Suzanne figured Sam would be more likely to hang a bell around her neck.

"I bet these bikes are really catching on, huh? Have you sold many?" she asked.

"Truth be told, I've only sold two so far. One to a nice young lady from Jessup who actually rode it home," Kuyper said. "The other sale . . . I gotta say it made me kind of nervous."

Suzanne's ears perked up. Mr. Kuyper had a suspicious customer?

"It was a young boy, couldn't have been more than ten. But he'd read all about these e-bikes and was desperate to start hitting the hills with one. I thought he was too young for all that power, but his dad was adamant."

By the time Suzanne arrived at the Cackleberry Club it was midmorning. She parked in back, reminding herself that this was where they'd have to set up the grill for tonight, then pushed her way into the kitchen. There was an apology on her lips for showing up so late but Suzanne never got a chance.

Petra heard the door click open, turned with a smile on her broad face, and said, "Toni tells me you two are the heroes of the hour! That you single-handedly—or would it be doublehandedly?—brought down that truck hijack ring!" She flew across the room and gave Suzanne a giant bear hug. "Good for you."

"I'm not sure everyone sees it with as much positivity as you do," Suzanne said. "Sheriff Doogie was . . ."

Petra waved a hand. "Doogie probably feels embarrassed that he didn't figure it out himself. I mean, Mayor Mobley was parading that Stryker fellow all over town, talking him up like he was Mr. Big Boss. And now he turns out to be a crook. A common thief."

Toni heard the commotion and ran into the kitchen. "I told Petra all about our big adventure last night." She was fairly bubbling with energy.

"About getting up on the roof, and cranking open the skylight, and discovering all those stolen goods," Petra said.

"And almost getting caught," Suzanne said. The night wasn't all fun and games, but that hadn't dampened Toni's spirits.

"And I told her about that flamethrower trick you did with the lighter and hairspray. Whoosh!" Toni threw her arms up in the air. "Scared the crap out of Stryker and company and really saved our hides."

"I'm just bursting with pride for you brave ladies," Petra said.

"Maybe you should name a sandwich after us," Toni said. "Call it the Hijack Pepperjack Special."

Petra aimed a finger at her. "I like that."

"Or a cocktail. The Hijack Highball."

"So the murders and pharmacy robberies are solved?" Petra asked. "Stryker was behind everything?"

Suzanne shook her head. "We don't know that at all. Doogie and his officers still have to poke through the warehouse and look for evidence of pharmaceuticals."

Petra's smile slipped. "Here I thought we were all done with this nonsense."

"Maybe we are, maybe we're not. That's up to Sheriff Doogie to figure out," Suzanne said.

"So you're bowing out of the investigation?" Petra asked.

"I think I almost have to," Suzanne said. "Doogie's upset with me for horning in so much, and Sam . . . well, the less said about that the better."

"Oh." Petra seemed disappointed.

"But the good news is, I picked a whole bunch of morels for you. They're out in my car," Suzanne said.

"That's terrific," Petra said, moving back to her stove, where a pan of bacon sizzled. "I can't wait to start working on my sauces."

"Sauces plural?" Suzanne asked.

"A basting sauce for grilling the fillets and then a morel sauce for when we serve them."

"Yum," Toni said. "Why don't I run out and grab everything? I got two dozen loaves of French bread in my car that I gotta bring in as well." She ducked out the back door.

"So . . ." Suzanne hung over Petra's shoulder. "What's on the morning menu?"

"Hangover hash, for one thing," Petra said. "That's always wildly popular after a boozy Friday night."

Suzanne couldn't help but chuckle.

"Along with biscuits and gravy, scrambled eggs and chicken sausage, avocado and salsa omelets, and blueberry banana bread."

Toni came tripping in, carrying the basket of morels and an armload of French bread. She set everything down on the butcher block counter.

"When I stopped at the Kindred Bakery to pick up the French bread, Jenny was all excited about the raid last night. Said it's good to have things back to normal."

"But now Suzanne is saying it's not." Petra turned to look at Suzanne. "That things are still up in the air."

"Like I said, we'll have to wait and see," Suzanne said. "Let Doogie finish his investigation."

"Somehow that doesn't sound like you," Toni muttered under her breath.

"I can't . . ." Suzanne started to say. Then she thought about Sam's stiff warning to her earlier this morning and said, "I just can't."

"Okay, girlfriend," Toni said. "We'll circle back to this later. For now let's *carpe* this friggin' *diem.*"

Suzanne and Toni waited on a few customers, took orders, made small talk, and acted like they'd forgotten about the hijackings, robberies, two murders, and last night's crazy adventure.

But they really hadn't.

As Toni plated a cinnamon roll and Suzanne poured a glass of orange juice, Toni said, "What about those two dingbats next door?"

"What about them?" Suzanne said.

"Could one of those boys be the killer?" Before Suzanne could reply Toni added, "Or maybe one's the killer and the other's the robber."

Suzanne shook her dead. "Don't know."

"But they're supposedly ex-druggies. So aren't you burning with curiosity to see if they've relapsed?"

"My ears are still burning from the lecture I got from Sam."

Toni patted her on the shoulder. "You'll get over it, hon. You always do. Hey, do you know why the black widow spider eats her mate?" She gave Suzanne a conspiratorial wink. "To stop the snoring."

Suzanne delivered her coffee, then ran into the kitchen to pick up an order of scrambled eggs.

"Did you know we have an owl hooting out there in one of those trees?" Petra asked. "Doesn't he know it's morning?"

"I don't think owls are always strictly nocturnal," Suzanne said. "Maybe this one didn't get the memo."

IT wasn't until late morning that Doogie came tromping in. He looked around at the café, saw there were only a few lingering customers, then headed for the counter.

Suzanne was there in a flash. She put a cup of coffee and a slice of custard pie in front of him and said, "Is it over?"

"Maybe." Doogie shrugged.

"Either it is or it isn't." Suzanne wanted a solid definitive answer.

Doogie scratched his head. "We tore that warehouse apart at the seams and still didn't find any pharmaceuticals. Not even an aspirin in the first aid kit."

Suzanne's heart did a flip-flop. "So you think the truck hijacking and the pharmacy robberies are two separate crime sprees?"

"I ain't saying that just yet. It may only be a matter of time before Stryker cracks under pressure or one of his guys dimes him out. Nobody wants to go to prison to protect a crooked boss."

"And if the truck guys aren't involved in the pharmacy robberies?"

"Then we're back to square one," Doogie said. He picked up his cup of coffee, blew on it, and took a slurp. "There's some other tricky news, too."

"What's that?"

Doogie heaved a sigh. "It wasn't the same gun."

Suzanne was on red alert. "What do you mean?"

"We got an early ballistics report. The weapon that killed Harold Spooner wasn't the same gun we found at Noterman's house. They were both 9mm but the ballistics were different."

"What does that mean?"

"It means that Noterman was killed with his own gun."

"Murdered," Suzanne said.

"Oh . . . probably."

"And when Harold Spooner was shot at the hospital? And Ginny?"

"A different 9mm gun," Doogie said.

"So a different guy?"

"Could be," Doogie said.

"So everything is still up in the air."

"These investigations take time," Doogie said. "You have to work your way through them, pick apart every nit and nat." He took another slurp of coffee just as the front door banged open. He turned in his seat to see who'd walked in just as Suzanne glanced that way, too.

"Carmen," Suzanne said. She took one look at Carmen's face and thought, *Uh-oh*.

"Suzanne Dietz," Carmen screamed in a shrill raise-the-rafters voice. "And Sheriff Roy Doogie. Just the two co-conspirators I was looking for." She came barreling across the café, lips pulled tight, an angry gleam in her eyes, high heels clacking against the floor like castanets.

"Carmen," Suzanne said again. She had a sinking feeling she knew what this impromptu visit was all about.

"How *dare* you arrest Robert Stryker!" Carmen screeched. "He's a kind, wonderful, innocent man. A prominent businessman."

"Who just happens to have a warehouse chock full of stolen goods," Doogie said. He didn't seem to be taking Carmen's performance all that seriously.

"The man is innocent!" Carmen cried. "Innocent until proven guilty."

"Correct," Doogie said. He looked at Suzanne and said, "Ya think I could get a chocolate donut with sprinkles?"

"Coming right up," Suzanne said.

"Go ahead and make a ridiculous mockery of his arrest," Carmen said in an icy-cold voice. "Suzanne here is caught breaking and entering, but Robert Stryker is the one who gets arrested. Don't you see? He's a *victim*. Honestly, I can't believe the *unfairness* of it all!"

"Stryker was basically caught red-handed, Carmen," Suzanne said. "With piles of stolen goods." She wasn't going to stand here and listen to this verbal assault. If you let her, Carmen would chatter like a chipmunk all morning long. And there was work to be done.

"The best advice I can give," Doogie said, "is to hire a good lawyer for your friend." Doogie's eyes twinkled. "Or, if he can't afford one, the court will appoint a public defender."

"Can't *afford* one!" Carmen sputtered. "Can't afford . . . ? Just who do you think you're . . . ?" Carmen's eyes crossed as if she were about to have a fit and her mouth snapped shut. Then she gathered herself together, spun on her heels, and flounced out of the café with as much dignity (very little) as she could muster.

"I think you offended her," Suzanne said.

"Aw, you think so?" Doogie showed his eyeteeth when he smiled.

CHAPTER 31

"THIS Petit Paris dinner is going to be fabulous. Probably the best event we've ever done," Toni announced. She wasn't just animated, she was dancing around the café like a prima ballerina. "Maybe not as exciting as catching all those crooks last night, but from a business standpoint, the most successful dinner ever!"

"I sincerely hope you're right," Suzanne said. "Because we're for sure stretching our culinary chops with this menu."

"Oh, Petra can . . ."

"What can Petra do?" Petra asked as she slid through the swinging door into the café.

"I was just about to say you can outdo any cook, chef, or grill master in six counties," Toni said.

"Better than Koppelman's over in Cornucopia?" Petra lifted an eyebrow.

"Well, their *chateaubriand* is awfully tasty," Toni allowed. "But your menu tonight is . . . it's . . ." She was fishing for the right word. "Showier!"

"Thank you, I think," Petra said. "Now." She looked around the empty café, which looked just like . . . an empty café. "What do you two have up your sleeves for decorating? How are you going to make the magic of *Gay Paree* happen for us?"

"We've been working on that," Toni said. "Suzanne printed out the menus to look like little French passports."

"Excellent," Petra said. "And all those flowers sitting in my cooler?"

"We're going to use as many pink and white flowers as possible," Suzanne said. "Put them in crystal vases, use pink tablecloths, maybe even accent the flowers with some pink and black feathers we have left over from . . . well, I don't know what event that was. Maybe our Mardi Gras party."

"I get the drift," Petra said. "And it all sounds *trés* Parisian. Okay, my menu is whispering to me, so I'm going back in the kitchen to start whipping up a few delicacies."

"You're still going to hang bunches of flowers from the chandelier again, right?" Suzanne asked Toni.

"Oh yeah. And I think we should tie pink and white frou-frou ribbons on all the chair backs."

"We've for sure got to use the Fleur De Lys white stoneware," Suzanne said. "With crystal goblets for the wine."

"And you have the paper napkins with the Eiffel Tower images on them?"

"Yes, and I also ordered a few French berets for the men and scrounged a tape of Edith Piaf songs to play on our sound system."

Toni rolled her eyes. "Oo la la."

Suzanne shot an index finger at her. "Girlfriend, you just said a mouthful. But now we better hurry up and get busy."

Suzanne and Toni spread tablecloths, arranged flowers, set tables, added candles, laid out the passport menus, and added touches of playful French décor.

"Whew," Toni said, "I've never been to Paris but this place is genuinely starting to look like a Left Bank bistro."

"Believe it," Suzanne said. She'd just untangled a string of tiny white twinkle lights and was wondering where to put them.

Then the front door banged open and Junior stuck his head in. "Knock knock," he called out. "Are you ladies decent?"

"*Junior!*" Toni scolded.

"Got a big surprise for you," Junior said. He was grinning like a Halloween pumpkin.

"Hold everything," Suzanne said, staring at him. "You really did it? I mean, you actually got it done in time?"

"Come on outside and take a gander at my handiwork," Junior said.

Suzanne and Toni trooped outside after Junior.

"See?" Junior swept a hand toward a low, flat trailer that hung off the back of his combination pickup-camper. It held a five-foot-high credible scale model of the Eiffel Tower.

"*Voulez vous* . . . uh, le Eiffel?" Junior asked.

"Holy smokes!" Toni cried. "You did it. *How'd* you do it?"

"Aw, I got all these thin scraps of wood at the lumberyard for, like, free. And then I just started gluing them together," Junior said. "Kind of criss-cross like. And then, this morning, I found a can of gold spray paint and painted the whole thing gold."

"It's wonderful," Suzanne said, because it really was.

"Just amazing," Toni said. She looked at Suzanne and said, "I guess we should award Junior a participation trophy after all."

"And now I know what to do with that string of miniature lights," Suzanne said.

Toni saw movement inside Junior's truck cab and said, "Who've you got sitting in your truck there?"

"That's Kidd," Junior said.

"You've got a *kid* in there?" Toni sputtered. "Are you crazy?"

"No, it's *Captain* Kidd," Junior said.

Drawn in by their bizarre exchange, Suzanne said, "I know I shouldn't ask, but who exactly is this Captain Kidd?"

"It's not a who, it's a what," Junior said. "It's a goat."

"Pray tell, why do you have a goat?" Toni asked.

"I traded Chubs Schwingler for a set of tires."

"And you got a goat in return?" Toni was clearly flummoxed.

"It was a good deal because . . . well . . ." Junior shrugged. "The goat's not much and the tires were practically bald."

"What are you going to do with a goat?" Suzanne asked. They all moved over to Junior's truck and gazed at the small white goat that stood imperiously on the front seat. It looked back at them with eyes like liquid blue marbles and said, *Baaah.*

"Dunno. I thought I'd stake Kidd out in back of your place for now," Junior said. "Let him graze a bit so he doesn't rip the insides out of my truck. Besides, after we move the Eiffel Tower inside, I wanna hang around and help you guys with your fancy dinner." He rocked back on his heels. "Can I? Huh?"

"Sure. But keep that goat away from our back door, okay?" Suzanne said. "We're going to be in and out all evening grilling steaks."

JUST as Suzanne was in the kitchen, peeling hardboiled eggs for Petra, Jimmy John Floyd knocked on the back door. He opened it slightly and poked his head in. "Petra?"

Petra whirled around and said, "There you are. I've been on pins and needles all day, waiting for our big delivery."

"Well I got it," Floyd said. "Every last lick that you asked for. Including that fancy French cheese."

"The Brie," Suzanne said.

Floyd nodded. "Even the fresh peaches. They're so good and

juicy you'll think you've died and gone to heaven." He paused. "Hey. Did you know there's a goat in your backyard?"

Toni had just walked into the kitchen. "That's Captain Kidd. Junior's goat."

"You're not going to . . ." Floyd made a slicing motion across his throat.

"Cook him?" Toni cried. "Oh no!"

"We're grilling steaks tonight," Suzanne said. She chuckled. "Sticking to our original menu."

Floyd looked relieved. "Well . . . good. Heh heh. I'll go grab your order and be back in a flash."

"Need help with those eggs?" Toni asked Suzanne.

"Nope. Almost done here," Suzanne said.

Floyd carried in two crates of produce and set them next to the butcher block counter.

"You have my caviar?" Petra asked. She'd been fretting about her egg shooters all day.

"Got you a nice domestic brand called AmeriCaviar. Small, crisp whitefish roe from the Great Lakes, not too expensive."

"Are we ever gonna live it up tonight," Toni said. She grabbed one of the tins of caviar and danced around. "Eat, drink, and celebrate our crime-fighting prowess. And the fact that Suzanne has been such a great little investigator."

"You don't say," Floyd said, mostly out of politeness.

"Oh yeah," Toni said. "Suzanne was the one who pulled Birdie's fat out of the fire when Doogie thought she robbed the hospital pharmacy and then, just last night, she solved . . . well, with my help, of course . . . the truck hijacking thing. The ringleader, Robert Stryker, is cooling his heels in jail right now."

"That's been solved?" Floyd asked. He touched a hand to his heart. "I've been worried about those hijackers while driving my route. Always nervous that they'd come swooping in after me."

"Now you're perfectly safe," Petra assured him.

"And just wait until Suzanne solves the murders of Spooner and Noterman as well as the pharmacy robberies," Toni said. She patted Suzanne on the back. "Honey, your investigating is paying off. You're getting close."

"Maybe too close," Petra said.

"But I thought those murders *were* solved," Floyd said.

Toni shook her head. "Suzanne doesn't believe the hospital shooter was Noterman. Sheriff Doogie may have swallowed that phony suicide hook, line, and sinker, but Suzanne didn't."

"Well, that's really something." Floyd gave a little shiver. "I heard about poor Ed Noterman and it sounded awful."

"It was," Toni said. "We peeked through the window and saw Noterman all limp and layin' in a puddle of his own blood."

Floyd practically gasped at Toni's horrific description.

Suzanne saw the consternation on Floyd's face and decided to cut Toni off. "Now that we have all our eggs and produce, we should let Mr. Floyd get on with his day."

"Right," Petra echoed. "Mr. Floyd, how can we ever thank you for all your help? For sourcing the caviar and out-of-season peaches and making a special delivery in the middle of the day? If our dinner turns out to be a whopping success it will be due in part to your good help."

"You know," Suzanne said to Floyd. "We could still squeeze two more people in tonight. Why don't you and your wife come as our guests?"

"Really? Wow." Floyd waved both hands at them as he started to back away. "Thank you most kindly, but I promised to take the missus to her sister's."

"You sure?" Petra asked.

His head bobbed. "Yup, but your offer surely is appreciated."

"Next time, then."

* * *

THEY were unpacking groceries and washing greens when a tremendous clatter, like drilling machines at a construction site, erupted in the backyard.

Petra was startled. "What's that?"

"Sounds like a freight train jumped its tracks," Toni said.

"I think our grill just arrived," Suzanne said.

Toni ran to the window and looked out. "You're right. It's Bud Nolden and he's dragging a humongous cast iron outdoor grill behind his tractor."

Now Petra had to peer out, too. "That's gotta be a twelve-foot-long grill. Should do the trick."

"And he's setting it up in back just like we wanted?" Suzanne asked.

"He's angled it in close enough for jazz," Petra said. "And, oh how nice, it looks as if one of those young men from the Journey's End Church has come over to help. Wait . . . is that . . . does that fellow have a bottle of beer in his hand?"

"Better not," Suzanne said. She moved next to Petra and peered out the window. In a disappearing act worthy of the great Houdini, the amber bottle was magically gone and Billy Brice was waving at them, a look of pure innocence on his young face. Tapping a foot, Suzanne frowned and said, "Hmm."

Petra turned back to her stove. "Gotta work on this basting sauce for the steaks. Oh, and Toni, did you remember to put out steak knives?"

"Um, nope," Toni said.

"Then you better do that," Petra said. "And Suzanne, do you need a primer on running that grill?"

"I'm going to bone up on it right now," Suzanne said. She was out the door in a flash and saying hello to Bud Nolden while Billy

Brice seemed to have disappeared in a puff of smoke. Or was that beer foam?

"Suzanne," Nolden said. He was a barrel-chested fifty-something with a kind, weather-worn face. Today he was wearing bib overalls and tan work boots. "I understand you're going to be grill master tonight."

"Hoping to anyway. What tricks do I need to know?"

Nolden lifted a hand and gestured at his rig. "Well, this baby is propane powered so it's fairly easy to operate. There are three distinct grilling sections, each with three different settings to make cooking easier. I suggest you keep the rare steaks at this end, your medium steaks in the middle, and well-done at the far end."

As Nolden demonstrated how to power up and adjust the various temperatures, Joey rode into the yard on his bike.

"Hey Mrs. D, hey Mr. Nolden," Joey sang out.

"Hi, kiddo," Nolden said in a genial tone. "What trouble have you been getting into lately?"

Joey dumped his bike near a tree and grabbed his nylon backpack and paintball gun. With its black finish and wide bore, Suzanne thought it looked a little like a high-powered automatic rifle.

"I just came from a paintball tournament," Joey said. "My team got second place!" He let out a whoop and lifted an arm in triumph.

"Good for you," Nolden said. "Won't be long before you're out deer huntin' with a real gun. A Winchester XPR or a bolt action Browning."

"Please don't encourage him," Suzanne said.

But Joey was so pumped he barely heard Suzanne. He inspected the grill, ran a hand along the gleaming front, then headed for the back steps.

"Aren't you forgetting something, Joey?" Suzanne asked.

"Huh?"

"The jumpsuit? The paintball gun?"

"Oh yeah," Joey said. He peeled off his jumpsuit and stashed his gun next to the back door. Then he glanced back at Suzanne and said, "Since this is such a fancy dinner tonight, is there a chance there might be tips?"

Suzanne couldn't help but smile. "I'm sure there will be, Joey."

CHAPTER 32

THE twinkle lights were strung on the Eiffel Tower, the candles lit, and all the tables looked *très* elegant. At the last minute, Petra had arranged for a string quartet from the Kindred High School to come in and play music, so Suzanne had to contend with those youngsters once they arrived. She set up a half circle of folding chairs along with a jerry-rigged music stand.

While the string quartet tuned up, when everything in the café looked perfect, Suzanne and Toni ducked into the Knitting Nest to change. Suzanne slipped into a black cocktail dress, Toni wore a white ruffled blouse with black slacks.

"We look good, huh?" Toni said, gazing into a wavy antique mirror.

"We look great," Suzanne said. "Now, if we can just pull off this dinner."

Suzanne had a serious case of the jitters as she fussed about the café, trying to make everything better than perfect. She'd settled on S. Aviron Beaujolais-Villages for wine at dinner, so she popped a few corks to let the wine settle and breathe. Now if she could only do the same for herself.

"What's the plan, Mrs. D?" Joey asked. He was wearing black slacks, a white shirt, and a black bow tie. Suzanne thought he looked cute as a button, even though he was still wearing his silver nose ring.

"You'll be carrying in the big silver trays with individual plates of egg shooters on them. Just follow me around while I serve."

"Got it."

"Once the dinner starts—it's going to be five courses tonight—you'll be mostly clearing the dirty dishes." Suzanne turned to see if the musicians were ready to start playing.

"I saw that guy again," Joey said.

Suzanne turned back to him. "What guy?"

Joey lowered his voice. "You know, the dope guy."

"And he was *selling* dope?"

Joey nodded.

"Where'd you see him? Outside your school?"

"Naw, over in Jessup. I was hanging out with some friends," Joey said. "At the McDonald's."

"A young guy?"

Joey shook his head. "Old. You know . . ." He pointed a finger at Junior, who was trying to figure out which way to hang a French flag. "Like him."

Smacky, Suzanne wondered, *could that have been you?*

WHEN the big hand and the little hand both hit six, the string quartet launched into a lilting number by Debussy and their guests began to arrive. Suzanne greeted each guest warmly as Toni checked off names and led them to a seat where place cards marked each guest's spot.

Jenny and Bill Probst came tumbling in, followed closely by

Reed and Martha Ducovny. Laura Benchley, editor of the *Bugle*, was next, then Gregg and Brett who owned Root 66, and Paula Patterson of WLGN radio and her husband, Norm.

More guests flowed in. Faces mingled with excited greetings as Suzanne fought to keep up with the ever-increasing crowd. She knew dinner was practically a sellout, she just hadn't realized how many people they could cram into the Cackleberry Club.

Sam arrived with a kiss and whispered congratulations for Suzanne. He seemed to have set aside this morning's little altercation for the time being. And when Suzanne told him to be sure and give Joey a tip, Sam responded with a conspiratorial wink.

Finally, when everyone was seated and the room was buzzing, Suzanne drew a deep breath, marched to the center of the room, and smiled. Conversation immediately died down and a spatter of applause broke out.

"*Bonjour* and welcome to our Petit Paris Gourmet Dinner," Suzanne said. "*Bienvenue à dîner.*"

This time everyone applauded.

She grinned. "And that's pretty much the extent of my French."

Now the guests chuckled.

"Toni, Petra, and I are thrilled that you all could make it and we can't wait to tickle your palates with the five-course menu we've created just for tonight."

A sea of encouraging faces looked out at her and Suzanne felt as though she was in a dream as she continued.

"As you can see by your menus, the *amuse bouche* we'll be serving is the appropriately named egg shooters. These are hard-boiled eggs, the yolks finely diced with baby onions, celery, and *crème fraîche*, and topped with a lovely black domestic caviar."

"*Nous aimons le caviar!*" someone called out. *We love caviar.*

"*Oui,*" Suzanne agreed as she continued. "This will be followed by an appetizer of duck wings *à l'orange* and a mixed field greens salad dressed with sherry vinaigrette. For your entrée we're grilling petite fillets precisely to your exact order and serving your fillets with a wild morel sauce as well as a side order of parmesan-dusted *pommes frites*. Dessert will be a peach and almond tart served with small cups of espresso. A French red wine—S. Aviron Beaujolais-Villages—will be served with dinner. And for those who prefer white wine, we also offer a California Sauvignon Blanc.

ALONG with the red wine, the egg shooters proved to be enormously popular.

"They like them," Toni whispered to Suzanne, as they circled past each other, refilling wine glasses. "The caviar's a hit, too!"

"I had a feeling there were more than a few refined palettes hiding out in this town," Suzanne whispered back.

As they served the duck wings and then the salad course, Suzanne and Toni took orders for the cook on everyone's steak. They figured they'd be able to manage medium-rare, medium, and well-done without too much trouble. And when Suzanne stepped outside with her tickets, she found that Petra had already thrown a dozen steaks on the grill.

"These are the well-dones," Petra told her. "I thought I'd get a head start on them." She waved a pair of silver tongs and said, "You have tickets on all the steaks, right?"

Suzanne checked her notes. "We need eleven well-dones."

"Okay, I've got twelve fillets cooking. An extra one for good luck, then."

"Works for me," Suzanne said.

"What else?" Petra put up a hand to straighten the chef's hat that sat atop her head.

"We need fourteen mediums and eleven medium-rare fillets."

"Got it."

Suzanne watched as Petra turned the fillets then basted them generously with her garlic and wine sauce. "Those steaks look delicious."

But Petra was starting to get a tiny bit frazzled. "I just hope my *pommes frites* are going to be . . ."

"I think it's time I take over grilling duty," Suzanne said. "That was our basic plan anyway. You need to be in the kitchen to troubleshoot and cook."

"Right on." Petra happily handed over the pair of tongs to Suzanne.

"Just tell Toni to keep filling the glasses with wine. Now go. *Go!*" Suzanne cried as Petra flew back into the kitchen.

Suzanne checked her watch, then reached into the nearby cooler and took out fourteen fillets. These would be her medium steaks. She moved to the center part of the grill and slapped them all down. Feeling quite the professional grill master, she smiled as they made a satisfying sizzle.

It was practically dark now with a yellow crescent moon dangling high in the sky and a string of twinkle lights strung in the trees (compliments of Junior). The small bulbs cast a bit of faint light, but the glowing orange flames and sizzling steaks made everything feel cozy and warm and at peace with the world. It was akin to sitting around a fire pit in your own backyard.

Moving down the grill, Suzanne took a quick look at the well-done fillets. They were cooking perfectly. Grill marks, a nice char, a sweet, smoky aroma from Petra's basting sauce.

As the flames danced and flickered, a hum rose in Suzanne's ears.

Hmm? Did I set my grill temp too high?

She checked it. Nope, everything seemed fine.

Suzanne could still hear it. A low hum. A constant drone. Nothing she could put her finger on exactly. But . . .

Suzanne started to feel strange. In the limbic part of her brain, the deep memory portion, something stirred. It reminded her . . . no that couldn't be right . . . of the sound she'd heard last Sunday night outside the hospital.

The HVAC system on the roof? No, that surely can't be it.

An uncomfortable tingle oozed its way through Suzanne's body. It started at the tips of her toes, then shivered up her spine until it fizzed in her brain. She recognized it as her spider sense kicking in. It meant imminent danger . . .

If it's danger, then where's the . . . ?

Suzanne reached for a steak to turn and suddenly looked up.

BOOM!

An ultralight aircraft was bearing down upon her. A single-seater craft with fixed wings, super lightweight frame, gasoline-powered engine, and, yes, a pilot. And it was heading directly at her, dipping lower, like the Red Baron zooming in for the perfect kill.

CHAPTER 33

ONLY it wasn't the Red Baron at all, it was Jimmy John Floyd. Tonight he wasn't wearing his black jumpsuit and mask. Or even his white deliveryman's apron. But he was carrying the same shiny black pistol he'd used to kill Harold Spooner at the hospital. And as he steered his ultralight aircraft ever lower, he was aiming that pistol directly at Suzanne's heart.

Suzanne gaped at him, practically paralyzed with fear. This wasn't a vision you saw every day, a buzzing insect of a machine zooming out of the night sky with a maniac pilot who was intent on killing you!

Panicked, Suzanne glanced around, hoping against hope to find a pitchfork, a shovel, anything to defend herself with. But there was nothing. Only the metal tongs she held in her hand.

Could she make it to the back door of the Cackleberry Club in time? Or should she duck down beneath the grill and take her chances? Her heart blip-blipped inside her chest, her mind spun dizzily. She felt overwhelmed and completely trapped. Floyd was a wild, predatory animal and she was the meat!

Only a few seconds had elapsed as Suzanne tried to bite back her panic and think what to do, but they felt like hours. Then a nearby voice shouted, "Hey there!"

She whirled to her right and saw Billy Brice standing there, a red rose in his hand. Then the red rose slipped to the ground and Brice was moving, running fast and low to the ground like an angry panther. He ran behind Suzanne, practically spinning her around, and grabbed for Joey's paintball gun that was propped next to the back door.

Like Buffalo Bill Cody in a Wild West show, Brice flipped the paintball gun around fast, took aim at the ultralight, and pulled the trigger.

BOOM!

A paintball smacked against Floyd's chest, spattering him with bright red paint. His ultralight faltered, seemed to hang in the air for a few seconds, then tilted crazily. Seconds later he had it under control again. He buzzed around in a circle, then came back for another try at them.

BANG, BANG, BOOM.

Three more paintballs exploded from the gun in rapid succession.

"Get down!" Brice shouted at Suzanne.

Suzanne moved as fast as she ever had, ducking for cover beneath the grill.

Blue, red, and yellow paint spattered the ultralight now and its high hum had turned into a low mechanized roar.

Suzanne peeped out. "I think you got him," she cried. "You shot him!"

But Floyd kept on coming and when Billy pulled the trigger again, there was nothing but a hollow click. He'd run out of paintballs!

"Ammo!" Brice yelled. "I need ammo!"

Keeping low, Suzanne skittered to the back door, pulled it open, and grabbed the first thing she could find. A carton of brown Maran eggs. Petra's favorite. She ran back out, flipped open the carton, and, standing next to Billy like some kind of World War II sapper, dropped two eggs into the paintball gun. Billy Brice aimed and fired.

SPLAT! SPLAT!

The eggs hit the wings of the ultralight, spattering yolks and white goop everywhere. Floyd yelled something—probably a curse—and kept on coming.

Suzanne tossed another egg into the paintball gun just as Floyd lifted his pistol, cocked the trigger, and fired directly at them!

Quick as a flash, Billy pulled Suzanne aside and stepped in front of her, trying to shield her. A split second later, he let out a high-pitched yelp.

"Oh dear Lord, are you hit?" Suzanne screamed.

Billy grimaced as he fumbled another egg into the gun, lifted it, aimed, and fired again.

This time the bright yellow yoke exploded directly in Jimmy John Floyd's face, virtually blinding him. Floyd screamed in fury, then wiped frantically at his eyes as his machine dipped and shook and faltered. Then his engine seemed to sputter and miss. And Suzanne watched, stunned, as the ultralight aircraft, with Jimmy John Floyd aboard, wobbled and shook like a wounded bird. Until it finally tumbled from the sky.

At that exact same moment, Billy groaned and crumpled to the ground.

CHAPTER 34

"SAM! Sam! Come quick!" Suzanne screamed as she tore through the kitchen, running past a stunned Petra and Joey, and popping out in the dining room. She knew her hair was horribly tousled, her face spattered with paint, and that she was waving her arms and yelling like a crazy woman. Didn't matter. "Billy's been shot!" she cried. "Floyd came at us with a gun!"

That brought the entire dinner to a standstill. Chairs were pushed back from tables, voices raised, the violinist struck an awkward chord, and all eyes were suddenly focused on Suzanne.

Sam's fork clattered to his plate and his chair tipped over backward as he leapt up. "Where?" he asked.

Suzanne reached for him. "Out back. Follow me!"

Now panic erupted among the guests.

"Gun!"

"Hide!"

"Set your phone on video recorder!"

"Let's go look!"

Suzanne and Sam raced through the kitchen, past a still-stunned Petra, a disbelieving Joey, and a goggle-eyed Junior, who'd just emerged from the cooler with a bowl of whipped cream.

"He's hit! Billy's been hit!" Suzanne shouted again as she felt a rising tide of panic. Was Billy dying? Was she responsible? And why had he so stupidly (bravely?) stepped in front of her like that? As they ran into the backyard, she tried to hold back her tears but found she couldn't.

But Sam was right there, calm and professional, kneeling next to Billy, his hand gently pulling up Billy's denim shirt to inspect the gunshot wound.

"It feels like my ribs are broken," Billy gasped. "I can hardly breathe."

"The bullet creased the side of your ribcage, yes. But . . . no, it's not lodged in your flesh," Sam said in a soft, reassuring voice. "It's a through and through. I'd have to say you got lucky."

"Doesn't feel like I did. I still hurt bad," Billy said.

"Ambulance is on its way," Petra said as she pushed open the back door and stepped out. "So is the sheriff." She looked over at Floyd, who was pinned under his ultralight and moaning, and said, "Hmph."

Billy groaned again and tried to tuck his knees up to his chin.

"Buddy, I know it hurts, but just hang on. I promise you're going to come through this," Sam said. "I don't see anything that's life threatening." He was checking the boy's respiration and pulse, keeping pressure on the wound with his hand, and gently reassuring him.

"His name is Billy," Suzanne said.

"Okay, Billy. I'm Sam. I know this gunshot wound hurts like hell. But we can take care of it, okay? You're not bleeding too badly at all." He looked around. "I wonder if I could get . . ."

Petra handed Sam a clean dish towel.

"I'm going to press this towel against the wound . . . there, let me . . . yeah, turn a little bit, that's the ticket. Are you still breathing okay? Just relax and try to take slow, rhythmic breaths. Soon as the ambulance gets here we'll drive you straight to the ER, irrigate the wound, take a few stitches, and bandage you up, okay?"

Billy tried to nod. "I guess."

"We'll get you some good pain meds and you can spend the night in the hospital. Tomorrow you'll have a hell of a story to tell your friends," Sam said.

Suzanne, who hadn't said much of anything, who'd hung back so Sam could take care of Billy, now spoke up.

"He jumped in front of me," Suzanne said in a trembling voice.

Sam turned and looked up at her. "What'd you say, sweetheart? I didn't catch that."

"I said Billy jumped in front of me. To, you know, block the shot." Suzanne was crying in between hiccups, her voice sorrowful and hoarse. She was trembling and her face was still white as a sheet.

Sam shook his head as if in disbelief. "He *what*?"

Louder now. "Billy jumped in front of me, Sam. He saved my life!"

"You jumped in . . . uh, you shielded Suzanne?" Sam gripped Billy's hand. "The woman I love?" Now he was the one who was struggling to talk. "I'm . . . Kid, I'm in awe. I'm forever in your debt."

Billy managed a slightly strangled smile and a weak thumbs-up. "She said there was a guy. I guess I'm glad it turned out to be you."

SHERIFF Doogie and Deputy Driscoll arrived some thirty seconds later, just behind the ambulance. While the EMTs huddled with Sam, Doogie strode around the backyard looking slightly bewildered.

"What the hell happened here?" Doogie asked. His vision clouded by the smoke from the grilling steaks, he waved a hand in front of his face. "Those steaks smell darn good but the ones on the end look a might crispy." Then he caught sight of the wreckage from Jimmy John Floyd's ultralight and he looked even more startled. "Good gravy, what's that? Some kind of UFO crash landed?"

"An ultralight aircraft," Suzanne said. Toni was standing next to her now, a reassuring arm slung around her shoulder.

"It crashed and burned right here in your backyard?"

"It belongs to Jimmy John Floyd. He tried to kill me," Suzanne told him.

Doogie reared back. "*Kill* you?"

"But he shot Billy instead." Suzanne pointed to the tangle of wings, propeller, and metal struts. "That's Floyd over there, all crumpled up under his aircraft."

A light bulb went off over Doogie's head. Suzanne could almost see it pop. "The OxyContin in the field," he muttered.

"Help," came Floyd's plaintive voice. "Somebody please help me." His pleas for help had been largely ignored until now.

"He's the one who robbed the hospital and shot Harold Spooner and Ginny," Suzanne managed to choke out. "Probably killed Ed Noterman, too."

Doogie walked over to where Floyd was lying, hitched up his gun belt, and peered down at Floyd.

"Is that all true, Mr. Floyd?"

"No! Of course not!" Floyd wailed. "These crazy people shot me down. I was minding my own business, just flying along—it's my hobby, you know—and they shot at me and caused me to crash my ultralight. There's . . . there's surely a lawsuit here."

"And you just happened to have a pistol in your hand," Doogie said. He walked a step closer and kicked it out of Floyd's hand.

"Now, if one of my crackerjack deputies took this gun over to the state ballistics experts, would they determine that it was the same gun used on Harold Spooner?"

All of a sudden, Toni let out a growl like a ferocious dog. She broke away from Suzanne, rushed over to Floyd, and tried to kick him in the ribs. Doogie caught her just in the nick of time and wrapped her up in a bear hug.

"Quit it," Toni cried. "Let me go. That dirtbag tried to kill Suzanne. And he shot Billy!"

"I'll let you go you when you calm down and act nice."

"I'm always nice," Toni said in a crabby voice.

"You gotta help me," Floyd groaned. "I'm hurt real bad."

"Help you?" Doogie asked as he released Toni.

"I . . . I think my leg is broken. My shoulder hurts, too."

"Uh-huh. And did you shoot that young man who's laying over there?" Doogie asked. He flipped a hand to indicate Billy Brice, who was being gently lifted onto a gurney. "And those people at the hospital? And poor Ed Noterman?" He pursed his lips. "Oh. Got nothin' to say for yourself? Looks like you're under arrest, Mr. Floyd."

Floyd muttered something under his breath.

"What was that?" Doogie asked.

"I said I want a lawyer."

CHAPTER 35

It was all over but the eatin'. Toni and Petra went back inside the Cackleberry Club and soothed the collected frayed nerves of their guests. They gave a semi-amusing CliffsNotes explanation of what had taken place outside, then served up additional glasses of wine (which helped enormously). After checking on the welfare of his goat, Junior set about grilling the rest of the steaks with Petra's chef's hat perched at a jaunty angle on his head. The dinner would go on.

A second ambulance arrived to transport Floyd and, in a moment of quick thinking, Suzanne hauled Joey out to look at him.

"Is this who you saw?" Suzanne asked. "Do you recognize this guy?"

"That's him," Joey said, confirming her suspicions. "He's the dirty dope guy."

And another piece of the puzzle dropped neatly into place.

"That's where the drugs were going," Suzanne told Doogie

after she'd sent Joey back inside. "Jimmy John Floyd was selling them on the street.

"Huh," Doogie said. He was holding a leash that was attached to a tan and white dog. Suzanne remembered the dog and thought his name might be Banjo.

"Isn't that Noterman's basset hound?" she asked.

Doogie nodded, looking a little sheepish.

"You took him in? Adopted him?"

"He's a police dog now. Been deputized and everything."

It was Suzanne's turn to say, "Huh." She'd never seen that in Doogie before, a genuine compassion for animals. But that was good, right? Actually, it was pretty darn wonderful.

"Suzanne?" Sam was calling to her. "There's someone who wants to say goodbye to you."

Suzanne rushed over to the ambulance where Billy was just about to be loaded into the back.

"Billy," she said. Some of the color had returned to his face and he didn't look quite as terrified as he had five minutes earlier. She put a hand on his shoulder, and said, "Thank you, Billy." There was a distinct catch in her voice.

Billy managed a grin and a half shrug. "That's okay. And you can call me William if you want. That's my real name, you know. My Christian name."

"I'd like that."

Billy curled an index finger at Suzanne as if he wanted her to lean in closer. So Suzanne bent forward, the better to hear him.

"I get it," Billy whispered to her. "Your guy. He's a good guy."

"Yes, he is." Suzanne reached out and gently touched the boy's cheek. "So no more roses, okay?"

Billy nodded. "No more roses."

"But here's the thing," Suzanne said. "Once in a while I'm going to drop by with a plate of sticky buns or butterscotch scones, if that's okay with you."

Billy looked happy. "You'd really do that?"

"Of course I would. For as long as you're here."

"You know what? I like it here. And I kind of think . . . that maybe I'm starting to do good."

Suzanne's words were a gentle caress. "I know you are, sweet William, I know you are."

Recipes from the Cackleberry Club

Suzanne's Egg Shooters

8 hardboiled eggs
3 Tbsp. mayonnaise
1 Tbsp. sour cream
1 tsp. Dijon mustard
¼ tsp. paprika
Salt
Pepper
5 Tbsp. caviar (about ¼ oz.)
Chives

Peel hardboiled eggs and cut lengthwise, reserving the yolks. Place yolks in food processor and add mayonnaise, sour cream, mustard, paprika, and salt and pepper to taste. Process until nice and smooth. Transfer mixture to a resealable plastic bag and snip off one corner. Pipe the yolk mixture into the eggs. Top each egg with a generous teaspoon of caviar and a snip of chive. Yields 16 egg shooters.

Hangover Hash

2 Tbsp. olive oil
2 cups frozen, cubed potatoes
1 cup crumbled sausage
¾ cup salsa
4 eggs
Avocado, sliced
Salt and pepper

In a large skillet add olive oil and potatoes and cook over medium-high heat. Cook until crisp, about 6 to 10 minutes, flipping potatoes over every few minutes. Add sausage and cook until browned. Flatten potatoes and sausage and add a layer of salsa. Using a large spoon, make 4 wells in the mixture and drop in the eggs. Cover and reduce heat to medium-low. Cook 4 to 6 minutes. Season with salt and pepper, top with diced avocado, and serve. Yields 4 servings.

Petra's French Toast Sticks

8 slices thick-cut Texas toast
4 eggs
1 cup heavy cream
2½ tsp. cinnamon

1 Tbsp. sugar
1 Tbsp. vanilla extract
3 Tbsp. butter
Maple syrup

Cut each slice of Texas toast into four sticks and set aside. In a large bowl, whisk together eggs, heavy cream, cinnamon, sugar, and vanilla. Dip each bread stick in the egg mixture, making sure you coat all sides. Set aside on a large plate. Repeat dipping process with the remaining pieces of bread. Heat a large sauté pan over medium heat and add the butter. Once butter has melted, place several of the coated sticks in the pan. Cook until golden brown, flipping over to brown all sides. Continue cooking all the sticks. Serve hot with maple syrup or jam for dipping. Yields 32 toast sticks.

Ham and Apricot Country Biscuit Sandwiches

8 country-style biscuits, made from scratch or purchased
Butter
4 slices of ham, cut in half
½ cup apricot jam
2 Tbsp. whole-grain mustard
1 tsp. Dijon mustard

Warm biscuits, cut in half, and butter both halves. Top each biscuit bottom with a half slice of ham. Combine apricot jam with the two mustards and spread mixture on top of ham. Add biscuit tops. Yields 4 servings (2 per person).

Breakfast Tacos

6 eggs
2 Tbsp. oil
1 lb. sausage
1 medium onion, chopped
½ cup cheddar cheese, grated
2 baked potatoes, chopped
1 pkg. flour tortillas

Using a large skillet, scramble eggs in oil, then transfer to a dish and keep warm. Crumble sausage into pan and cook until brown. Add in onions and cook for a few minutes. Add in scrambled eggs and chopped potatoes. Cook on low for 5 minutes. While mixture is cooking, warm flour tortillas. Fill tortillas with egg mixture and serve with your favorite salsa. Yields 6 to 8 tacos.

Peaches-and-Cream Pancakes

2 cups Bisquick baking mix
1 egg
1 cup milk
2 Tbsp. brown sugar, packed
¾ cup heavy whipping cream, whipped
1 can sliced peaches, drained (or 2 fresh peaches peeled and sliced)
Ground cinnamon

Beat together Bisquick, egg, milk, and brown sugar until well blended. For each pancake, pour ¼ cup of mixture onto hot griddle or greased fry pan. Cook until pancakes are dry around the edges, then flip and cook until golden brown.

To serve, top with whipped cream and peaches. Sprinkle with cinnamon. Yields 4 servings.

Blueberry Banana Bread

½ cup butter, softened
1 cup sugar
2 eggs
2 large ripe bananas, mashed
1½ cups flour
1 tsp. baking soda
½ tsp. salt
1 tsp. vanilla extract
1½ cups blueberries, fresh or frozen

Preheat oven to 325 degrees. Grease and flour 2 loaf pans. Cream together butter and sugar, then beat in eggs. Add mashed bananas. In separate bowl, measure out flour, reserving 2 table-spoons to coat blueberries. Stir baking soda and salt into flour, mixing well. Fold flour mixture into banana mixture and stir in vanilla. Sprinkle the 2 tablespoons of flour over the blueberries, then fold berries into batter. Transfer batter to 2 loaf pans and bake for 45 to 50 minutes. Yields 2 loaves.

Junior's Favorite Beer and Pork Goulash

2 Tbsp. oil
2 lb. pork cubes
1 medium onion, chopped
2 Tbsp. paprika
¾ tsp. salt
¼ tsp. pepper
2 Tbsp. flour
1½ cups beer
½ cup sour cream

Heat 1 tablespoon oil in a large skillet. Add pork cubes and cook 4 to 5 minutes, stirring frequently and browning on all sides. Remove pork to a plate. Heat 1 tablespoon oil in same skillet. Stir in chopped onion, cover, and cook for 5 to 6 minutes. Stir in paprika, salt, pepper, and flour and cook for 2 minutes. Add beer and stir. Return pork to pan, then cover and simmer for 30 minutes. Remove pan from heat and gently stir in sour cream. Serve immediately. Yields 6 servings. (Note: serve with crusty bread on the side.)

Orange Bars

1 large seedless orange
1 cup raisins
½ cup butter, softened
1 cup sugar
1 egg
2 cups flour, sifted

½ tsp. baking powder
¼ tsp. salt
1½ cups powdered sugar

Preheat oven to 425 degrees. Cut orange in half and squeeze out 2 tablespoons juice. Reserve juice. Place rest of orange, including rind, in food processor along with raisins and pulse until mixed. In large bowl, beat butter for 45 seconds. Gradually add sugar and egg. Beat until light and fluffy. Add flour, baking powder, and salt. Mix well. Stir orange mixture from processor into sugar, egg, and flour mixture. Spread in a 12" x 9" pan. Bake for approximately 25 minutes. Just before bars are done, mix reserved juice with powdered sugar until smooth. Spread on baked bars while still warm. Cool and cut into bars. Yields 12 to 15 bars.

Petra's Basting Sauce for Steaks

¾ cup olive oil
¾ cup dry red wine
1 Tbsp. lemon juice
2 garlic cloves, minced
⅓ cup onion, minced
1 tsp. sugar
1 tsp. salt

Combine all ingredients in a covered jar or shaker. Shake until very well blended. Baste onto steaks while cooking. Yield: Enough basting sauce for 5 to 6 steaks. (Note: As an alternative, this can also be used as a marinade to coat steaks 1 to 2 hours before cooking.)

Keep reading for an excerpt from
Laura Childs's next Tea Shop Mystery . . .

Haunted Hibiscus

Available soon from
Berkley Prime Crime!

Dark clouds bubbled across a purple-black sky, then lifted gently, like a velvet curtain in a darkened theater, to reveal the top two floors of a dilapidated old mansion.

"That's it," Theodosia said. "The place they dubbed the Gray Ghost."

"I can't say it looks particularly charming," Drayton said. "In fact, it's slightly off-putting."

Theodosia gazed at a corner turret that was bathed in green and purple lights. At one time the home had whispered wealth and taste. Not anymore. Now the exterior, the balustrades and finials, even the third-floor widow's walk displayed the battering it had received from a century of Atlantic hurricanes, salt-infused sea air, and industrial-strength humidity.

"Haunted houses generally aren't that attractive," Theodosia said. "But at least this one's being put to good use."

It was the week before Halloween, and tea maven Theodosia Browning and her tea sommelier Drayton Conneley were strolling down Tradd Street in Charleston, South Carolina, heading for the old Bouchard Mansion. It was a property that had recently been bequeathed to Drayton's beloved Heritage Society.

"The Heritage Society wasn't all that happy about inheriting this old place," Drayton explained. "But it was donated by one of the last remaining Bouchards. Written into his will. And you know our fearless leader Timothy is loath to turn down any sort of gift."

"Still, I love how your curators and marketing folks figured out to make the most of it," Theodosia said. "What an amazing idea to create a literary- and history-inspired haunted house. And then to launch it the week before Halloween?" She gave a little shiver of anticipation. "It's a fabulous concept. People will be standing in line." They rounded a tall hedge of crepe myrtle and arrived at the front walk where at least five dozen people were clustered, waiting to get in. "Actually, people *are* standing in line."

"Opening night," Drayton said as they shuffled up the sidewalk with the rest of the visitors. "So I suppose folks are curious."

"I sure am," Theodosia said as she gazed at the old place. Yellow light spilled out from tall, narrow front windows; inside looked to be a beehive of activity.

"You remember Willow French, Timothy's niece?" Drayton asked.

"Oh sure, I've met her a few times."

"She's here tonight, signing her new book."

"Willow's written a novel? That's wonderful."

Drayton pursed his lips. "It's not exactly a stunning piece of literature. Rather an anthology titled *Carolina Crimes and Creepers*. Supposed to be a mixture of true crime and some of our low-country legends."

"You mean haunted legends," Theodosia said, feeling another tingle. Even though she didn't believe-believe in spirits and ghosts, it was fun to pretend that Revolutionary War–era ghosts and headless pirates still stalked Charleston's narrow cobblestone alleys. Besides, there were plenty of folks who *did* believe in ghosts. Case in point, there were four different ghost tours that guided visitors to the Old City Jail, Provost Dungeon, and Unitarian Graveyard. As well as to a twisted old hanging tree where dozens of pirates had been executed.

Drayton glanced up at the dilapidated mansion where a swirling projection of ghosts and witches moved eerily across an outside wall. "Haunted, yes," he said.

The low country and Charleston in particular were a hotbed of legends and lore that included ghosts, hauntings, boo hags, spirits, apparitions, and spectral goings-on. Everyone who lived in Charleston knew about the haunted theaters and mansions, Lavinia Fisher, the Headless Torso, and the Weeping Woman of St. Philip's Church. And there were dozens more creepy tales that had been passed down through generations.

As they walked through antique wrought-iron gates, a ghoul with a green-painted face and a bolt through his neck tapped Drayton on the shoulder. "Tickets?" he rasped.

Drayton fumbled in his jacket pocket. "As a matter of fact, I do."

"This is going to be amazing," Theodosia said. She was already three steps ahead of Drayton and loved what she was seeing. Edgar Allan Poe lounged on the front portico; Washington Irving's Headless Horseman lurked in a window. And she was pretty sure she could see Lady Macbeth sweeping past the guests who were already inside.

"You're liking this, yes?" Drayton said when he caught up with Theodosia.

"Yes!"

Possessing a keen sense of adventure, Theodosia was in her early thirties and the owner of the Indigo Tea Shop on Church Street. She was also blessed with expressive painterly blue eyes, a fair complexion (it helped to be religious about sunscreen), and a riot of auburn hair that she worried sometimes looked slightly untamed.

Drayton, on the other hand, was sixtyish, dapper, a true Southern gent, and the model of conservatism. He was always appropriately dressed (tweed jacket and bow tie tonight) and had a personality that could veer from genial to slightly stiff. Drayton's idea of an exciting evening was attending *La Traviata* or holing up in his private library to read his beloved Dickens.

"I think this place is terrific," Theodosia said. She was excited and feeling a little bit giddy. "Who doesn't like Halloween, after all? Who doesn't enjoy a good haunted house, even if it is all costumes and theatrics?" She reached out, letting her fingertips brush against the rustling full-length satin skirt of a masked woman.

"Ah," Drayton said, catching up to her. "From the legend of Madame Margot." Then he took her arm and said, "Come on, let's go find Willow."

WILLOW French was young and pretty, with honey-colored hair that framed a smiling face. She was clearly in seventh heaven from all the attention she was receiving tonight. Seated at an antique library table, she smiled brightly as she autographed books and thanked everyone in her immediate vicinity for showing up.

The authoring business must be good, Theodosia decided. Dozens of people waited in line for a signed copy, Willow's table was stacked with double towers of books, and cardboard cases full of books filled the small parlor where she was seated.

"Willow," Drayton said, greeting Timothy's grandniece with a wide smile and a nod of his head. "I see our favorite author is in residence tonight."

Willow glanced up, recognized Drayton immediately, and grinned from ear to ear. "Uncle Drayton!" she shrieked.

Theodosia gave Drayton a sideways glance. *"Uncle* Drayton?"

"That's how Timothy has always introduced me to his grand-niece," Drayton said in a low, soft voice. "As though I'm a member of the family."

And it was abundantly clear that Willow *did* consider Drayton part of the family, because now she skittered around to the front of the table, arms flung wide, ready to give him a most exuberant bear hug.

Willow squeezed Drayton, uttered another high-pitched squeal, and, after a few giggles, eventually released him. "I was hoping you'd show up," she said breathlessly. Standing barely five two, with shining eyes and an impish expression, Willow looked even younger than her twenty-four years.

"I wouldn't have missed this for the world," Drayton said. Then, hurriedly, "You remember Theodosia, don't you?"

"Of course. You're the tea lady," Willow said, immediately reaching out to give Theodosia a quick hug as well. "Hey, thanks bunches for coming."

"This is a big night for you," Theodosia said as she returned the hug. "I understand it's your first big book signing."

Willow nodded. "I've been to a couple bookstores, but am I ever loving this. I wondered how my book would go over here, but it's been gangbusters so far. Sales are good with lots of friends dropping by to say congrats. One of the bigwigs from the Charleston Library Society even stopped by my table to tell me she'd ordered twenty copies from my publisher, who I hope is wandering around here someplace."

"I couldn't be happier for you," Theodosia said.

"We're delighted," Drayton echoed. "And of course we both want signed copies."

"I've got first editions that I can personalize for you." Willow hurried back around the table, sat down, and grabbed two books from a box on the floor. She flipped them open and grabbed a squishy marker pen. The large moonstone ring on her left hand flashed as she signed both books with a flourish.

"Has Timothy stopped by yet?" Drayton asked.

Willow nodded. "Oh yeah, he's around somewhere."

"I don't think Timothy was all that keen on this haunted house idea," Drayton said. "But judging from the crowd that's turned up tonight, I must say it's . . . well, speak of the devil!"

Timothy Neville ghosted into the room like a character out of King Lear. He was an octogenarian who was not only the power behind the Heritage Society, but also a board member of the Charleston Opera Society, occasional violinist for the Charleston Symphony, collector of antique pistols, and proud possessor of a stunning mansion on Archdale Street that was furnished with equally stunning paintings, tapestries, and antiques. Interestingly enough, all that knowledge and power was contained within a small man who was barely one hundred forty pounds and had a bony, simian face, yet possessed the grace and poise of an elder statesman.

"Looks like your haunted house is a rousing success," Drayton declared.

Timothy favored Theodosia and Drayton with a thin smile. "I wouldn't have dreamed this up in a million years. But my staff . . . all I can say is they're blessed with vivid imaginations."

"But in a good way," Theodosia said.

"Did I hear there was some some sort of property dispute?" Drayton asked.

Timothy gave an offhand wave. "One of the last remaining Bouchard relatives tried to contest the will, but my attorneys assured me it was ironclad. This place, such as it is, remains ours, lock, stock, and barrel."

"That's wonderful," Theodosia said. She was marveling at the crowds that continued to pour in. And then, as Drayton and Timothy remained locked in conversation, she managed to slip away. She definitely wanted to get a good look at the various literary characters in their elaborate displays.

And she wasn't disappointed. The folks at the Heritage Society had done a masterful job.

Edgar Allan Poe had his own writing studio—really, more of a dark garret—complete with quill pens, inkwell, antique desk, threadbare rug, old leather-bound books, and even a stuffed raven sitting on a perch.

Wearing a silver-gray floor-length corseted dress, Lady Macbeth stalked her way through the old mansion carrying a silver candlestick. Dr. Jekyll and Mr. Hyde had their own laboratory set up as well. And Sherlock Holmes had a wonderful study, complete with books, a messy desk, and a coatrack that held his tweed overcoat and deerstalker hat.

As Theodosia gazed into a mirror that reflected an image of Dorian Gray, she decided that she'd better get a signed book for Haley as well. Haley, her *compadre* and young chef at the Indigo Tea Shop, was a good friend of Willow's and would appreciate having one of the first editions.

But when Theodosia eventually wound her way back to the small parlor, Willow was no longer seated at her table.

Stepped out, I suppose, Theodosia thought to herself. *Maybe I'll pop back later in the week. I know Willow plans to do a couple more signings.*

"There you are," Drayton said.

Theodosia whirled around. "Have you seen Willow? Do you know where she ran off to?"

"She's probably being introduced around by Timothy," Drayton said. "He's busting his buttons over her. Or perhaps she's taking a break." He smiled. "Could have picked up a touch of writer's cramp from signing so many books."

"Tonight's been a real success for Willow. Really, for the Heritage Society in general," Theodosia said as they walked through the main parlor, then stepped outside onto the wide porch. A chill wind had sprung up, and she was suddenly cold. As she buttoned her jacket, they continued out into the front yard.

"I'll be the first to admit that I thought a literary haunted house was a half-baked idea," Drayton said as they walked past a horde of people anxiously waiting to get in. "But this was rather . . ."

A loud, collective gasp suddenly rose up from the moving crowd, drowning out the rest of Drayton's words.

Puzzled at the burst of noise, Drayton shook his head and said, "What?" just as a woman's high-pitched scream rose like some kind of ungodly yodel and pierced the night air.

Both startled and curious, Theodosia spun around just in time to see something—could it be a body?—dangling out the window of the third-floor tower. She grasped Drayton's arm and pulled him around as well. "Drayton, look up there!"

"My heaven!" Drayton exclaimed in a shaky voice, as all around them the cacophony of screams and shouting continued to build and build until the noise seemed like an explosion.

"It's some kind of illusion!"

"How terrifying!"

"Oh no, it's really happening!"

"Help her! Somebody please help that poor girl!"

At first glance, Theodosia thought it had to be part of the entertainment, some special effect that had been rigged to frighten people. A woman's body, dangling from a rope, motionless and frozen in the harsh purple and green lights.

But that would be too terrible, wouldn't it? And this looks positively . . . real.

And then the body twirled slowly and horribly, twisting around so everyone could finally see the dark-purplish tinge to the woman's face, the dead, sunken eyes, the long blond hair whipping frantically in the night wind.

That's when a rocked-to-the-core Drayton suddenly clutched at his heart and gasped, "Dear Lord, it's Willow. Someone's hanged her to death!"

WHILE dozens of stunned visitors whipped out their cell phones en masse and flooded Charleston's 911 system with distress calls, Theodosia short-circuited the lot of them. She immediately called Pete Riley, police detective second grade, trusted first responder, and boyfriend extraordinaire.

Riley picked up on the third ring. "Well, hello there," he said in a leisurely tone of voice. He had caller ID, so he knew it was Theodosia. What he didn't know what how upset and terrified she was.

"Riley, I need you to come quickly!" Theodosia said in a tight voice. She tried not to sound crazed or hysterical, just focused every part of her being on holding it together.

"What's wrong?" Riley knew Theodosia well enough to realize there had to be some sort of emergency.

"At the haunted house . . . the one the Heritage Society is sponsoring, there's been a . . ."

"Hold a sec, will you?"

"Riley!" Now Theodosia did cry out in frustration. Why had he cut her off like that? What could be so all-fired important? Especially now when she needed him the most.

A few seconds later Riley was back on, his voice crackling with alarm. "I just received an emergency text from dispatch. Theo . . . are you calling from the haunted house on Tradd Street?"

"Yes!"

"Then stay put. I'm on my way." And just like that Riley was gone.

Drayton stared at Theodosia with alarm in his eyes. "While you were talking, the police just . . . They're already here. Two officers ran upstairs to see if . . ." Drayton's words ended in a guttural choke, as if he'd run out of air. Then, "Did you get hold of him? Riley? Is he coming?"

Theodosia breathed out slowly. "He's coming."

"We need to find Timothy," Drayton said. "To tell him . . ." He touched a hand to the side of his head. "Gracious me, what do we tell him? *How* do we tell him?"

At that exact moment, a sharp, strangled scream rose up from inside the haunted house.

"I think he already knows," Theodosia said.

THE EMTs arrived next. Hauling a gurney and emergency packs, they charged into the house and up the stairs to the third floor. Then three more squad cars came screaming in, the officers immediately rushing into the haunted house to try to round up visitors and herd everyone outside.

"Timothy," Drayton said as they watched the frightened visitors pour out. "He's still in there. What must he be feeling? We've got to go in and help him!"

Together, Theodosia and Drayton fought their way through the surging, almost hysterical crowd. They pushed their way back up the front walk, reached the porch, and then slipped inside. They found Timothy standing in the parlor where Willow had been signing books only minutes earlier. His face was twisted in anguish, his narrow shoulders hunched. He looked as if he'd just been sentenced to death.

"You people need to go outside," an officer barked at the three of them.

"The woman . . . she's his grandniece," Drayton said.

The officer's face fell. "Oh," he said, stepping away.

Theodosia, Drayton, and Timothy stood there, too stunned to even speak to one another, as yellow-and-black crime scene tape was strung all around them and more officers arrived.

Finally, Detective Pete Riley came flying through the front door.

"Riley!" Theodosia cried as she rushed into his arms.

"You saw it happen? You've been here the whole time?" Riley asked her.

Theodosia nodded, savoring his warm embrace. Then she took a step back and gazed at him. "It was awful. I thought maybe . . ." Tears formed in her eyes. "I guess I don't know *what* to think."

Riley just nodded. He was used to dealing with distraught people. Used to investigating homicides and serious crimes. At age thirty-seven, he was one of the up-and-coming detectives on Charleston's police force. A tall, intense man with an aristocratic nose, high cheekbones, and cobalt blue eyes. Theodosia, of course, simply thought of him as Riley, her Riley. He called her Theo, and she called him Riley. It was as simple as that because it suited them.

"What's going to happen now?" Theodosia asked.

"This whole place is a crime scene, so we're going to follow standard procedure," Riley said. "We'll detain as many people as possible and get statements from them. At least that's what the boss ordered."

"The boss?" Theodosia said.

"Tidwell."

"You've already talked to him?"

Riley nodded. "He's on his way over. Should be here any minute."

Theodosia glanced at Drayton and Timothy. "I should stay here with them. Maybe I could . . ."

"No," Riley said. "Let's get you outside right now before things get really ugly." He walked Theodosia to the front door and down the steps into the large front yard. Harried-looking officers wielding pens and clipboards were hastily asking questions and writing down the names of as many witnesses as they could round up.

"What are you going to do?" Theodosia asked Riley.

Before Riley could answer, a large, bulky man strolled out of the shadows and into the garish green light. It was Detective Burt Tidwell, the head of Charleston PD's Robbery and Homicide Division. He was as wide as a soccer mom's van and as touchy as a puff adder.

"Riley," he growled.

"Yes, sir."

"After we conduct a thorough search of this so-called haunted house, I want you to go over and search the victim's apartment," Detective Tidwell said in his trademark baritone. Hesitating for a moment, Tidwell cast a quick, almost sardonic glance at Theodosia and added, "That's if you're not too busy here."

"I'm on it, sir," Riley said. He snapped to attention as Tidwell pushed past them, his large belly protruding from between the lapels of his ill-fitting tweed jacket. Though Tidwell was irascible, overweight, and overbearing, he was undeniably the finest investigator on the force. As a leader who inspired utter confidence, his men would probably leap into a volcano for him. They'd probably follow him into the pit of hell.

Theodosia watched, fascinated, as the crowd parted for Tidwell as if he were a visiting dignitary. She'd butted heads with the crusty Tidwell before. And though she didn't always get along with him, didn't always see eye to eye, she did respect him.

Theodosia turned back to Riley, put a hand on his arm, and said, in an urgent voice, "Let me go with you."

Riley half smiled as he shook his head. "I can't do that."

Theodosia was not about to take no for an answer. This was far too important.

"Please," she said. "For Timothy's sake. You'll be haphazardly looking through all his grandniece's personal belongings. And I'm positive it would be a great comfort to Timothy if someone he knows and trusts went along with you."

"No can do. We can't have civilians poking around and contaminating a crime scene."

"You think that's a crime scene, too?" Theodosia asked. The idea hadn't occurred to her. Now the notion of checking out Willow's apartment seemed almost tantalizing.

"I suppose I won't know until I get there," Riley said.

Theodosia stared at Riley, a combination of nervousness and excitement sparking in her eyes. "I'm not exactly a civilian, you know. I've been down this road before."

"I get that. It's just . . . tonight, no. It's simply not possible." Riley brushed his lips across Theodosia's forehead and was gone. Strode deftly through the crowd and back into the haunted house.

Five minutes later, Drayton emerged. He had a hangdog, defeated look on his face.

"They threw me out," he said to Theodosia.

She touched a hand to his shoulder. "Timothy's talking to the investigators?"

Drayton nodded. "Trying to anyway. He's awfully upset."

"They'll see he gets home safely," Theodosia said. Then, "There's nothing we can do for him here."

"I suppose you're right," Drayton said. "But I still wanted to . . .

Oh no, will you look at that?" His eyes drooped heavily as he glanced out toward the street.

Theodosia followed Drayton's gaze and saw that one of Willow's books had been discarded in the gutter, its spine broken, pages fluttering crazily as they were ripped out, one by one, by the chill wind that was now battering in from the Atlantic.

Be sure to watch for Laura Childs's next
Cackleberry Club Mystery

Eggs Over Uneasy

It's the week before Suzanne's wedding and the strangest things are happening!

And watch for Laura Childs's New Orleans
Scrapbooking Mystery

Cadmium Red Dead

An excavation in the French Quarter reveals a terrible crime that pulls Carmela and Ava deep into a mystery.

Find out more about the author
and her mysteries at laurachilds.com
or become a Facebook friend at
facebook.com/laurachildsauthor.